Friends

Allison,

It was great to
meet you, Enjoy
the book.

Love Janet

Friends

6 Women, 6 Cultures

One Humanity

A Novel

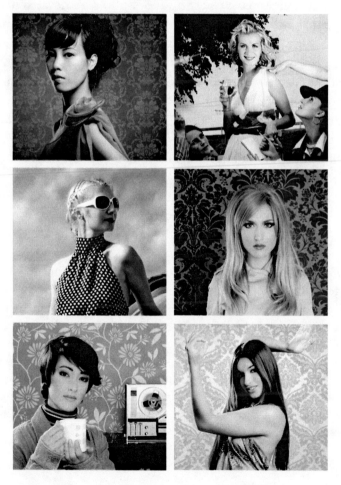

Janet Love Morrison

First Published in Canada 2012 by Influence Publishing

Graphic design and layout: Nara Subramaniam
Portrait Photographer: Brian Harris

Dedication

This book is dedicated to
Janet Agnes Morrison (nee Love)
Ewen Morrison
and Master Dhyan Vimal

Acknowledgements

To those who trusted me with their stories,
and to those who supported and inspired me,
I sincerely thank all of you for participating in the creation.

With love from Love

Epigraph

Let the rose bloom to its highest glory
not only for itself
but for another too
the heart of a friend who loves mankind.

Master Dhyan Vimal
Founder
Friends to Mankind

01

January 1970, the old cliché *Out with the old and in with the new* was resonating with some, while with others the inauguration into the new decade wasn't the least bit significant.

Huxtable had been entertaining the thought of moving downtown Vancouver for several months. It was where he considered all the action to be; he knew he was done with suburbia and the ordinary salon shop banter he was listening to day after day. He delighted in the thought of working in a salon where women of sophistication were his clients and conversations revolved around the latest trends and styles from Toronto and New York. Yes, it was time to leave Riverville.

Standing at the reception desk Huxtable said quietly to his colleague, "George, I've decided I'm going to sell the salon. I wanted you to be the first to know. I'll give you an excellent recommendation to whoever buys it."

With the broom in hand, George was completely non-reactive, "Well, good for you, I'm not too surprised. You've seemed to be leaning towards making a change. You've created a lot of success here in Riverville, I'm sure good fortune will continue your way."

"Success? Why yes, I guess I have been successful here. I'll be honest, it was tough in the beginning, getting used to living in a small town, but I saw it as an opportunity to create something on my own. Its been good, but I am a city boy at heart you know. I started this business because I wanted to be my own boss, now I'm thinking that working for someone else isn't so bad. Leaving all the bill paying and headaches to someone else sounds rather appealing. Now I think just putting in my time and leaving at the end of the day will be heaven. I want to live downtown, I want to feel that pulse again."

"Maybe I'll buy it," considered George.

Startled, Huxtable questioned, "Really? You're 19 years old! You haven't been married more than a year and your wife Marthina is expecting! Life is a lot different as an owner George. Right now you get to come and go and you don't have to be concerned about the overhead or competition moving into town, are you sure you're ready to take over? You haven't had any business experience; the bank may not see you as having enough financial credentials. You have to make money George."

While Huxtable continued to rave on about the dark side of owning a business, George's beliefs were profoundly different.

It was an opportunity. He'd have to create the new; it was something to get excited about; not to negate.

Asking politely George said, "Do you mind if we tell the ladies? I'd like to ask them something."

"Certainly, they have to find out sooner or later."

George leaned the broom up against the wall, turned off a couple of dryers and announced, "Sorry to interrupt you ladies," as he noted they were in a heated discussion about something. "Huxtable has decided to make a change in his life and sell the shop." Startled looks came from everyone all around, before they had a chance to think too much George asked, "Would you still come here if I was to buy it?"

A chorus of *Yeses* instantly confirmed the fact.

"Of course we would," supported Bermudadas. "I know what it's like to take over a business and I'll be here."

"You're so young and you haven't any business experience, but I would give you a chance," pondered Manjira.

Turning to Huxtable he said, "Well, I'll talk it over with Marthina to see how she feels, and then let's sit down and discuss the facts."

Surprised by George's confidence, Huxtable wholeheartedly agreed, "Okay, I've got a price in my head, I won't go lower than $6000. Give me some time to talk to the bank and my lawyer. I need some direction on how to move forward."

George smiled, "Thank you ladies." With that Huxtable and George returned to the reception desk while the women continued their heated conversation about the recent news surrounding the women's liberation movement.

"Getting back to our subject of the day Manjira," stated Bermudadas, "Women pretending to be men is nonsense. It's just creating another idea. Women wearing men's clothes and being masculine is just ridiculous. It's a loss of grace. I'm all for women getting liberated, but as I see it, with the way it's going, all the movement is doing is creating bitterness between both sexes."

Manjira, sitting near the reception desk, argued, "Well, what do you suggest? What brilliant idea do you have for women to gain equality? You've had the luxury of being born and raised into a family not seeping in tradition Bermudadas. In my culture we can't flippantly get divorced the way you want to and then go around partying and flirting with every man we come in contact with. Tradition is engrained into Eastern cultures; we don't even date. Marriage is arranged and yes, I know you Westerners think it's awful, but there are advantages and disadvantages. As I see it those women protesting for liberation are doing what they have to do to get their rights and all the power to them."

Pulling a long, dramatic drag from her long, slim, black and gold cigarette holder, Bermudadas' eyes narrowed and everyone listened intently for her reply. "Well, I'm not saying I know better or the West knows better, that would be rude. I'm just saying that in regards to women's lib, imitating a man is stupid. I believe women around the world need liberation, but not by imitating men. All it's doing is creating hate towards men. It's doing to men what they did to us. I feel this is ugly. I believe women just want to be appreciated for what they are," as she sucked another long drag.

Negar, sitting next to Manjira in the reception area, negotiated, "I can understand what you're saying Bermudadas, but try to …"

Rebecca interrupted Negar, "We have traditional roles here too."

"Please, let me finish Rebecca," said an aggravated Negar. "As I was saying, try to understand that it takes great courage for women in some parts of the world to stand up to their families. It isn't easy. From birth roles are defined. In some countries women wish for their first born to be a son. If they have a daughter they live in fear that their next child will be *just another girl*. You can't imagine the pressure." That subject was close to home as her and Karim weren't able to have children.

"Women must stop being ashamed being born women," Bermudadas stated. "Is there an acceptance among women that to be born a man is luckier than being born a woman? I won't be insulted because of my gender and I'm not here to live out anyone's idea, I'm here to live out my idea."

No one spoke.

"Again," she continued, "All I'm saying, is that I agree women need liberating. I just don't agree it's through imitating men or taking revenge on men. That's creating more violence. I think it would be wiser for a woman to become a wilful woman, not imitate a man. To me the movement comes across as revenge. Women have become the chauvinistic ones; its become aggressive. I feel their anger is perpetuated by the inability to act."

Saffron's dryer shut off, she pushed the cone up and perked up at this morning's topic of conversation.

"Well, in fact," said Rebecca, happy at last to have her say, "Women here in Canada fought for their rights too. Look at the suffrage movement here in Canada, by 1916 women finally got the vote in some provinces. What they did took sheer guts. The ballot created an awareness of equality and through the vote women began to study and practice law. From that moment in time male candidates couldn't rely on attaining votes getting drunk in a bar, suddenly they had to seek approval from women to earn their political positions. I'm fourth generation Canadian, second generation Riverville, and women in my family have always voted since it became the law."

Manjira now taking the floor so everyone could hear her, "It's not just about the right to vote. I'd like to know how a woman, who has been raped in the developing world, where the judicial system is incapable and ill equipped of enforcing the law is able to seek justice? The evidence is generally destroyed and she risks being raped again by the investigating officers. In many nations, those so-called citizens who serve society only pretend to protect and serve the people; quite often they're the felons. Here in Canada there are shelters for women and a justice system that has much more credibility.

When I was 15 my parents sent me to India to live with our relatives for a year, they wanted me to have a taste of where I came from, and believe me - some of those women live in a different world. Not all women of course and every situation is different."

"I don't have all the answers Manjira," Bermudadas offered. "Perhaps as women we have to take responsibility to teach people who we are."

Pondering Rebecca said, "There isn't a women's shelter here in Riverville, I guess we don't need one."

Looking at Rebecca in utter disbelief Bermudadas said, "Just because we don't hear about it doesn't mean violence against women isn't happening in your backyard, get your head out of the sand woman, domestic violence is everywhere."

Then, turning back to Manjira, "And as I see it, anything that is done where your will is violated also constitutes as rape. I'm just trying to make the point that the women's liberation movement isn't the way to gain equality. I don't know about the countries your families come from. I'm sure it's damn tough. As I see it, we must always be in a state of inquiry. And maybe it's time we went beyond our own culture's thinking. We were born women, we will die women; we don't live in anyone's shadow. Women around the world can be so much more. The fact is, from birth feelings and behaviour are labelled masculine and feminine. Girls are hugged more, and boys are raised to be tough. Eventually young girls believe and accept that emotionally they are the weaker sex. Parents have a tendency to have more concern over baby boys dressed in pink than baby girls dressed in blue. This tells me that the male identity is more important than the female identity. Come off it, do girls really want to wear pink ribbons in their hair? I never made Constanze wear pink unless she chose it. And let me ask you this, did Neil Armstrong walk on the moon last summer for men or for humanity? For humanity. Did Sir Edmund Hillary reach the top of Mount Everest for men or for humanity? For humanity. Yes, as individuals they got the joy, but every human being on the planet got to rejoice with them. The whole subject of gender identity needs to be addressed with intelligence. We are supposed to be living in a civilized world. Women need to challenge the conditioned behaviours attributed to them by society."

Saffron, now joining the discussion stated, "Compared to my parent's generation in Korea, my father was ahead of his time. In fact, my mother was adamant that I wasn't raised in a traditional environment like she was. There was a time when she didn't even want to teach me how to cook for fear that that's all I would know. In her day, and my grandmother's day, women did all the cooking and served the men. Women ate when the men were finished, they didn't even eat with their husbands. When I grew up there were household chores; but they were never gender-based chores. My father washed dishes, vacuumed, and naturally carried out other tasks. My brother did domestic work too. I mowed the lawn and piled firewood. We all had jobs, but that's exactly what they were; just jobs. As a child I believed this was normal; that all men made domestic contributions until I went to my friends' homes where their fathers didn't do much around the house. I think we have to be careful not to conclude and divide East and West. My father grew up in a traditional Eastern home, but he never enforced that when he became a father here in Canada."

Lucy who had been sitting quietly in George's chair was all ears. George noticed she was listening carefully as he was putting the final touches on her new, long-layered shag haircut that framed her face so nicely.

"Well, that's rare Saffron," said Manjira. "What you need to understand Bermudadas, and most Western women do too, is that many Asian women of my generation who were born here in Canada are caught between two worlds. We're always balancing the responsibilities and roles of two cultures. On one hand, I've had to battle the stereotypes of outsiders who expect me to be a submissive, obedient Indian woman. And I've had to deal with my mother who demands that I fulfil the role of the dutiful daughter following our culture's values and morals. Then, on the other hand, I've always had to compete with others and be assessed by Western standards. It amazes me how Western writers are experts on Asian women. They're portrayed as charmingly passive, delightfully petite, and sexually accommodating. This notion derives from Western fascination with Asian women humiliated throughout our history by practices such as dowry giving and a life as a courtesan. And finally, when we rise above these stereotypes and excel in education and professional life, we are then dismissed as being too driven by Western values and standards. Our mothers constantly remind us of what they think our priorities should be – that one's home takes priority over one's career. They do not understand our drive to attend competitive universities or plan for a demanding profession, as though they are afraid that no one will marry ambitious, accomplished women. They perpetuate a society that is male-dominated; a society where men provide for the family and women care for the home. Our mothers seem to think we embrace everything Western, but fail to realize that it is possible to balance between two worlds and not feel pressured to choose between them. Our mothers have not had the same experiences and temptations; they need to understand why their advice will never work for us. Accepting a role designated for us will only take us farther away from our self-respect."

"I get what you mean Manjira, sometimes I face similar challenges with my mother," agreed Saffron.

"I used to feel a sense of guilt," Manjira continued, "That no matter how much I achieved, I've disappointed my mother who cannot fully appreciate my achievements. Everyone looks for acceptance and it's hardest when your own mother does not see the reason you are so driven, why you push for goals that you have set for yourself. Some women, Indian friends of mine, choose to stay at home and follow traditional expectations. Conventional feminism stresses the idea of the empowerment of women to give them a choice over their lives. But this choice should include the decision to stay at home and raise a family. I do not contest the decisions of these women who choose this life, but I am rebelling against the expectation that all Indian women, or Asian women for that matter, want this. These stereotypes are not merely harmless misconceptions, they give a false notion of reality and justify irrational expectations. They exert a damaging pressure on women like me who attempt to shatter these stereotypes."

Negar helped to explain, "In the East, from birth many women have bought that they are second-class citizens. As I see it, women must reject that they are sub-species. Why are women apologizing for being born female? That's where I believe change begins. As all of you know, Karim and I can't have children and it is devastating in our culture. Living here takes that pressure off, but over there it's like a terrible taboo."

Manjira stated, "Femininity is a weakness, so many women live in fear." Looking at Lucy she informed her, "In India women live in fear of the blonde woman."

Lucy's eyes bulged at hearing that. She always thought her golden locks where so ordinary, "Really? I can't imagine why."

Bermudadas explained, "Because it's different sweetheart, in some cultures being fair skinned is considered to be better than having dark skin. It's so ridiculous." Turning to Manjira, "Femininity isn't a weakness. Feminine attributed qualities aren't weak. In fact, they need to be made a priority. Femininity extends to the male gender as well. As I see it, feminine qualities such as compassion, joyfulness, and resilience are the future. When these virtues become prevalent in the world and are used with clarity, confidence, and grace; there will be a whole new perspective of life on this planet - for all people of all cultures."

Saffron looked at Bermudadas in a way she never had. "Wow, Bermudadas, that actually makes a lot of sense. I've never thought about all that. When Daisley and I have children I want to have a girl and I want to make sure she has the same opportunities as any boy."

Bermudadas who was on a roll now nodded and continued, "Women need to support women and together create a new awareness, a new universal energy. Women need to take responsibility for their own lives, quit bitching about their men, quit blaming and be a part of their own solution. Let me ask you, have we as women taken responsibility to teach people who we are? And women need to be aware, with freedom comes responsibility. And, not to offend you Manjira or Negar, the way I see it, women need to go beyond their culture's own thinking process. It's now time for women around the world to move away from this past conditioning. I see that as moving forward, not running around shouting, blaming and being angry with men. Bloody hell, I love men!"

"Well ladies," said George, "Perhaps what is really needed is liberation for both men and women."

Everyone looked at George wanting clarification.

"What do you mean George?" asked Saffron.

"It seems to me that perhaps both genders need liberation from the collective mind and all its conditioning. Men and women aren't superior or inferior to each other, they are both unique."

"Now isn't that profound?" nodded Bermudadas in agreement.

Huxtable, precisely on time with his rotations, took the break in conversation as an opportunity to keep everyone on the move and on time. The two men had developed a strong efficient working rapport and Huxtable appreciated and liked that.

"Okay," he ordered, "Rebecca and Lucy you're done. Bermudadas to George's chair, Saffron to mine, Manjira and Negar to the sinks."

Everyone stood up and started shifting and the conversation faded to a lull. As George was finishing up with Lucy he made a proposition.

"Lucy, if everything goes through with the bank, would you be interested in working with me? I could really use the help."

Surprised, she lingered, "What could I possibly do?"

"Well, you could help out at the front desk, answer the phone, book appointments, wash the client's hair, make and serve coffee, and just help out when something needs to be done. Perhaps you could start out part time and after you graduate this spring you could take on full-time hours."

"I'm not sure. My father works full time and I have a lot of responsibilities at home between him and my younger sister Karen. Maybe I should ask my father first."

Sensing her indecisiveness George mentioned, "Why don't you check with him and let me know?"

She sat expressionless, "But it should be okay. I hope I won't let you down."

Negar piped up, "This could be something totally new for you Lucy. What a great opportunity, you can make a few dollars."

Agreeing full heartedly Rebecca stated, "Oh yes and working with George you'll have a lot fun." Lucy had remained so quiet through Bermudadas and Manjira's dialogue that Rebecca wanted to let her know she wasn't forgotten. She had known Lucy's mother Pearl; she had died from breast cancer. Like everyone else in the room she used to come here every Friday morning. All the women felt compassion for Pearl's two daughters Lucy and Karen. Her own daughter Elizabeth and Karen were classmates in elementary school and had become good friends. Even at eleven years old Karen was confident and out going while seventeen-year-old Lucy was melancholy and submissive. Over the years Pearl had brought the girls in to get their hair done too, she was pleased that Lucy continued the tradition. Rebecca felt it would help in the healing of her loss. In fact, she remembered the day when Pearl had told Lucy, *When you're feeling sad, go get your hair done and you'll walk out as a different person, it will help.*

Over last month's Christmas holidays Rebecca knew Lucy's father, Dan Cassidy, had spent more time in the Riverville Pub with his friends than with his young daughters. Plus, she knew for a fact, that a Lions Club Christmas hamper had been delivered to their home so she knew there wasn't a lot of money in the family for extras.

By chance her husband Lance and Elizabeth had delivered the hamper to the Cassidy home. Elizabeth was startled when Karen had opened the front door - both were surprised at the unexpected meeting. Elizabeth had later reported to her mom that the Cassidy home seemed like a cemetery. *Well dear*, she advised, *don't say anything to her at school as she may feel uncomfortable.*

Coming back to the moment Rebecca added, "And as an added perk you'll get free haircuts!"

"Okay," Lucy answered quietly and nothing more was said.

Driving home that evening in his 1961 Mercury Montcalm, with Otis Redding's *Sittin' On the Dock of the Bay* playing on his eight-track stereo, George reflected on his future and his clients. They were certainly an interesting bunch of women; different ages, different belief systems, and all intertwined with different cultures – and that is the beauty of this country he thought. The ones who really stuck with him were: Bermudadas, the experience junkie who needed the outside world to stimulate her; Rebecca, devoutly religious and wanting to help everyone; Negar, the peacemaker; Saffron, the artist in love; Manjira, the leader who loved being the authority, demanded attention and constant approval; and Lucy, who appeared to be deeply troubled.

"Well," he mused to himself, "What a year of drastic changes. I left Saskatchewan, moved to the West Coast, went to hair dressing school, met Marthina, got married, and now I'm going to own my own salon and soon be a father."

George then reflected back to his first day on the job; Bermudadas had been his first client ...

02

"Damn, you look like you just got out of high school."

"Well, that's not too far from the truth Ms. Beppolini," he said smiling.

"Just call me Bermudadas darling, all the men do, don't they Huxy?"

Huxtable cringed at hearing *Huxy* it was so degrading to his breeding and esteemed heritage; however, he never dared to tell her.

Not waiting for a reply she informed George, "Now, just so you understand, I see my hair as an accessory. I keep my hair long and I like my fringe to be long and feminine looking. I get compliments all the time about my long black locks. Men love my hair and I love men!"

A little over an hour later Bermudadas' jet black hair was shampooed, set, and dried. George's first client had had no inhibitions about sharing the details of her private life. She was 33 years old, conceived while her Italian-Canadian parents were on their honeymoon in Bermuda, thus Bermudadas, born in Toronto, married at 18, now separated from her husband, and her 15-year-old daughter Constanze was referred to as the kid. Her parents still didn't know she was separated. *What's the point in stressing them out? Besides mother always said, there will be no divorce in this family.* She spoke Italian and French, played the piano and for a while considered singing as a career, loved to cook and entertain, drove the latest '69 Mustang, and loved to party. She had been the owner of the local travel agency for five years, and before that she had been an airline hostess for Ward Air where she met her husband Richard, a pilot.

"I'm heading up to ski at Whistler Mountain this weekend, I'm leaving right after work, it's going to be fabulous!" she announced to everyone in the salon - which included: Huxtable at the reception desk who was collecting payment from Rebecca Barnicot his first client; Saffron Kim, the mayor's wife who was thumbing through the Eaton's Christmas catalogue while waiting patiently for George; and Negar, Huxtable's second client who was sitting in Huxtable's chair waiting for the final touches.

Everyone perked up as her voice carried throughout the entire salon and above the radio, "I'm dating a ski coach, he's a classy bastard. Last weekend we went to see *Butch Cassidy and the Sundance Kid.* What at movie! Redford and Newman, what a pair of handsome outlaws!" Laughing she said, "This weekend the kid has the house to herself, she'll probably have a rocker of a party, the little bugger better have the place cleaned up before I get back!"

Rebecca, a devout Baptist, still standing at the reception desk had years ago considered changing her regular Friday morning appointment time to avoid Bermudadas. She considered her raunchy, vulgar, and appalling. Instead, she decided she would try to save Bermudadas' soul, so she kept her regularly scheduled time with a secret intent to convert her.

"Bermudadas, do you really need to use such coarse language? Referring to Constanze as a little bugger just isn't loving." She wanted to manipulate Bermudadas into seeing her abrasive personality, besides it just wasn't right for a woman to use such foul language. She knew she could change her and sooner or later she'd be going to church with her, after all, it was for her own good.

Bermudadas peeled with laughter, "Oh relax Becs, of course I love the kid, I just want to encourage her to live in the present, have fun, be spontaneous, we never know how long we're going to be here.

After she graduates from high school I've been encouraging her to go backpacking in Europe and see the world. She can get there for free through her father's benefits, so why not? By the way how are your two twin buggers and lil' miss Elizabeth?"

Although Rebecca was 40, seven years older than Bermudadas, her twins Rachel and Keith were in the same grade as Constanze. They had grown up together. They had gone to the same schools, were in the same plays so it was circumstances that had brought them together reflected Rebecca, it certainly wasn't choice. Bermudadas was the only person she allowed to call her Becs; it created a bond and was part of the long-term plan. Cringing again at the foul language she answered, "They're busy with their studies, they're both on the honour role, and busy leading our church's youth group. I want my children to learn to be generous, thoughtful, and attentive to others. "

"Bloody hell woman, don't you Baptists ever have any fun? You wear your plain conservative clothes, flat practical shoes, no make up, no dancing – don't you ever dance, celebrate life? If you want to be religious that's perfectly fine, that's your choice, that's your personal belief, just don't trespass my beliefs. You keep on polishing your halo and I'll keep on celebrating! I grew up with next to nothing, so I'm making up for it now. I don't deny myself anything. I am unashamedly living the good life. And let me tell you something, because I know what it means to be poor, I'm grateful for everything I have today. Anyway, tell your twins my daughter is having a party this weekend, send them over for an initiation into real teenage life!"

"I know you see our lives as boring, but in our house we do have some wine from time to time. After all," she said with a twinkle in her eyes, "Wine is the first miracle!"

Everyone had a laugh and Huxtable added, "Maybe you'll even be out dancing one weekend Rebecca!"

"You just never know Huxtable!" she answered. Then, looking at Bermudadas, "I just don't understand why you haven't told your parents that you're separated. What happens when they call or want to come out here for a visit?"

"Oh they send birthday cards to Richard and when they call I say he's in the shower or at work. His family knows we're separated, but they live in North Vancouver, so they're not going to be running into my parents any time soon. He lives in Richmond now, close to the airport, and he sees the kid on weekends if he's not flying. He's a good father."

"I just don't get it. It's teaching your daughter how to lie."

"No, it's teaching my daughter not to hurt people. If my parents found out they'd be devastated. They'd be so concerned, *Who is going to take care of her?* My mother won't sleep and my dad will have to deal with her. That's their generation. I can take care of myself, but they don't see the world like that. My intent is from a place of love, I'm perfectly capable to take care of myself and the kid, I don't want them to worry."

"Well, it just all seems a little odd," as she reached for her coat on the coat rack.

George, more interested in finishing up with his first client than all the bantering and personal information, continued to backcomb her hair.

Suddenly, "That's not how you do it school boy!" Bermudadas' humour dampened as she grabbed the brush from his hands. "Watch and learn, this is how Huxy does it. You don't know what you're doing. You're taking way too long. I'm supposed to be at the agency by now."

Everyone froze - except George. Huxtable suddenly thought he was going to lose George on his first day.

Surprising everyone he said, "Well Bermudadas, the universe is always perfecting itself, so I shall personally work on that too."

Putting the brush down a startled Bermudadas answered, "Well, that's that. See you next Friday school boy."

From the coat rack Rebecca coaxed, "Hurry up Bermudadas, I'll walk to the agency with you, I'm headed that way too."

A short while later, after Rebecca and Bermudadas' departure, Negar looked up from writing her check out at the reception desk and offered, "You know George, Bermudadas is quite brash, but there's a sweetness under that armour. To be honest, I like being around her. She's so energetic and lively, she's living life to the fullest and she's never afraid to try something new."

"Oh sure," a carefree George replied from the sink while wrapping Saffron's shoulder length black hair in a towel, "I don't take anything personally."

"There's Negar, our peacekeeper," came a sarcastic voice through the door. It was Manjira Das. "I'm so glad I missed that trollop this morning. Who is she sleeping with this week?"

"Now Manjira," said Negar as they met at the coat rack, "She's human like the rest of us and she's had her challenges in life, it's not for us to judge. And, quite frankly, you've made a lot of money from all the contacts she's given you." Not waiting for the nasty reply she knew would be forth coming she opened the door and called out, "See you all next Friday. The cheque is on the desk Huxtable."

"Thanks Negar, see you next week," he answered.

The door closed and Manjira declared, "She'll change her tune when Bermudadas ends up sleeping with her husband."

Huxtable nodded in agreement as that's what one did with Manjira; heading for the sinks she introduced herself to George in passing.

"My name is Manjira Das. My husband and I are the owners and operators of Das Catering Company. Are you married? If you ever need catering for a wedding or any other occasion, I'm the one to talk too. We have the freshest food; our presentations are all about style. We can accommodate small parties from four and up; we've catered everything from small company lunches to huge traditional weddings. For larger parties we have rented china and serving staff available. We have a custom menu of both Eastern and Western cuisine, or we can mix and match."

Absorbing all her information George politely answered, "Let's see what the future holds, thanks for telling me. Okay, to the chair Ms. Kim!"

Persisting Manjira advertised, "We're the best there is and the only one you can trust in this town when it comes to catering. Our food and service is dependable. When we moved to this town I didn't care what business we went into as long as we made money, the bottom line is turning a profit and making money. Right Huxtable?"

"Of course Manjira, so you'll be paying your tab today?" he teased.

"I'll pay my tab next week, I forgot my check book," she retorted.

As Saffron was getting settled in George's chair he said, "Now Ms. Kim, is there anything particular you'd like done this morning?"

"Please call me Saffron, my Korean name is Eunmi. In my fourth grade art class I decided to change my name to Saffron. I was so stubborn, I didn't answer to anyone unless they called me Saffron, and I just love the colour saffron. Everyone thought it was just a fad, but it just felt right, so I changed my name myself," she answered.

"Why not? Good for you. I heard you're an artist."

"Yes, I'm an art major, my medium is acrylics. I'm passionate about art history and anything to do with art. I love colour, as I'm sure you can tell from my clothes! I love pop art, Andy Warhol, the fashion of the sixties, mini-skirts and hot pants are just so much fun to wear, I wear them all the time. I design and make many of my own clothes too; I want everything I do to be an expression of my love for colour. I've been told I'm quite Bohemian, I take that as a compliment!"

Interrupting them from the sink Manjira persisted bluntly, "Are you married George? Have any kids?"

He smiled, "Well, yes, I'm a newlywed. My wife Marthina and I have been married for almost five months." Getting back to Saffron, he asked again, "So, what will it be today Saffron?"

George and Saffron started to cultivate a client-stylist relationship and not having met any Korean-Canadians before, George was curious as to how Saffron's family ended up in small-town Riverville.

"Well, in 1920 shortly after the independence rallies in Korea, my father managed to get to Hawaii where he became a plantation worker. He wanted to get away from the Japanese occupation of Korea, which all began in 1910. Plus, he's the second son and in Korea where birth determines a man's station in life, he chose to get away from the rigid hierarchy. Once my mother was allowed to join him, they moved to California and then they immigrated to Canada just before

WWII. Sometimes they suffered from racism; however, they always believed one day the war would be over and life would still be better in North America. They believed all their challenges were opportunities."

"Wow, good for them, that's remarkable. Where does your father work now?"

"My father is a landscape architect, he has an office in town, but he works all over the Lower Mainland. I'm the first generation in my family to be born in Canada, my younger brother is living and working in Toronto right now. At first my parents were very strict with us, they said we were to speak English only in our home. My father believed if we were going to make Canada our new home we needed to be fluent in the language. It wasn't until I was eight or nine that I started to study Korean. We went to classes after church on Sundays. I speak enough to get by; I wish I was more fluent. My husband Daisley has been studying Korean ever since we met, he's still working on it, he always does his best to speak Korean with my parents."

"Daisley, that's an interesting name, I don't think I've heard it before," mused George.

"Yes, many people say that. His full name is Daisley Michael. His father's family originally came from England; actually, both sides of his family are from England. He's the new mayor. I'm not sure if you know, he's only been in office for a couple of months."

"No, I didn't know. Good for him, I'm sure life in politics will be challenging."

"Definitely, but he feels up for it, he really loves his job. Most people weren't in favour of our mixed marriage, plus he's almost ten years older than me, but we're in love! And when I told him before we got married that I wanted to keep my last name, he was so understanding, it was perfectly fine with him. He said whatever makes me happy makes him happy. For as I see it, in the past women were always recognized through being someone's wife or someone's daughter. I chose not to take Daisley's last name because I want to be me, not an extension of being someone's wife. Many people were shocked, but Daisley understood. He loves me."

"Oh please Saffron," moaned Manjira. "You're just 25 years old, what do you know about love? Wait a few years and then talk to me about love and your perfect husband."

"I believe in lasting love Manjira and I am devoted to communicating my belief through my art. Many artists use art as a therapy and end up selling misery. I want to convey love, to provoke people to open their hearts. As I see it, if you love someone, in your presence you allow him or her to be them self. When I paint, I'm giving a piece of me. I'm sharing. And besides, look at Negar and Karim. Negar is just so, so sophisticated, she's a goddess. She dresses so elegantly and has such poise and grace. She's tall and slender, and her Mary Tyler Moore hairstyle is always perfect. And it's not just her looks, she's just so nice, I just adore her. She's so perfect and so unpretentious. They've been together for years and they're still together. They have something truly special."

"That's because he's always away on business," came a sour answer.

George, interested in the cultural diversity of his clients asked, "How did they end up in Canada?"

As she was settling down into the stylist chair next to Saffron, with Huxtable hovering over her, Manjira supplied the answer for she was anxious to be the authority of the moment, "Karim first came from Iran to Vancouver as a university student. He's at least ten years older than her too. I think he studied finance or business. Anyway, after the new 1962 Canadian immigration laws, he returned with Negar because of the potential investment opportunities. My parents came from India after the First World War to make money, nothings changed; we all came here looking for a better life. Anyway, Karim deals in Persian carpets, silks, furniture, and I don't know what all else. There are very few people from Iran in the Vancouver area; most Iranians immigrate to Montreal. He's very successful, I think he does well because his stuff is unique." Something switched in her brain as she studied at herself in the mirror, "Huxtable, don't I look good with these new pearl earrings? They go so well with this dark blue Chanel suit. I bought them at the new Lougheed Mall that just opened, don't they just ooze success?"

Not waiting for an answer, she self-admired herself in the mirror while Huxtable stifled the real answer he wanted to give.

Later on, with Saffron under the dryer, George lit a cigarette between clients and took in the pulse of the salon. He felt quite at ease, everything felt right. He was going to enjoy working here. After a short pause, he stubbed out his cigarette. Feeling revived, he kept busy sweeping the floor, making and serving coffee, and pushing the magazine trolley to the ladies under the dryers until his next client showed up. He had checked the appointment calendar and discovered her name was Lucy Cassidy.

Wearing worn out runners with frayed laces on her feet, Lucy was dressed in a drab, brown polyester button-down shirt tucked into her high-wasted blue bell-bottom jeans. She sat with her shoulders bent; face frozen in misery. Intuition told George this one was troubled and complicated; he knew he'd have to draw a conversation out of her.

"So, Lucy, where do you work?" as he started to comb out her shoulder length blonde locks.

"I don't. I'm in high school, grade 12."

"Oh, no classes today?" as he tightened the collar of the plastic plum coloured apron around her neck.

"Yeah, but I always skip Friday afternoons. No one cares and the classes are boring. What's the point in going to school anyway? I'm stuck in this deadbeat town."

Somewhat surprised that she had concluded her life situation at such a young age George said, "Things may seem a little challenging now; however, you're young and life is really all about choice Lucy. I moved here from Saskatchewan, I'm just a few years older than you myself, and if I can move somewhere new and create a new life you can too."

Her vacant eyes told George there was more going on than just boredom; however, he suggested, "High school isn't the easiest time, perhaps after you graduate you'll see things differently."

"I doubt it," came a sceptical answer.

"Well Lucy, this is how I see the world. Sometimes life wants to teach us something, so existence throws us a test. We choose to fall or to rise. It's all about how we rise. Being a teenager is a big time of changes and sometimes we don't have the tools for today's world. You can become more than you think. We're all possibilities. Lucy, don't you see that you're a possibility?"

"A possibility for what?"

"Let me tell you a story. Do you know where Bali is?"

"Yes, it's an island, part of Indonesia, we studied it in World Geography last semester."

"Okay, well on the island of Bali there is a unique type of bumblebee. The locals use the bee as a parable, a story to teach a life lesson. It's quite big, maybe twice the size of the ones we have here. Anyway, its wings aren't very big in comparison to its body. The locals say by the laws of physics the bee's wings shouldn't be strong enough to carry its body - yet it buzzes around like it's the king of bees, it doesn't know it has any restrictions. What I'm saying is, you don't know your strength yet, or how high you can fly. Life can be quite beautiful, and it's all about choice. Just be patient and give yourself some time."

Silence descended through out the room, only the hum of the traffic going by could be heard. Huxtable, Manjira, Saffron, and Lucy all stared at George and listened carefully; they were all drawn into his story telling.

He continued compassionately, "Align yourself with living not with destruction. Maybe start with this … ask yourself, Am I existing or am I transforming? And see what answer you get."

Manjira's commanding voice broke in, "He's right Lucy." Turning to George, "I keep telling her she's got her whole life a head of her and to quit whining." Then, turning to Huxtable she reminded him, "Make sure you tell any new clients that my office is just down the street."

"Manjira," weary from years of her bulldog personality he answered, "I have your business cards right here next to the phone, I always send them to you, and you know that."

03

By the time the cherry blossoms along High Street were blooming at the end of March - the deal was sealed. Huxtable was living his dream downtown Vancouver and George was now the owner. New gold lettering, *George's Salon*, adorned the front door. After receiving the okay from her father, he hired Lucy part time and she agreed to work full time once she graduated from high school in just a couple of months. Negar took over managing the books and he got into a rhythm of staggering his clients so he didn't have to hire another stylist right away.

On his first day as the new owner he stood in the middle of the salon breathing in the combined chemistry of yesterday's perm solutions and cigarette smoke. The shop was wide and deep. The savvy black and gold décor oozed style. The natural daylight streaming in from the front ceiling to floor windows balanced well with the florescent lighting. To the left of the entrance was the black faux leather reception desk with a glass countertop exhibiting the latest array of hairpieces. To the right a black arborite coffee table surrounded by a few strategically placed chairs and a steel coat rack met the client's needs when they first entered the salon. Looking towards the back, light artificial wooden panelling with posters exhibiting the latest chic hairstyles covered the walls. On the right there were three work stations complete with big round mirrors mounted on the walls. Between the mirrors, glass shelving held bottles of specialized hair products in neat rows with all the labels facing forward in perfect unison. And at the very back were two matching black sinks with white towels neatly folded on glass shelving above; however, the piece d' la resistance was to the left - three of the most modern hairdryers. "Sweet ..." George whistled.

The cone shaped dryers attached to the reclining black vinyl chairs were the industry's latest models: they even had ashtrests built into the armrests.

Although outwardly George carried confidence and excitement of becoming an entrepreneur, inwardly he had moments of panic. His wife Marthina was due to have their first child in the fall and he was anxious about making enough money to support his family and keep the business sustained. Finally, he came to the conclusion that he had acted on the belief that he could do it and now he had to surrender and trust that all would be okay. He had done all he could do, and everyday he was aware of what he had to do, so now it was time to rest into his new life and responsibilities and have some fun.

His first week as shop owner was a celebration – all week long clients brought in new plants, chocolates, they offered encouragement and congratulations while promising to bring in new clients. And on Friday morning Rebecca's homemade bran muffins and Manjira's catering leftovers continued to sustain the ambiance of merriment.

"Well George, you did it," announced Manjira. "Did everyone see the new magazine rack I bought for George?" She held it up for all to see, it was a shinny brass plated magazine stand. "I thought it would be perfect next to the table in the waiting area, then there's not so much clutter on the table."

Seated in one of the dryer chairs Rebecca sarcastically voiced what everyone felt, "Yes, Manjira we all saw it and we all think you're a kind, wonderful giver."

Immediately picking up on her provoking tone Manjira glared at her and asked, "Well, what did you give George?"

"Toilet paper!" answered Rebecca. "Toilet paper?" repeated Manjira in utter disbelief.

Everyone was laughing and George added, "I must say it was a bit of a surprise, but she did bring in a big box of toilet paper. What a great gift!"

"Well, I just wanted to give you something practical, 24 rolls!" she added, still laughing.

Manjira laughed a long and said, "Well George, the shop is yours and now you'll make all the money."

Feeling compelled to define his beliefs on success George eyeballed her and said, "Success isn't all about making money Manjira. There are many ways to measure success. As I see it society's understanding of success is dualistic; rich and poor, it's always about profit. The world is divisive due to society's definition of success. Many, many times people have been exploited for another's attainment of success. For many people, success is used to try and dissolve their past. I've never thought much about how society measures success. If I may, I'd like to quote Gandhi, *The world has enough for every man's need, but not enough for every man's greed."*

She retorted, "Well, I work to make money, and I'll do what I have to do to make it. The world is a hostile, hard place George."

"That may be your view Manjira; however, I choose to participate in creating right success and sharing my success with others. War and violence feed the ego and nations at war celebrate different ideas of success. Just look at Vietnam right now. If I want to become rich, as I see it, I must play a role in someone else's life to become rich. For me, one measure of success is the twinkle in my clients' eyes when they leave the shop," he explained with a grin. "Now that is abundance!"

As her hair was done and she was feeling isolated by everyone in the shop, Manjira was ready to leave in defiance, "Well, I share my success. My staff receives presents."

"Yes," said Rebecca, "Believe me, we all know, but that's all a big ego trip Manjira, you always make sure everyone knows when you've given them something. You're giving to make yourself look good. That's not giving."

"Well, that may be how you see it, but my staff appreciate it. On that note I'm off to work. I have three people working full time, three on call and I contribute to the local economy, so don't think I don't do my part. I pay them first and myself last so I'll have to put today's charges on my account George. I'll pay you at the end of the month." And she was out the door, almost running over Saffron at the entrance, before anyone could reply.

A few moments after she left Rebecca commented, "That woman is just so blunt, I don't know how her staff put up with her. My neighbour Joy works for her; she supervises for Manjira and she's always doing things that aren't a part of her job description. Joy does what has to be done, but I tell her Manjira takes advantage of her. It seems to me that Manjira lacks consideration for them. Joy said she's low on her own accountability, yet she demands it from everyone who works for her. And, listen to this, Joy told me Manjira pays her bills late on purpose, can you imagine? Then Joy has to deal with all the angry phone calls and her staff is made to feel like beggars on payday. She's a power tripper. To quote Abraham Lincoln, *Nearly all men can stand adversity, but if you want to test a man's character, give him power.* That woman shouldn't have any power over another."

Negar mediated from her seated position at the dryer, "Well, maybe Joy should speak up, I'm sure Manjira would listen. Try to understand she's coming from a different perspective and perhaps she's doing what she has to do to survive. We don't own a business, so I don't feel it's right for us to judge her." She had a cigarette resting on the ashtray, George's receipts spread on the footstool, and the ledger balanced on her lap. She had happily offered to manage George's books. She had gotten into a regular routine of working on the tallies after George had finished her hair. Plus, she enjoyed the extra time in the salon. Her name was on the school district's substitution list, but she didn't get a lot of hours teaching, so it was a nice way to spend her time. She didn't like to be alone in her house day after day.

Jolting her back to the present moment, Rebecca countered, "Well, maybe so, but the way she bullies people just isn't okay."

"I know, I agree, maybe just try to see if from her side."

"And I can't believe she has an account here. I know it's not my business, but why can't she pay every week like the rest of us?" Rebecca injected.

Not wanting to engage in a confrontational dialogue, Negar consciously changed the subject, "Who knows ... anyway, George, you need to do a better job of keeping track of your expenses. I need more information with all your receipts. You can help me out by writing on the back exactly what the money was spent on. And I can't seem to find Ned's last invoice."

"Okay, thanks Negar. I'll take a look for it at home, or maybe it's in the car. And by the way, what's my allowance this week?"

"You get ..." suddenly Negar realized he was teasing. "You get the same as you always do - money for coffee and cigarettes! Before I leave you need to sign a few checks for me and I'll drop them off at the post office."

A curious Lucy asked, "How do you know so much about book keeping Negar?" as she guided Saffron to the sink.

"As you know I'm an English teacher Lucy, but with Karim away so much I take care of all our household bills and with his business background he's taught me an efficient way of bookkeeping. And by the way, you're doing a wonderful job of keeping the daily log in order, you're lucky to have her George, she's caught on fast."

"Oh, thanks Negar," blushed Lucy, not comfortable with receiving compliments.

At that moment in waltzed Bermudadas wearing a new colourful jersey wrap- a-round dress with a matching scarf tied around her neck, big gold hoop earrings and cork platform shoes, "Three months into the '70's and I'm loving the new decade, it's wonderful!"

"Go on, just tell us what is happening Bermudadas. Get it done with, " piped up an irritated Rebecca as she stood up and moved from the drier to George's chair. She was getting so annoyed with Bermudadas' grand visions and story telling. *She's got such a romantic idea of the world* she thought to herself, *She's never been committed to one career or one man, what a way to live life*, and she, Rebecca, disapproved so much. She had finally given up on getting her to church.

"Well, Mrs. Volunteer Queen," Bermudas was quick to pick up on Rebecca's cynical query, "Last year we had Woodstock, the first man on the moon, the world is full of fun and opportunity. And do you know what the Trudeau government introduced on January 1st?"

Not waiting for an answer she continued, "A new divorce act, now that makes me happy! Mr. Trudeau has got my vote for as long as he's in politics!"

"What has changed?" asked George, as Rebecca was getting comfortable in his chair.

"Well, before 1968 the only grounds for divorce were adultery or cruelty. Now, there doesn't need to be a fault on either side, so finally Richard and I can get divorced and I can move forward. By the end of the summer I'll be legally single again! Look out all the single men!" she stated with grand elatedness.

"As if not being divorced has inhibited you Bermudadas," stated Rebecca. The celebration energy was sliding downhill fast. "And are you finally going to tell your parents?"

"Now that's just nasty Becs, and no, I won't be telling my parents," retorted Bermudadas. "You know, society is happy when you're in a relationship but when you're divorced society is the enemy. I made a choice - either have the guts to do what was right for me or remain miserable and attempt to live up to society's expectations. It's a tragedy that everyone always wants to fit into society."

"So true," said Negar, "Women seem to need outside approval to be women. If they're married then quite often they're conditioned to believe that they'll be more accepted into society."

"And that's just sad, I consider the marriage to be doomed if a woman is not herself. Why would a woman be in a relationship if she's not authentic? What kind of a life would that be?" said Bermudadas. "I'm not for divorce. I am for love. Let me make that perfectly clear. I'm not suggesting that every woman who is unhappy in her marriage should pursue divorce. But really, look at how many women remain in damaging relationships, it's brutal."

Lucy looked over at Bermudadas, an instant cloud shrouded her and George noticed.

"Well, you just seem so flippant in your relationships," ridiculed Rebecca.

"You and your purity, we all know you want to save the world. You're such a wanna-be martyr; do you do everything because you really want to help others? Sometimes your kindness seems to be nothing more than an ego trip to me, *Look what I do everyone*. You have this built in philosophy of suffering, you want everyone to think you are sacrificing so much for the rest of the world. As I see it, I will never do anything that goes against my life force. All of us should have the courage to live by our hearts, do whatever makes us happy, not prescribe to society."

"Ladies, ladies," injected Negar before Rebecca could reply.

Then suddenly Bermudadas remembered something. Pulling a wooden oval plaque from her purse she said, "Here George, read this!"

Accepting the plaque he read it out loud, "Don't take life too seriously, you'll never get out of it alive anyhow."

Everyone laughed and George remarked, "Thank you Bermudadas, why don't you do the honours and find a place to hang it up?"

"I will do just that George!"

Putting the plaque down on the reception desk, Bermudadas started scanning the walls for a place to hang it while Negar continued, "Back to what you said on divorce Bermudadas…"

"Yes," she answered, still scanning.

"In Iran divorce is so rare. And if a woman does get granted a divorce she's then considered easy and men see them as nothing more than targets just to have sex."

"Really?" asked an innocent Saffron. "What if she's been abused or her husband has had an affair?"

"That's just how it is, you have to understand it's such a different culture. There is a saying in Farsi, I'm not sure if the translation is accurate, it's something like, *You go to your husband's house in a white dress and you leave in a white dress.*"

Everyone looked at Negar with an odd look, "I don't get it," Lucy said quietly as she wrapped a towel around Saffron's head.

"Well, when you're married you wear a white dress, so, when you arrive at your in- law's house to spend the rest of your life you're dressed in white. Then, when you die, your body is wrapped in white fabric when you leave."

A chorus of *Ohhsss*, followed.

"The parable means you're there for life. Let me explain, in many Eastern cultures, the woman must leave her family and all the security she has grown up with to live with her husband and her new in-laws. That takes sheer guts. The changes for her are profound. She is now under the mercy of a new mother-in-law. Her husband remains in his comfort zone, his life situation isn't nearly as life altering."

"Well, that culture certainly wouldn't work for you would it Bermudadas? What happened to the ski coach? You haven't said much about him recently," Rebecca asked.

Not emotionally reacting to Rebecca's question she answered, "Oh, he started seeing a racer chaser. Some floozy who brags about all the ski racers she's slept with. One day he's telling me we can't get too serious and that we need to keep things quiet because he's sorting out his own divorce, then I find out he's openly dating her. Well, it's his karma."

"What is karma?" asked Lucy looking at Bermudadas.

"It's a self-addressed envelope sweetheart. Any wrong act is going to come back and kick you right square in the ass."

"Don't change the subject, so what exactly is your definition of relationship Bermudadas?" mused Rebecca, who was clearly feeling bitter with Bermudadas because she had rebuked all her efforts to change, "This should be interesting."

"Actually," Bermudadas continued, "It was more a case of him not offering information, so in his mind he's done nothing wrong. He means nothing to me."

"Now suddenly he's nothing is he? Before he was everything. All you ever do is blame Bermudadas, you don't take any responsibility for your role in anything - yet you profess women need to stop blaming men. You can be such a hypocrite," Rebecca was fed up with being soft and kind with her.

Negar piped up once again to soften the air, "There's no reason for everyone to get so upset. Love and relationships is a big can of worms for us all. We're never taught what it all means, we only start learning once we're in it. It's not as though there's a course called, Right Relating 101!"

"Love. What is love?" asked George. "Well, ladies before we engage in that dialogue, as I'm sure it will be lengthy, Lucy can you please escort Bermudadas to the sink? You're a little early Bermudadas, once I finish with Saffron I still have to comb out Rebecca."

"That's fine George. Hey, how is Marthina surviving being pregnant?"

"She's just fine, thanks for asking."

"Good, tell her I say hi and don't hesitate to let me know if she needs anything."

"Will do, thanks Bermudadas. Well Rebecca, to answer your question on behalf of the male gender, as I see it the possibilities to define love are as diverse as the universe. Movies, novels, music, poetry, and art differentiate love through the passion of the director, the writer, the musician," and looking at Saffron, "the artist. Do you have the guts to define it? I don't."

Saffron innocently agreed airily, "It's not so simple. We're all at love's mercy. There are many different types of love: romantic love; love thy neighbour; and friendship love. And then there are the connotations of: in love, to love, or for love."

"Let me throw this out there ladies, I think the word love is used too flippantly. Men have misused the word to get women into bed and women have misused the word to make men feel guilty."

"Now just hold on George," bellowed Burmudadas.

Gathering up all the receipts to allow Saffron the drier Negar calmly said, "I think there is a lot of truth to that, we are all responsible for our actions. I have to agree with George, both genders have abused each other."

No one, except George, noticed that Negar's words stung Lucy. She wrapped Bermudadas' hair in a towel, excused herself, and went to the bathroom while everything and everyone carried on.

"Okay … Saffron, under the dryer, Rebecca it's your turn," smiled George as he spun the chair around to face her.

"For a young man you talk as though you have a lot of experience regarding love," challenged Rebecca. "Actually," she continued, "Other than knowing you're from Saskatchewan, we really don't know that much about you George."

"Well, my ancestors are from Russia."

"Russia!" exclaimed Rebecca, "How interesting. Where?"

"Leninakan, but the city has gone through a couple of name changes. It used to be Gyumri; when my relatives left it was called Alexandrapol and today it is known as Leninakan. The area is known as Armenia and it became a part of Russia in 1813. When my ancestors came to Canada they ended up in Saskatchewan and started homesteading."

"It's so interesting how we all ended up here," said Saffron.

"Yes, indeed it is," agreed George. Then he continued, "Most of us, at one time in our life, have had our hearts broken Rebecca. Women who have been dumped in relationships believe that they have lost love. Men who have been dumped in relationships feel they've lost their manhood. Women cry so much about giving so much. Men measure success, women measure love. Women claim they can love more than men, but women also have the capability to take more. It appears to me that the women who claim to love, who claim they are loving, end up taking shamelessly from their partners."

"Did you hear that Bermudadas?" cackled Rebecca. "Taking shamelessly from their partners. I believe in a traditional relationship. I will never leave my husband and he will never leave me."

"And you're so sure of that are you Becs? Longevity; do you honestly think your husband will stay with you forever? Is there any guarantee?

No relationship is secure and that's the reality," countered Bermudadas who stood up and walked over to sit in the salon chair next to Rebecca.

In her mind a bitter Rebecca thought, *As long as you stay away from him.*

Quietly, Lucy reappeared and began fussing about with the magazine trolley and making coffee. George noticed her re-entry. He kept trying to solve the Lucy mystery of Dr. Jekyll and Mr. Hyde. He had decided to sit back and not be intrusive on her private life; she'd open up in time he figured. He knew she was troubled, it was more than losing her mother, but until he knew the facts he didn't want to assume anything.

Negar interrupted his thoughts, "Well, as I see it, in the beginning love will do many things to you and in that knowledge understanding, compassion, and tolerance take on new definitions. When Karim is away I can get very lonely. When we first came to Canada, he wasn't away that often. I just wish he was around the house more, it gets so lonely."

"Well, in some relationships that would be a good thing!" laughed Bermudadas as she lit up a cigarette. "I believe you must love, respect, and honour yourself before attempting to love another. Be happy yourself, don't look for someone to find happiness."

"Listen to the wizened one! I guess that's come from all your experience!" chided Rebecca.

"I believe my happiness is my responsibility. And as I see it, taking on the responsibility to make another happy must be a horror."

"Have you ever been alone Bermudadas?" asked Rebecca.

Not sure if the question was authentic or a slight, everyone awaited an answer, "I don't mourn being alone," she stated. "I made a choice. I did what was right for me. I don't need someone to feel complete."

George stepped in, "I have met women whose parents literally ostracized them from their families because they felt the community was judging the entire family. I find it incomprehensible that parents and extended family members turned their back on their daughter for choosing to escape a bad marriage. No one seemed to ask the women how they felt – their families were more concerned with an apparent loss of face. They valued their neighbour's reactions more than their own daughter's safety, mental health, or happiness. Can you imagine how alone those women felt? Why do people use society to define who they are?"

Bermudadas added, "Well, I know my parents would be horrified. The fact is they would be concerned what the neighbours would think, so that's another reason I just don't bother to tell them. I will never understand why people put so much emphasis into what other people think. My happiness supersedes anything society dictates. Does a woman get married because of love, or because family and society demand that she get married?"

"I think that depends a lot on where you come from and how you're raised," offered Negar.

George threw out another question, "Are people more interested in the idea of marriage or are they really interested in relating; being in union with another?"

Rebecca stated, "I don't know, but from what I see partial definitions of love are propagated in movies, in novels, in daytime soap operas and seven out of ten songs are about love. These mediums do nothing but fabricate fallacies about love. What does that teach young people of today? What do you think Lucy? Do you have a boyfriend? An admirer to take you to grad?"

Lucy froze, the attention was too much; unable to verbally answer she shook her head and continued to fold the clean towels.

"As I see it," said Saffron, hoping to take the unwanted attention from Lucy, "I believe the virtue of love is never having to beg. Perhaps both genders need liberation from begging. The ego wants someone to beg. If your action isn't right from the beginning, then everything will go wrong. We need to watch our intent, both men and women need to stop reducing themselves in the name of love, it's self betrayal."

"I agree," said George. "It seems to me that when one is in love, it's about acting in total consideration of your partner …"

"And your partner of you … " injected Saffron.

"Yes, Marthina has a mind and a life of her own. Love isn't about giving up your individuality, it's about respecting and celebrating each other's individuality without the desire to turn them into something else."

"I agree George," offered Negar, "And I think it takes great courage to love truly, to be vulnerable."

"Oh, I bet Manjira would have loved to have been here to hear this conversation," laughed Bermudadas. "She would be bullying us all into thinking just like her because she knows best! Oh well, I guess she does come from a different way of thinking, I shouldn't be so hard on her. Well, you can go on and on, I just know that for me, I chose to live here and now. I'm all for living in the present moment and I'm not into getting so serious. Everything in my life is great. I'm excited about the new Vancouver Canuck hockey team; it's their first season this fall in the NHL, just think of all those handsome hockey players! I'll be going to the games!"

Eyes pinched together Rebecca queried, "Will you ever get serious Bermudadas? Are you going to live your whole life wearing rose colour glasses and jumping from man to man? You need a financially stable traditional man."

Hooting with laugher she replied, "Don't rain on my parade Becs, life can change in a day, so I'm going to live it to the max. You go to church and do your thing and I'll live my life and do my thing."

"I will never understand you Bermudadas."

"Well, perhaps you need to accept me for who I am and not judge me. And just quit telling me what to do, I'm not telling you what to do am I? George, I decided where the plaque should go."

"Where?"

"Right here beside your mirror."

"That's perfectly fine." Smiling inwardly to himself, George continued to listen to their banter and pondered how unique it was for these women from such different belief systems to all end up in his shop. This is the soul of Canada he thought, a country built on immigration where opportunities abound and cultures meet. It almost seems like a healing: a healing where these women come together to discover themselves through recognizing their beliefs and understanding another's. Smiling to himself he decided that everything is perfect in its way. The universe truly arranges itself; everything comes together very naturally.

04

Summer arrived and everyone's schedules changed and adjusted with their kids at home. It wasn't until September when the new school year began did everyone's routine settle back into its old Friday pattern.

George and Marthina were now the proud parents of a baby boy. Marthina was at home being the full-time mom and the proud father kept updated photos in the shop. Just before opening one morning, as George was taping up the latest baby photo on the mirror of his workstation, Lucy walked in severely hung over.

Barely able to choke out a *Good Morning*, she muttered, "I'll be ready in a moment George."

Coolly, George nodded. After she went into the bathroom George sat down in his chair, spun around a couple of times, and pondered the situation. Lucy had barely graduated in June. Her final grades reflected the disorder of her life. Concurrently, she wasn't taking care of her health and she was coming into work hung over on a regular basis. It wasn't just time-to-time anymore. George had hoped it was a phase that she would pass through once she graduated, but he was wrong. It was time to talk and the timing was perfect because they weren't expecting any clients for another fifteen minutes.

Lucy closed the bathroom door behind her and as she walked towards George he spun the chair beside him and said, "Have a seat Lucy."

She sat down, completely mute.

"Lucy, is the way you are, the way you want to be?"

"No."

George waited for her to speak more, but nothing was forthcoming. "Okay, how do you want to be? How do you want your life to be?"

"I don't know," came a blunt answer.

"Let's look at what your life is showing you, okay?"

Silence.

George interpreted her non-verbal answer as an *Okay*. "What are the facts about your life Lucy?"

"I live in a big house where we all come and go, it's not a home like before. My sister is beautiful, she's always with her friends and nothing seems to affect her. My father works hard, but he's an asshole. He drinks and parties his fucking face off with his friends, nothing gets done around the house. Beer bottles pile up and the place stinks of pot all the time. He wants me to be successful, to do something with my life, but I don't want to give him the satisfaction."

Now we're getting somewhere thought George.

Suddenly, with a loathing in her eyes, she gloated, "Last night he and his work friends got drunk and he told me in front of them that I will never be anything. I know what he's doing, it's his sick way of trying to motivate me, but it's not working. Our living room smells like a bar, I just take their booze and they don't even know it."

Finally getting an understanding of her home life George asked, "Where do you drink?"

"In my room, or I go down to Lions Park by the river."

"You're drinking alone?"

"Sometimes alone, and sometimes my friend Sherry comes with me, it's no big deal. I like being alone, no one can hurt me. And besides, anyone who likes me must have something wrong with them."

"Well, Lucy, it seems to me you're drinking to ease your anxiety about something. What are we going to do? Have you decided this is all there is to life?"

"I don't know. I give up, there's no hope. What can I do? This is my life."

"Have you reached a point of hopelessness or are you going to rebel?"

"I try to get up in the morning, I try to get here on time, but then the old habit of rolling over just kicks in."

"Well, as I see it Lucy, that's personal betrayal. The first clarity you need to get is, *I can be the way I want to be.* You have to work at it Lucy. Can you do that, or are you going to give up?"

"I don't even know how I want to be. I could never go to university."

"Well, let's look at it. As I see it, success means you simply give the best of you. You don't have to have a university degree to be successful. Let's take it slowly. What can you do right now?"

"I don't know. I don't want to live at home anymore."

"So, what do you have to do to get your own place?"

"Oh, I could never move out. I don't have anything."

Here we go thought George, *Dr. Jekyll and Mr. Hyde.* "Don't allow that to determine your situation. Have you decided the way you want to be cannot be achieved?"

No answer.

"What you need to see is, *I can be the way I want to be.* Accepting where you are right now is the first step, the beginning. Can you say to yourself; *I know the path forward, the work that is required, I can arrive there?*"

"But I don't know where I'm going."

"Well, right now you have a good full-time job. If you are interested, maybe you'd like to go to hairdressing school. As you know, some days I could use another stylist around here.

Would that interest you?"

"Maybe."

"Well, try moving from the defeated mind to the able mind. A defeated mind is the mind that begins with negativity based in fear. Try to live from an able mind … then, when you are the way you want to be you have order. It's time to move to a new reality Lucy. Don't drop out of life. Get yourself right."

A shadow passed over Lucy. She's still not telling me all, thought George. Sensing the conversation was over and not wanting to pry anymore he explained, "I need you to be here on time Lucy. I need you to be sharp and doing your job as best you can. Like you did when you first started. Can you understand that?"

"Yes," misery still flowing in her veins, "I'll try to do better George." Unable to meet his gaze, she slid off the chair and walked to the reception desk to check the day's appointments.

A couple of hours later George couldn't help but wonder what was going on that day, everyone coming in seemed unhappy - not just Lucy.

Saffron, who came in early as always, was looking absolutely gloomy. Rebecca's hair was done, but she hung around to talk to Saffron. The two were sitting beside each other in the reception area and without too much effort Rebecca had managed to find out why she was miserable.

"Last night at the Chamber of Commerce dinner, you should have seen Bermudadas. She was dressed to the nine's, she had an ostrich feather boa and she was flirting with all the men. I've never seen that side of her. In fact, she cozied right up to Daisley and he didn't seem to mind." Imitating Bermudadas she mimicked, "*Oh Mr. Mayor, Riverville must have the most handsomeness mayor in the Lower Mainland and what you're doing for this town is so fabulous!* And then to me she chided my outfit, asking me which thrift store I picked out my dress. I designed and made my own dress, I felt so worthless, so out of place being there with all those business people. The whole evening just seemed like a lie, everyone selling their bullshit projections. Then, when the evening was winding down, she was talking everyone into going to the Swinging Lantern, that new pub down by the river. I could tell Daisley wanted to go, I had to remind him he was the mayor and it might not be a good idea to go party hard all night. I just felt so insignificant. I have an art show next year and I can't even pick up a brush right now."

"I saw the whole performance myself. My company did all the catering by the way. It was typical Bermudadas," said a boisterous Manjira from George's chair. "And what did I say to you several months ago? Let me remind you, you have a romantic idea of what love means young lady."

"Once again, you're oozing with compassion Manjira," snapped Rebecca. "Now Saffron, first of all, don't allow what Bermudadas or what anyone else says to influence whether you're happy or not. Bermudadas is so out of touch with how another feels, she's probably completely unaware that her flirting hurt you."

"Right," laughed Manjira. "Earth to Rebecca … I'm sure she knows exactly what she's doing. She's out to sleep with your husband young lady, if she hasn't already, and you're a fool if you didn't see that coming. I told you so."

Saffron's whole body reacted in pain. She sat completely vulnerable and speechless.

Lucy behind the reception desk was stunned. Negar doing the books from the dryer sat stunned. Rebecca was stunned. Even George was taken back by Manjira's bluntness.

"Well," said George, in an effort to rescue the moment, "Saffron, why don't you just talk to Daisley? Tell him how you feel. From what you've always told me, you like to settle things right away and communication seems to be a strength you have."

"Oh yes, now you're getting advice from someone who hasn't even been married as long as you," snapped Manjira. "All of you live in la-la-land with your relationships."

"How dare you conclude us all in one wide sweep Manjira," Rebecca stood up and walked over to her, hands on her hips, clearly ajitated. "Correct me if I'm wrong, but I do believe Lance and I have been married longer than you and your husband. We've been married for 21 years. We were married at 19, which is young, but we're still together. Relationships by their very nature are fragile and vulnerable. You profess to be such an expert on relationships; well actually, you profess to be an expert about everything. Regardless, the fact is you're a control freak and you manipulate people to do exactly what you want. I can't imagine being married to you."

Negar jumped up, walking over to Rebecca she suggested, "Let's talk about the weather shall we?! You know when we first moved to Vancouver, one of the first things I noticed was how much Canadians love to talk about the weather!"

A hesitant laughter resulted in Negar's attempt to bring about peace. Manjira was speechless and as Rebecca had had her say, she went back to sit next to Saffron.

"Okay Manjira, you're done!" Sensing her feelings of isolation George quietly suggested to her, "Manjira, if you don't have to rush out, why don't you stay and have a coffee for a change? Sit and chat for a while."

"Maybe I will," she answered with a twinkle in her eye, "Then they won't get to gossip about me!"

In a louder voice George said, "Okay, let's see, I'll comb out Negar, Lucy can you please shampoo Saffron?"

"George, just before I sit down, I'm trying to balance your cash flow and I seem to be short $50?" asked a confused Negar.

"Oh, take a look in that big dictionary under the phone, it's tucked in there," he laughed. "I brought in that old book to hide the money at night."

"In a dictionary?" she asked.

"Well, I figure if anyone ever breaks in, they'll be looking in the cash drawer. I leave a little there, but the big bills I stash in the dictionary."

Everyone shared a laugh and Manjira shook her head in disapproval while she wandered to the coffee trolley, "Did you learn that in Business Class 101?"

"No Manjira, I learned that in Street Smarts 101!"

"You know George," as she found the money in the dictionary, "I first walked into this salon almost eight years ago when Karim and I first moved to Canada and its been a place of comfort for me. I never dreamed I'd end up doing the books or spending so much time here."

"Iran sounds so exotic, I don't know why you would pick Riverville," stated Lucy as she adjusted the water temperature to wash Saffron's hair.

"It's a different world there Lucy," she said as she was getting settled in George's chair. "Like everywhere there are good things and bad things. In the beginning coming to Canada was like a different planet. You'll laugh at this, I was so used to having maids in Iran; it was such a difficult adjustment. In fact, I was helpless to do anything on my own."

Flabbergasted Lucy was stunned, "Maids? You had maids?"

"Yes, but you have to understand Iran is such a different place. Everyone has maids; it's common for the middle class. When I first arrived here I was so useless around the house. It was damn tough at first, but not only that, the cultural differences were a massive adjustment. In Iran I was used to having so many family members around me all the time, it was so overwhelming. And when I moved here, I went from one extreme to the other - from being smothered to being alone. I was 23 when we moved to Canada. We can't have children and living here with that fact is probably easier than being in Iran, but I've had my moments. Some days I was so depressed and miserable. The adjustment was more than I thought it would be, and with Karim away so much, I couldn't bare the loneliness. It was like a bad dream. I tried to make friends, but I never felt like I belonged. I was so nostalgic about my past, it became an illusion, I made it more than it really was. I actually started to drink, I was in a fog. I decided life was fated, I was ridden with anxiety. I cut myself off from everything. I was adamant about not looking at my life situation. When I'd meet people I would go out of my way to be accommodating, sometimes I would just be nice because I didn't want to be alone. I was trying to understand life in Canada. I felt so displaced. Then I started to see how unhealthy that was. It was such self-betrayal. I was taken advantage of, but I only have myself to blame. I just wanted to be accepted, it's like my personality changed. I allowed it to happen. Then something happened, this will sound crazy, but one day I got a flat tire and I had to change it on my own – and I did it!"

"You got a flat tire?" repeated Lucy. "I'm confused."

"Yes, and that was a beautiful life lesson. I figured out that if I was capable of dealing with changing a tire I was capable of dealing with my life. That's when things changed for me. I became more independent. Independence is what women want, but when faced with it, it's something altogether different. And the funny thing is, when my father taught me to drive in Iran the first thing he made me do was change a tire. I was so frustrated with him. I just wanted to get behind the wheel and drive, but no, he made me change a tire. He said, "You have to know what to do if you're alone and get stuck on the side of the road. Well, several years later his lesson made sense. Then, after that, life here began to get a lot better. A Canadian friend would call, or I'd come here, or I'd get a few days teaching. It was quite choiceless actually. The fact was our life was here and I had to deal with it. Then, I figured out that I'm perfectly capable to deal with my loneliness and eventually I became strong in my aloneness."

"What do you mean by aloneness?" asked Lucy.

"Let me see if I can explain, as I see it, being lonely is negative, it means you can't be alone, you hate being by yourself, you always feel something is missing. Aloneness is actually a positive connotation. I see my aloneness to mean that I have strength. I'm not hankering to be with Karim like before, I can be with myself and that's okay. I still have a long way to go, but I know I'm moving forward because it's easier to be alone. I'm not as emotional when Karim leaves. And, I actually started to realize that I like to do things on my own, I love gardening. It's like gardening re-charges me. Aloneness has a beauty, it's silence, it's peace. I'm not sure if all that makes sense or not."

"Well, you can always come to my place Negar," offered Rebecca. "Sometimes I would love your peace and quiet. With two young teenagers and a third one up and coming our home can drive me nuts some days. Actually, I should come to your place where it's quiet!"

Everyone had a laugh while Rebecca continued, "You won't believe this, last Saturday morning Lance went off to the barbershop, and Rachel went with him, she still gets that old barber Ken to cut her hair. She's such a tomboy at 16. I want her to come here, grow her hair long, but she insists on keeping it short for all the sports she's in. Well, I guess I shouldn't complain, it's nice the two of them have the time together. But I just cringe at the thought of her sitting on a barber's stool with old Ken cutting her hair."

Addressing Saffron at the sink Negar said, "Marriage changes so much Saffron. I'm sure you're seeing it in your relationship. Suddenly you're balancing a multiple of responsibilities, maintaining the house, your career, the in-laws. You're role-playing. Men have to adjust too, right George?"

"Absolutely. And you're married to the mayor Saffron, so there's more pressure. As I see it, the challenge for most is that society demands we love in a particular way. Society tells us how to judge another's relationship."

"Yes," added Manjira as she sat down with her coffee, "And the West loves to tell the rest of the world what love is: flowers on Valentine's Day, sappy movies, soap operas. Those mediums do nothing but fabricate fallacies about love. It's all a fantasy. The East has a wealth of knowledge on the subject of love, but the West professes to know best. All this new age self-help literature - what nonsense."

George nodded in agreement and continued, "And let's face the fact that many women get married with the belief that they are taken care of and they won't have to worry about making their own choices. A man cannot be the solution to a woman's life situation. From what I've witnessed too many women live their lives through men, they lose their souls. Think about it. I agree with Bermudadas when she said a few months ago that taking on the responsibility for another's happiness is madness. What a massive expectation. If a woman or a man can say, *My happiness is my responsibility*, then I feel there is a greater possibility for the relationship to work. Perhaps men just need a gentle reminder that instead of feeling saddled by their relationships, their wives can once again be there joy. A lot of women want men to rescue them, and as I see it, that is giving your responsibility away."

"I agree George," said Negar. "A lot of women do want to be rescued instead of taking responsibility for their own lives. Perhaps it's conditioning."

"Yes, and perhaps to live in dignity the work is to un-condition the conditioned," he stated.

"To be honest, I know I'd be happy if my husband was around more," said Negar stubbing out her cigarette as George held up the hand mirror and spun her around to look at her hair.

"Where is he now?" asked Manjira, now settled in one of the dryer chairs.

"He's in San Francisco. He's looking into a partnership with a distant cousin; they want to break into the American market. I'm just so weary of him being away so much, but I know he's working so hard for us and I keep reminding myself of my flat tire."

"Let me ask you something ladies," said George. "What is it women truly seek in a relationship? Is it the idea of marriage or could it actually be love? I have to agree with Manjira, we do need to discard imagination. Quit pretending we're living in a romantic novel, expecting the men in your lives to behave like Prince Charming. When was the last time we all took at look at our lives and instead of grumbling about what we don't have, we became aware of what we do have? Are we a grateful people? That only seems to happen when someone close to us dies or gets ill."

Everyone in the room went silent as they thought about it.

George continued, "That seems to be the time when we suddenly become thankful for all the gifts we take for granted: health, family, the air we breathe, freedom of speech, clean water to drink. Think about it. As I see, it gratefulness is a quality of seeing truth."

"I'm grateful for how hard Karim works," Negar said lighting up another cigarette as she walked back to the reception desk to finish the week's tallies. "But sometimes I get bitter because I just never see him. When he gets home on the weekends I should be happy, but sometimes I get angry with him, then I feel guilty, it's a vicious cycle. I try to keep the peace, but then I just check out and fall back to my fears and patterns of when we first arrived. I thought when we first got here that Karim and I would have so much time together, it would be just us. That was a big illusion. I guess it really doesn't matter, the universe is unfolding as it should."

"Well, as I see it, it does matter," said George. "What you want is important. When you say *It doesn't matter* it sounds like you're saying *You don't matter*, and you do matter Negar. Bravery is when you are courageous enough to be you. And in the darkest night courage comes."

Avoiding George's insight she continued, "When Karim first started travelling, I was getting so tired of speaking English all the time. Now when he's home we don't even seem to be aware which language we're speaking in; English or Farsi. That first year was so difficult. I missed being with my family and friends, listening to my grandmother's stories, the markets, and the street vendors. All those things I took for granted in Iran. I had to construct a new me when I arrived here, it was something I wasn't the least bit prepared for. The life strategies that I lived by in Iran couldn't be used here. Sometimes I wonder how others created and survived their sense of life in Canada. I experienced frustration, anxiety, anger, stress, sadness ... it was tough, but here I am, eight years later and I can truly say Canada is my home. Now, when I go back to Iran for holidays, it feels like reverse culture shock! It takes me a few days to get back into life there. I'm aware of the beauty of both countries, I have a deep appreciation for the richness of both worlds."

"Good for you Negar," said George. "Any life trauma is a blessing."

"A blessing?" queried Lucy.

"Yes, any life trauma is a blessing," George repeated. "This life is perfect for learning. An easy life doesn't teach us anything. Let life teach you, don't take it as pain, take it as kindness. Any life situation where we feel unsettled is an opportunity to ask; *What is my life showing me?*"

"You know Negar, all of us came from somewhere," Rebecca stated. "Canada is a nation built on immigration from around the world. You're not the only one to experience all that. When immigrants first came to this country they couldn't even dream of returning home for a visit."

"I know Rebecca," said Negar restraining herself.

George said, "Okay, Saffron you're next. Then, turning the conversation back to Negar, "Are you getting many hours teaching these days Negar?"

"It varies from week to week. I've had a few shifts at both the junior high and high school levels. I love to teach, it gives me some sense of worth. I worked so hard to get Canadian accreditation, but I don't want to make a full-time commitment and fortunately because of Karim I don't have to work. I do it for something to do, but I really love it when I'm in the classroom."

"Have you thought about a hobby or some volunteer work? You may enjoy that."

"I have, I just haven't gotten pro-active about it."

At that moment the door swung open and in marched Bermudadas, "Hi everyone, how do you like it?! Isn't it wonderful?!" Spinning around for all to see, "It's the new Vancouver Canuck hockey jersey, the colours blue, green, and white are to represent the water, forests, and snow surrounding Vancouver. Their first game is next month, the ninth, against the Los Angeles Kings at the Pacific Coliseum." In her hair a matching blue scarf held her ponytail in place and her bell-bottom jeans revealed her slim figure. "I plan on getting a date with one of those handsome players before the season is over!"

"I imagine you will have dated the entire team by the time the season is over Bermudadas," suggested Manjira.

"Always sharp with the comebacks aren't you?"she laughed, "You're just jealous because you're stuck with one man Manjira!"

"Hi Bermudadas," George greeted her.

"Hi George, how's that wee babe of yours?"

"Just fine, thanks for asking."

"And Marthina, how's she liking motherhood? Is there anything you need?"

"We're all fine Bermudadas, I'll be sure to let you know if there is anything we need. Okay Rebecca, you're ready for the dryer, Saffron to the chair and Bermudadas to the sink. Lucy, after you've washed Bermudadas' hair, would you mind checking the stock? Ned will be in later this afternoon to take an order."

"It's done George, I wrote it out yesterday," she answered as she got a couple of towels down and began to wrap one around Bermudadas' neck and snap in the plastic plum apron.

With *Yellow Submarine* by the Beatles playing in the background Bermudadas continued while she settled back into the sink, "It's so depressing that the Beatles broke up, at least I got to see them at Empire Stadium in '64. What a party that was! Hey Saffron you and your handsome hubby should have come to the Swinging Lantern last night, what a rocker. Riverville's finest business community all getting hammered, well it's good for the economy! The town's future was all decided over a pool table!"

An awkward silence fell, finally a brooding Saffron snapped, "Well, going to the Swinging Lantern to play pool and drink isn't what we're about."

Sensing Saffron's irritation Bermudadas retorted in her usual flippant style, "Oh relax woman. It was just for a few laughs, lighten up."

"Don't tell me to relax!"

"What are you so worked up about?"

No reply. Finally it was Manjira who spoke up, "Maybe she doesn't appreciate you flirting with her husband. Most wives don't you know? And the Swinging Lantern? I heard all the hippies go there and smoke pot."

"Oh, my goodness! Hippies and pot smokers! You people are so stuck in your *You know best beliefs*," laughed Bermudadas. "But Daisley? Is this what is bothering you Saffron? Daisley and I have known each other for years sweetheart. He married you. He was quite the partier in his twenties, now he's so serious, I guess that's what happens when you become the mayor." *And he's obviously never told you about our little affair all those years ago*, thought Bermudadas to herself, who was married herself at the time.

Turning in George's chair to meet Bermudadas' gaze she confronted her, "He's not in his twenties now and he has a lot of responsibilities."

"As I see it, having fun is what life is all about Saffron. As I've said before, we don't know how long we're here for. I'm living in the moment, that's much more satisfying than living some romantic idea. Why so serious? What good can come from being so serious? Lighten up."

"Don't tell me to lighten up," snapped Saffron. "Is life always a party for your Bermudadas? It's as though you always have to party, like an ego trip to show off or something. What are you afraid of? Being alone? Afraid of missing out on something? Being deprived?"

"Well, I don't allow life to get me down," turning to Lucy she said, "That's something you need to work on Lucy." Lucy's face balked. "Even as a child I was optimistic, this is how I am, take it or leave it."

"Well, I'll leave it thank you very much," answered Saffron. "I don't see life as one big party. I'm not escaping life through drinking all the time."

Saffron's sharpness caught everyone watching on the sidelines by surprise. Lucy who was wrapping a towel around Bermudadas' head just wanted to run and hide.

Bermudadas poked Saffron, "Afraid Daisley isn't going to be around forever? Talk about fear, a little fear of abandonment perhaps?"

"You just stay away from my husband Bermudadas."

Laughing loudly and shaking her head, "Okay, now the truth comes out. Don't worry sweetheart, Daisley isn't my type, he's too worried about his image. Where as I just don't give a damn what any one thinks about me."

At that moment the door opened and Ned walked in wearing a yellow turtleneck and a stylish navy suit with double-breasted buttons. "Good Morning George ... ladies!"

"Good Morning to you too Ned, aren't you looking handsome today!" piped up Bermudadas.

"Ahh, well," he smiled, "One must create an image in this business. I see you're going to be a Canuck fan!"

"But of course, the first game is next month. I'll be there cheering loudly!"

Gesturing George said, "Ned, you can put the stock by the sink if you like and I believe Lucy has this week's order ready for you."

"Great ... hi Lucy" as he strolled through the shop, nodding to the ladies with his schoolboy smile. He was quite happy George had handed over the responsibility of ordering all the supplies to Lucy. He looked forward to seeing her every second week, but she clearly didn't seem to be returning the enthusiasm. He figured one day he'd corner George and get some information about her, maybe she had a boyfriend. He wasn't that much older than her, maybe six years at the most he guessed.

As Lucy and Ned were going over the order, the energy of the room shifted. Saffron was clearly not going to engage with Bermudadas any further, she had said what she wanted to say and Bermudadas was content to leave it alone too.

"Okay, thank you Lucy," Ned smiled at her and headed back to the entrance. "Thank you George. No dainties today ladies? Are you all watching your figures?!"

"Definitely not Ned! They're right here, under the paper," said Rebecca.

"Oh thanks," as he took a bite from an oatmeal cookie and headed for the door.

Negar was ready to go and then she remembered, "Oh, I brought my camera everyone! I've been taking photos of our home, Riverville, our neighbours … I'm making a little photo album to send to Iran. Can everyone stand together for a photo? Would you mind taking it Ned?"

"It would be my pleasure!"

"Saffron, stay where you are in George's chair and we'll gather around you, come on everyone!"

One by one the ladies all got up and gathered together with George standing next to them.

"Okay, ready ladies?" asked Ned as he held the camera into position.

"Yes," answered a smiling Negar.

"Everyone say … I love Ned!"

Everyone burst into laughter and Ned snapped the photo.

"Thanks Ned," said Negar as he handed the camera back to her. "I'll make copies for everyone. Okay George, I'm off. I'll do your deposit and see you next week."

"Great, thanks Negar"

"It's time for me to leave too," said Manjira. "I'll walk to the bank with you Negar. Then it's time to get to the office, I have a busy weekend. A wedding tomorrow night and a funeral on Sunday."

"I'm ready to head out too," said Rebecca. "I'm off to the church, we have a thrift shop meeting."

"Allow me ladies," flirted Ned as he held the door open.

Laughing loudly they all left the salon, leaving Saffron and Bermudadas in the shop with George and Lucy. *Well,* thought George, as he wasn't convinced that this entanglement between Saffron and Bermudadas was over, *let's see how this plays itself out.*

05

Several weeks had passed and it was now late November. Saffron and Bermudadas were civil to each other, yet everyone noticed there was a shift in their friendship. Bermudadas appeared to be on eggshells around Saffron; which surprised George as it wasn't inline with her character. Saffron confided to Rebecca one morning that she had noticed a change in Daisley, which he deflected by saying he was overloaded at work. Everyone knew Bermudadas had a new boyfriend, the town pharmacist, so Rebecca had been trying to convince her to let go of the idea that anything was going on; when in fact Daisley and Berumdadas were having an affair.

"What a year the world has seen," commented Rebecca as she was thumbing through the paper on Friday morning, "Last month the October Crisis involving the *Front de liberation du Quebec* and the Trudeau Government; American forces in Vietnam moved into Cambodia; Greenpeace and Earth Day were born. Jimi Hendrix died. Our world in Riverville seems quite ordinary in comparison to all that world news."

"Ahh," said George, "Yet there is so much extraordinariness in the ordinary."

"What do you mean?" asked a hung over Lucy.

"Well, Ms. Lucy, moments of extraordinariness can be found in moments of ordinariness."

At that moment, as if it was an omen, the power went out. Cries of surprise were heard around the salon as the place descended into a gray darkness. George did a quick visual check to find Lucy rinsing the shampoo out of Bermudadas' hair; Saffron and Rebecca sitting in the reception area; Manjira under one of the dryers who had reacted instantly by flipping up the cone; and Negar in his chair.

He put his scissors down and announced calmly, "Everyone just relax," while he stepped outside to take a look. The wind had been howling up and down High Street since he arrived early that morning. The entire street was out of power. Several people were also stepping out of the other near by shops to take a look. Everyone appeared stunned. George's first thought was *Get some candles.*

Opening the door to the salon he called, "I'll be right back ladies!"

George ran across the street in hopes that the hardware store would let him in. He dashed through the pelting rain, the clerk let him in, and he returned half soaked to the salon with the goods in hand.

He had a grin on his face as he announced, "Let there be light!"

"Give those to us George," said Negar, "We'll use the ashtrays as candleholders."

With the candles lit and everyone settled, George advised, "The traffic lights are out and with the high winds it would be wise for everyone just to stay put for now."

"Agreed," stated Manjira, her sediments were echoed around the salon.

Teasing Negar he said, "So, let's all relax, grab a coffee before it gets cold and talk about the weather!"

Soon everyone had settled into a circle, taking up seats and drawing close to each other.

"This is kind of fun," said Bermudadas. "I wonder what the schools are doing, oh well, I'm sure the kids will be fine. What do you think Becs?"

"Yes," she answered, "I'm sure Principal Matheson will have everything under control, he's an old army chap, they'll be fine."

A concerned Manjira said, "Well, hopefully their teachers will make it an adventure so they won't get scared. I'm sure every parent is calling the school to see if their child is okay, I'll wait awhile, their phone is likely to be jammed with calls."

George looked around and reflected that after a year of working in Riverville; Fridays were truly different. It had become the morning social with Rebecca bringing in something homemade to eat; Manjira sharing some catering leftovers; Saffron coming in early and generally everyone was upbeat for the weekend.

Lucy interrupted his thoughts, "I don't get what you meant about ordinariness George."

"Oh right … well, think about it, just going for a walk by the river may appear ordinary, yet do you stop to appreciate the abundance of nature? I believe, myself included, that we take our backyard for granted. This might be an ordinary salon, but meeting all of you has definitely made my life very extraordinary!" he laughed shaking his head.

Negar added, "You know, I felt that way about nature when I first arrived in Canada, I loved all the natural beauty. If I really stop to think about it, now I take it for granted. I get what you're saying George."

"Right now Mother Nature is out there having a great time reminding us to appreciate Thomas Edison and the light bulb! The storm has created an awareness in us to stop and be grateful. Having said that, we don't have to be the scientist who is going to dazzle the world and be extraordinary. As I see it we just need to be ourselves and get our individual worlds right. And by getting right I mean being awakened to the fact that we are the creators of everything that happens in our lives.

Have you noticed how people love to go on and on when something good has happened in their life? They love to claim that they made it happen, but when something goes wrong they'll find someone to blame. Everything that happens to us is our creation: good and bad. As I see it, once we accept responsibility for everything that happens to us, our world falls into order."

"Let me see if I've got this," asked Saffron. "Are you suggesting that I am somehow responsible when bad things happen to me?"

"Yes, you are. And you may want to be careful when you label something bad. As I see it, it's alchemy, an opportunity to learn, to see what life is showing you. That's why we truly need to be conscious of our beliefs and live in awareness. So, when so-called bad things happen, it's not necessarily bad if you have the eye to see it as an opportunity to look at yourself and transform. Every problem ... actually, I don't like to use that word, let's say every challenge is an opportunity to learn about ourselves. It's like being a mirror to you, self-mastery over your life. Life is about creation: not a problem to be solved. It's quite natural actually. Let me ask all of you ladies, do you believe your beliefs create your reality?"

"Give us an example George," asked Manjira.

"Sure, okay, when I bought this salon from Huxtable, I could have sat in the belief that to continue the salon's success would be difficult and to make money was going to tough. Yet I didn't. I held the belief that the salon would be a success, that I would make money. I've owned it for about nine months now and it's a success."

"That's so true," said Negar with a smile, "I can attest to that because I've been doing the books."

"As I see it we need to stop listening to negative people, they kill our possibility, they can plant negative beliefs in us. We need to look carefully at the beliefs we live our lives by. Then, it's about discovering your own hidden possibilities, your individuality, learning to accept you, encountering you, and then growing and transforming. It's all rather organic actually. Let me ask all of you ... don't you want to live your life as the choser? Don't you want to realize your own will? To be free from the collective consciousness, to live in society yet not allow society to define you? We all grow up with so much conditioning and traditional beliefs. I'm not saying tradition is bad, all I'm saying is that it needs to be a choice. And for it to be a choice, we need to be aware of what beliefs we are living our life by, to wake up. "

"How do you start?" asked Saffron.

"Maybe a place to start is by looking at your fears. Fear is a by-product of not accepting what is. When you have a clear view of what is, then you can move forward with a recognition of what has been your entrapment."

"Fear?" Lucy asked with her head pounding from her hang over. She was quite happy the power went out so she could sit down and do nothing.

"Lucy, from observing you all this time I feel you believe your life is crystallized, that you can't be anything more than what you are, you live in a fear of being abandoned. You mistrust your own common sense, you see the world as a threatening and dangerous place, and so you're fearful most of the time. Learn to trust your instincts, you can take care of yourself, find your courage."

Lucy sat stunned, as though hit with a sword. Not saying a word, she repeated George's words in her head knowing he was right.

"What about me George?" asked Negar tentatively.

"Negar, you believe your efforts don't matter, you just want to keep the peace, you live in fear of separation. You avoid conflict of any kind. You negate your feelings of negativity to keep the peace, you suppress how you really feel. Be honest with what really matters to you. Perhaps you need to see that the more you develop as a person the more you'll be able to contribute to others. Sometimes we need to assert ourselves, that's just a fact."

Everyone sat in silence either looking out the window or staring into their coffee cup.

Without any coaxing he continued, "Manjira, you're obsessed with control, you have a fear of submitting to others, you fear that no one will listen to you, that you'll be taken advantage of, so you grab as much power as you can. You're overbearing and intimidate people who get your way. Why don't you assist people to rise, be compassionate, kind, and inspire others? Those attributes are not weaknesses."

Manjira jolted as though hit by lightening herself.

"Saffron, you have a fear of being defective, that something is missing. You don't have to try to be special, and because you compare yourself to others you miss what is there. Instead of wanting to matter to everyone, perhaps ask yourself if they matter to you. You get stuck in your emotions, look at facts for clarity."

Nodding her head in awe at the truth of George's words, she sat silently.

"Bermudadas, you want everyone to think you're okay. You overindulge in pleasure, you're addicted to the highs in life, and you avoid feeling any pain, getting serious or heavy. You don't have to be *Up all the time* to be accepted. You have a fear of being deprived; thus, your ever present *Out there lifestyle*. Why don't you practice being still and observant, and see the restfulness and wisdom in that?"

Pulling a drag off her cigarette, Bermudadas was too stung to reply in the moment.

"Rebecca, you have a fear of being unloved. You're always meeting another's needs, you need to be important in other people's lives to feel worthwhile. You want to rescue the world. You have spent your life altering yourself to please others, you keep a scorecard for all you do for others, and then you get upset and angry thinking that you're not appreciated for what you do for them. You don't have to give to be accepted, you are loving."

"As I see it, with all of you, fear prevents you from looking at yourself, and if you don't look and see your truths how can you rise to be more? Explore who you are, don't live in a conclusion of who you are."

Rain pelted against the window while everyone sat in shock at the truth of George's words.

"I can see your fears in you because I have witnessed them in myself and I've worked not to allow them to determine me. I'm sharing what I see in you because as I see it we need to question everything in life: myself included. We need to be aware of our daily lives, our beliefs, our attitudes, our overall outlook on life and use every experience as an opportunity to evolve, to rise."

"And you're saying all this begins with looking at my beliefs and accepting that I'm the creator of everything that happens to me in my life?" asked Saffron.

"Exactly."

The only thing to be heard was the wind and rain battering against the window.

"Now, how did you get to be so wise as to see all this in us?" asked Rebecca.

"Well, I've had my share of life experiences too Rebecca. I may be young, but I've had my journey too. I've learnt a lot from my parents, my ancestors. I'm just sharing this with you, but don't take my word for it, you have to know it for yourself. Don't believe anything you can't verify for yourself. Figure it out, do you want to transform? Really, don't we all want to rise to be more, to be the best we can be in whatever we do? Every day when I walk through that door I rise to be the best stylist I can be; when I go home the best father, husband. And I don't mean the best from a competitive or comparison mind, the best I can be as a human. Saffron, just be the best artist you can be, don't worry about comparing and see how your brain rests."

"I get it, that makes sense," she agreed.

"Can you give an example of a belief held by society?" asked Negar.

"Sure, does everyone know who Roger Bannister is?"

"Yes," said Saffron, "We learnt about him at school when we studied the 1954 Commonwealth Games held here in Vancouver. I was in elementary school at the time. He's the English runner who became the first man to run a mile under four minutes; he did it a couple of months before Vancouver. Then, at the games, the mile became the big event as Landy the Australian and him were competing against each other. At the entrance to Empire Stadium there's a statue of them now. Anyway, they were running shoulder to shoulder when Bannister glanced over his shoulder to see how close Landy was; that was his mistake, Landy passed him and won the gold. That race is now known as *The Miracle Mile* because they both ran it in under four minutes."

"That's right. Now, understand this; for years and years sports writers and others claimed that it was impossible to run the mile under four minutes.

Well, in May 1954, in England like Saffron said, a few months before the Commonwealth Games in Vancouver, Bannister ran the four-minute mile at 3:59.4. He debunked the belief that it couldn't be done. He shattered it. Now, stop and think of Bannister's psychology. His belief system didn't fall to the negative. He obviously believed that he could break the world record and he did exactly that. Why I'm telling you this story is … your mind needs to come to its own, not the collective. Bannister had sheer guts; he wasn't going to be conformed to an old belief. You can do the same in your life, find your own voice. We live by so much conformity that our uniqueness dies. We conclude ourselves and we conclude others."

"Well, I've never been stuck in conformity," announced Bermudadas. "I've pretty much always done what I want to do."

"That's probably true Bermudadas," agreed George. "But let me ask you this, is that truly you or are you trying to prove something? You party hard and drink a lot …"

"I've always said your drinking is vulgar," stated Rebecca, happy that George was condemning alcohol.

Looking at Rebecca he said, "I'm not saying it's bad from the righteousness, holier than thou belief you're operating from Rebecca. Don't slot me into that." Then turning to Bermudadas he continued, "I'm suggesting that perhaps you need to look at why you drink," glancing at Lucy he was also using this opportunity for her to look at herself too, "Alcoholics aren't in contact with their truths. It puts you to sleep so you don't feel, then after a while it's the next drug. So as I see it, whatever drug you're using, it's keeping you miserable and there's no moving forward. If you have to take drugs and drink a lot it means your normal time is hell."

In her defence Bermudadas said lightheartly, "I drink and party because it's fun. I don't want to be stuck doing the same old thing all my life, there's too much to experience out there. I'm not an alcoholic or anything like that. And the new man in my life loves to have fun, we're always going out. We're thinking about going to Hawaii next spring, Don Ho here we come! Tonight I wanna to go that new bar in Port Moody, they've got a hot band playing."

"Well, that's your choice Bermudadas. I'm not going to tell you what to do, all I suggest is that you look at it. And you Lucy, why do you drink?"

The room was silent. The ladies all knew Lucy was becoming more and more troubled. They knew she was coming into work hung over on a regular basis, but they just didn't know if they should intervene in her private life. Rebecca's efforts to help her through her religious beliefs had backfired. Rebecca had considered talking to Lucy's father, but she knew he spent his time between the Riverville Pub and the Swinging Lantern and most likely wouldn't be receptive to her concerns. She thought he was a miserable bastard. Rebecca never understood how sweet Pearl allowed him to carry on the way he did for so many years. Everyone waited. The wind and rain could still be heard outside, the candles were burning down with their light reflecting off the glass.

"Because life isn't fun."

"Well, if your life isn't fun, believe me, you aren't fun. You are more than this person who is showing up for work hung over on a regular basis."

Everyone froze. No one was used to George speaking in such a harsh tone, especially with Lucy.

"Perhaps it's time you took a hard look at your life Lucy and see what your life is showing you. When you wake up and feel miserable Lucy, don't escape it. Your need to escape your pain must dissolve. Look at where your energy is moving, is it falling or rising? If you can get one moment of clarity things will start to change."

"I'm okay," she said.

"No you're not. Once again you're smoothing things over. If you say *I'm okay* you're perpetuating the lie. The source of your misery is your feeling of powerlessness. When we experience misery, it's life demanding us to meet life. The need to transform the source of your pain is what needs to be awakened. Try perceiving misery as a point of growth, an opportunity to encounter yourself. Misery is a wake up call. Look around and see the facts of your life, then look at the beliefs you're operating from and you'll soon witness for yourself that your beliefs are creating your reality. The evidence is in the facts of your life situation. Rise to have the ability to create how you want to live, participate with life. Have personal mastery over your life. As I see it, it's a process of seeing life as a creation, not a problem and then having the ability to create the reality you want to live by."

"That sounds like a lot of work," said Lucy.

"Well, it's your choice Lucy. Your life is a misery because you failed to act. What is preventing you from acting? Do you have the capacity to learn?"

As Lucy wasn't offering an answer, Saffron said, "It actually makes a lot of sense."

"It's a natural process. It starts with discovering one's own individuality and transcending it, moving from struggling to living life itself, to becoming a creator. It is not a haircut change it's a soul change. Are you afraid to show your real self Lucy?"

Silence.

Saffron finally broke the stillness. "I like that …"

George continued, "You need to drop the victim mind Lucy. People suffer pain from anticipating the pain. If you can, see that everything in life becomes an opportunity for you to grow and transform. It's coming to see you are truly something more and to do that, it has to be your choice."

"Well, perhaps life is fixed, that it cannot be changed," challenged Manjira.

"Well, I guess if you believe that Manjira then that will be your reality, your trap. As I see it, going beyond your fixed state is living in personal mastery."

"What he says makes a lot of sense actually," said Saffron. "I do compare myself to others and I do always think there is something missing in me, that I'm not good enough. I get full of doubt. I have an art show next year and I'm so worried if people are going to like it or not."

Rebecca countered, "I've got twenty years on you George, and yes, you may have a point about some things, but you don't have a psychology degree, who are you to be telling us what to do?"

"I'm not telling anyone what to do Rebecca. I'm just sharing what I have discovered. I've gone through some realizations myself at one time or another. Why do you think I can recognize what you're all going through? I'm just revealing what I see because I believe we can all rise to be more. And when we rise to be more as individuals, humanity will rise, and I believe we can all agree that humanity can be more. You don't have to agree, that's perfectly fine, and it's your choice. My intent is only from a place of friendship.

As I see it, it's good to keep being challenged in life. We all have two points, the higher and the lower. We constantly live in this duality, the lower and the higher. In the lower nothing is right. You see yourself being pulled back to the old. Don't you see that Lucy? Your old habits - the old routine - the old reality. But whenever you push yourself to the best, you have a peek of something new. The path is to remain at your best and to make it your base. And once you have reached that best you see the next height. You will always have this duality, the lower and the higher. The lower is when you are fallen. The higher is when you have risen. The idea is to remain in the risen state and to make that your normal state and the moment you make it normal you see your next height."

The room went quiet and George suggested, "I'm going to go for a walk down the block to see if I can get any information, maybe I'll pop in at city hall. Does anybody mind if I step out for a short while?"

"No George, you go ahead," answered Negar, "We'll be fine."

George put on his coat, grabbed his old umbrella, stepped outside onto the sidewalk and headed for Riverville's city hall. The ladies all sat in silence pondering what he had said in relation to their own lives.

"What he says makes a lot of sense actually," said Negar.

"Perhaps," said Rebecca, "but it's a different way of thinking." She was busy comparing her religious beliefs to what George had said and her brain was getting confused.

Lucy sat staring at the floor. Silence again.

"Well, I don't need a twenty-year-old telling me what to do," stated Manjira.

"He's not telling anyone what to do Manjira. And in fairness to him, we've known him for a while now, he's just stating how he sees things. And men always see things differently. I feel inspired from what he said, it's making me think," stated Negar.

"Well, you just go a head and think. I have a business to run and I don't have the time you have to sit here and go on about this nonsense." Getting up she walked to the window and started pacing, "When will he be back? I want to get to work. All he has to do is comb my hair out, he doesn't need electricity for that."

"Oh, relax woman," said Bermudadas. "Sit down, this is an opportunity for you to drop your controlling mind. You can't do anything about the power being out, your kids will be fine and your husband is with your staff, so settle down."

With a rising intonation Manjira scoffed, "Now, I have the party girl telling me what to do! Who's next? I heard there is a new salon opening on the north side of town, I'm going to give it a try."

"Go ahead, go take your projections to the next place and sell them all your bullshit," retorted Bermudadas. "Perhaps, to quote George, *You should look at what life is showing you.*"

"Let's talk about you Bermudadas. Are you still hitting on Daisley? Or have you slept with him already? I saw you two having lunch at the café on Monday, things seemed quite cozy. Are you dating two men now? The pharmacist and the mayor? The pharmacist seems sweet, he seems like a nice chap, obviously he hasn't heard about your reputation."

Saffron froze. She had pushed all her fears of Daisley and Bermudadas to the side, now everything surfaced again. Daisley hadn't mentioned he had seen Bermudadas.

"Well, think what you want Manjira, but I'm having fun and you can judge me all you want. I certainly don't need your approval." Looking at Saffron she said nervously, "We just happened to run into each other, so we had a quick coffee." She had never wanted to hurt Saffron – and neither had Daisley. They had first met years ago, shortly after she was married to Richard. She had quit working for Ward Air and started working at the travel agency, long before she bought the business. A part of her was happy to leave the airline as she knew they were going to have a family and she would need to quit eventually. By working at the agency she was still connected to the travel industry and it was entertaining after all. Daisley had walked in one afternoon and the chemistry was obvious. He was single, had just graduated with an engineering degree from the University of BC and wanted to be a part of the new consciousness; for him life was exciting. Bermudadas was captivated by his energy and with Richard being away so much it didn't take long before they were sleeping together. For Daisley it was perfect, she was married; he didn't have to make a commitment. They both blew off any guilt. It all ended when she got pregnant, which, even until today she wasn't sure who the kid's father was, but she buried that thought years ago. Her pregnancy was an accident. Richard and her hadn't ever really talked about having kids, they were going to wait until they were older. That was so many years and men ago that she hadn't thought of Daisley anymore - until she saw him at the Chamber dinner. Almost 16 years had passed and they started up the relationship all over again. They both knew morally it was wrong; he was married and she had a new boyfriend.

But what the hell, she had thought – except she'd become racked with guilt when she'd see Saffron at the salon. She had thought of changing her regular Friday morning appointment, but then that would look suspicious. Compared to all those years ago, it was harder to meet privately now. He was the mayor and she was now a business woman; they had to be careful. *It's not as though I want to marry him,* she justified to herself, *it's just for a good time.*

Breaking her thoughts the door opened and in walked a soggy George, "Well, I spoke with someone at city hall and the power should be on in about two hours. Let's see …. I can comb you out Manjira," as if reading her mind, "the rest of you can decide what you want to do, go and come back later or stay, it's up to you. Bermudadas, your hair is still damp, I can put the rollers in if you like. Negar, your hair won't be dry for a while and I'm sure you don't want to go out with a head full of rollers! Anyway, I'm fine with whatever you'd all like to do. I'll be here."

"Well, let's get my hair done and then I can go see what is going on with my children and my business," said Manjira as she sat in George's chair.

"Okay."

"Oh, before I forget," said Negar reaching for her purse, "I have copies of our group photo for everyone. They've been in my purse all this time and I just keep forgetting to give them out."

"Let's see," said George.

Negar walked around the room handing them out and there was a moment of silence as everyone stared at the photo. George went to the reception desk looking for the tape, "I'm going to put mine right here!" He put it next to the plaque Bermudadas had given him months before that read, *Never take life too seriously, you'll never get out alive anyway.*

"Okay Manjira, let's get you all beautiful and ready for your day!"

The power came on within the hour, earlier than expected. Manjira was gone; Saffron and Rebecca had left with an intent to check in later; Bermudadas and Negar were under the dryers; and the salon felt unusually silent.

George started to fold towels while Lucy made fresh coffee. George watched her carefully. He hadn't meant to hurt her, he hoped his words would provoke her to see that she had the power to rise. He knew it had to be her choice. He also believed that there was much more going on with her than anyone knew. As much as he had tried to bring her into his confidence, she never cracked.

06

"Sliced bread was invented the year I was born!" laughed Rebecca with rollers in her hair. "That was 1928! How's that for a life altering event?!" She was going through the *World History Almanac* she brought in that cold and clear December morning. As a point of interest, she was reading out loud what happened in the year everyone was born.

"I was born in 1952," said Lucy, who paused with the broom in her hand. "Other than Princess Elizabeth becoming the Queen of England, I don't know what else happened that year."

"I was born during WWII, Roosevelt, Churchill, Stalin, and Mackenzie King were the leaders of the times," reflected Saffron from George's chair. George was adjusting her new hairpiece. Glancing at Bermudadas' reflection in the mirror she didn't want to be in the same room as her, but she wasn't going to allow her to ruin her Friday mornings. Intuitively Saffron knew something wasn't right. Daisley was different, aloof, but she wasn't sure if it was because of his work or if it was because of her. He had to attend so many social engagements as the mayor and she never wanted to go; they were social engagements that seemed to always end up at the Swinging Lantern. It was becoming an issue in their relationship. For him it was fun, for her it was a burden. She was starting to wonder if there was something wrong with her, she knew he expected her to participate more in his political life. He got frustrated every time she asked him what was wrong, so she quit trying to communicate with him. As a result she had withdrawn to protect her feelings. Something was off in her friendship with Bermudadas too; she was also different towards her.

Her fear of losing Daisley to Bermudadas was slowly eating away at her. Her suspicious mind would go crazy and then settle, and then go crazy again. She was caught in a horrible cycle, and it was spiralling deeper and deeper.

Breaking her thoughts Negar said from the reception desk, "That's interesting Saffron. I believe Amelia Earhart vanished somewhere over the South Pacific Ocean in 1937, that was the year I was born."

"She was the first woman to fly solo over the Atlantic Ocean wasn't she?" asked Lucy.

"That's right," nodded Negar.

"Well, I have you all beat," chided Bermudadas from the sink. "Guess what? I know for a fact Alcoholics Anonymous was formed the year I was born! I love it!"

The salon erupted with laughter. Even Saffron had to crack a smile.

"What about you George?" asked Rebecca. "What year were you born?"

"1951. It's interesting that you should ask. My grandfather always said, 'Study the year you were born and learn about the consciousness at the time, it will reveal something to you about yourself', I always thought that was quite fascinating."

"Wow, that is … you're such a puppy George," teased Bermudadas.

"Agreed!" said George. "I'm not up on the international affairs of the day, but I do know in 1951 the two movies *African Queen* and *An American in Paris* were released and that Nat King Cole, Tony Bennett, and Perry Como were the singing stars of the day, my mother used to play all their albums."

"1951, that was the same year the Shah of Iran married his second wife, Soraja. What a wedding! It was in February on New Year's Day, but she couldn't have children, so they were divorced by 1958. He married his third wife, Farah Diba in 1959. They're still together."

"Hold on, you celebrate New Year's in February?" asked Lucy.

"Yes, since we moved to Canada Karim and I get to celebrate two New Years'! December 31st with everyone here, and … well, let me explain; you see, the Iranian calendar follows the lunar cycle so New Year's falls on the Spring Equinox. It's called *Nowruz*, it means new light, it is the first day of spring; therefore, it's the first day of the year in our culture."

"Oh, I like that. So how do you celebrate?" Lucy continued her questioning, "Is it the same as here, at midnight everyone goes crazy?"

"No, it's different. Astronomers calculate the exact time of the Spring Equinox - to the exact second. Before hand we will have set the table with our finest linen and the table is always laden with seven foods that start with the letter S …"

"The letter S?" repeated Lucy.

"Yes, well they start with S in the Persian alphabet, they're called *Haftseen*. The seven *Haftseen* items are: *sabzeh* which is wheat barley, or lentil sprouts growing in a dish to symbolize rebirth; *samanu*, which is a sweet pudding made from wheat germ to symbolize affluence; *senjed*, which is dried fruit to symbolize love; sir, which is garlic ..."

"Garlic?" interrupted Lucy.

"Yes, garlic, it symbolizes medicine. The next is *sib*; an apple that symbolizes beauty and health. Let's see …" as she counted to herself. "Ohh, number six is *somag*, it's kind of a red spice and the colour symbolizes the sunrise; and finally, number seven is *serkeh*; vinegar, which symbolizes old age and patience."

"Why are there seven items?" asked Lucy.

"Well, the number seven has been regarded as magical in the Iranian culture since ancient times and it symbolizes heaven's highest angel."

"Oh," nodded Lucy as Negar continued. "A slightly less traditional *Haftseen* may include; *sekkeh*, coins which symbolize prosperity; and *sonbol*, which is a hyacinth symbolizing the coming of spring; a mirror, symbolizing truth, the reflection of the real world; and finally, a lit candle, symbolizing enlightenment and happiness. Many families sit at the table watching the countdown on television or listen to it on the radio, then at the exact moment an announcement is made and then we say 'Happy New Year' to each other, kind of like how people sing *Auld Lang Syne* here, then we eat and celebrate. The older generation gives money to the younger generation, but the age doesn't really matter. And it's similar to here, you know, how everyone goes to visit their relatives, except in Iran the younger people must visit the older people first and then the visit is reciprocated. Oh, and a few weeks beforehand we plant wheat or lentil seeds in a pot, the growth symbolizes the new year."

"Oh, that's so interesting," said Lucy.

"Since we've moved here, its been a little different. We celebrate with Iranian friends, or that's when we'll go back to Iran to be with our families."

"I understand what you mean Negar," said Saffron. "New Year is an important family time for us too, well I guess it is in every culture, just the traditions are different. Our Korean new year is called *Seollal*. We celebrate it twice, *Gujeong* on the first day of the lunar calendar, *gu* means old and *jeong* means the full moon. And *Sinjeong*, the first day of the solar calendar, Sin means new. *Sinjeong* is from the Japanese influence when they colonized Korea. On *Seollal* we need to be aware of what we say, of what we do, we need to be careful as it's the first day of the year and so we need to initiate it consciously. We have plenty of food too, another similarity in all cultures! We eat rice cake soup and another interesting part about *Gujeong* is it's to celebrate being one year older, not our birth year, but our psychological year. In the morning we visit the graves of our ancestors to honour and worship our them and to pray for prosperity in the coming new year, elders give the younger people advice, we play games, it's a lot of fun. We prepare beef, fish, rice cakes and fruit dishes, my parents still carry out the same traditions since we've lived in Canada."

To herself Lucy remembered all the fun that her mother created over the holidays: the food, the laughter, the love. It was all a distant memory now. After her mother died, she had tried to re-create that for her sister and her father. As hard as she tried to please her father, nothing could ever be the same. Then, Negar interrupted her thoughts.

"I don't know what the future holds for Iran. My brother told me recently that the defence budget has been increased and our relations with Iraq are going sour," she explained with a look of distant worry. Then, smiling she said, "Did you know that one of the world's oldest declarations of human rights was discovered in 1878 at an excavation site in Babylon?"

"No, I didn't," answered Lucy, as everyone else said the same.

"Well, it goes back to around 530 BC, Cyrus the Great wrote it, he is known as the founder of the First Persian Empire. His declaration was found in a cylinder and in it Cyrus describes how the locals were treated. I can't remember it all verbatim, we studied it in school, it goes something like this, *May Ahura Mazda, the supreme divinity, protect this land, this nation from rancor, from foes from falsehood and from drought.* He is also known for the respect he had for other cultures, their religious faiths and traditions. In fact, the United Nations is currently translating it into all the official UN languages."

"Really? Wow that's so interesting. We never studied anything about him here," said Lucy as she stood the broom against the wall and started to get Bermudadas ready to shampoo.

"Well, as a school teacher I know there's only so much that can be taught in a day. Anyway, that's our history lesson for this morning's class!" joked Negar.

Everyone laughed and Bermudadas added, "You won't be giving us a test will you?!"

"No," she laughed.

"Switching the subject, has anyone see Manjira? I haven't seen her for ages."

"I saw her at the Remembrance Day service last week," said Bermudadas. "We didn't chat too much, just small talk. She was getting ready to celebrate *Deepavali* with her family."

"What is *Deepavali*?" asked Lucy.

"Well, she could explain much better that me, but it's called the festival of lights. From my understanding *Deepavali* commemorates the return of Rama and Sita to their kingdom of Ayodhia after 14 years in exile. The people of their kingdom celebrated their return by lighting lamps. There is much, much more, you'll have to ask her to get the story right. She usually invites everyone over and they have traditional clay lamps lit up along their windowsills and the food is incredible! All her relatives are there and it's a lot of fun. She gets all dolled up in her sari; she looks stunning in a sari. I love the Indian sweets her mother makes. They really share their culture, it's wonderful. Anyway, like I said, we didn't chat too much at the cenotaph last week. It's not really the time or place to be social."

"Yes," said Negar, "I saw her there too, but she hasn't been here in the last month has she George?"

"No," he confirmed. "The last time I saw her was that day when the power went out … okay Saffron, one more bobby pin and you're done, the length of your fringe is perfect now. Its grown out just right. Rebecca, you're next, I'll comb you out. Perhaps Manjira didn't care for my insight."

"Well, we all know you meant well George," said Negar as she took a seat in the reception area.

"I ran into her at Shop Easy last week," said Rebecca. As she got up from the dryer, she put the book down on the footstool and proceeded towards George's chair.

Saffron stood up and sat down again next to Negar. Feeling better about herself with her new hairpiece she started going through her purse to find her wallet.

Rebecca went on, "She mentioned that she's been trying out new salons in the area."

"Really?" said Bermudadas.

"Yes, I was just as surprised."

"I have to confess that I do miss her," laughed Bermudadas as she put her head back and relaxed in her chair while Lucy ran the water.

"I think we all do," said Negar.

Bermudadas closed her eyes and thought about Daisley. She had felt Saffron's frostiness these past few weeks. Racked with guilt, in that moment she decided to tell Daisley its over. *I'll call him as soon as I get to the agency.* Besides, she was enjoying spending time with the pharmacist and what if he found out. *I don't want to hurt anyone.* Both her and Daisley never intended their one drunken encounter to continue. It happened shortly after the Chamber dinner. They had run into each other at the Swinging Lantern. The kid was at Richard's for the weekend and they ended up at her place. *And what about the kid? What would happen if she found out? Bermudadas, she told herself, this time you've gone too far. If this got out, the kid might want to go live with her father; this could push her over the limit. She'd be mortified; they'd both be humiliated. Yes, time to end it. I'm not a teenager, I have responsibilities and even though I don't care what people think, I have to think of my daughter first.* Constanze was the one person she never ever wanted to hurt. She was playing a dangerous game and she knew it.

"Well, we can always count on you for the latest gossip can't we Rebecca?" smirked Bermudadas, keeping her eyes closed, "You need a job."

"Being a full-time mom and wife is my job. I want my children growing up knowing I'm at home doing everything I can for their well being, and to see how rewarding volunteer work is. I want them to grow up in a traditional home and good morals."

"I know, I know. I've been listening to your song for years Rebecca," answered a bitter Bermudadas.

"Okay, Rebecca, you're due for a perm next week, so allow yourself some more time," said George.

"Okay George," she answered.

"I'll write that down right now," said Lucy as she finished wrapping Bermudadas' hair in a towel and headed for the reception desk.

"Thanks Lucy," said George. He had noticed she was trying harder around the shop, yet she was clearly still drinking and recently her clothes started to smell of pot.

"I'm subbing all of next week George, so I'll need to change my time too," said Negar.

"Great, where?"

"At the high school, I've had these classes before, they're good kids. It will be nice to have them for a whole week. And subbing is perfect, their teacher has all the lesson plans ready for me, I love that part of subbing!"

"Good for you, well just come in when you can."

Turning to Lucy she said, "If there's space Lucy, I'd like to come in late Friday afternoon instead."

"Sure," she had lengthened Rebecca's time and was sharpening the pencil, "What time?"

"Let's say four o'clock, is there room?"

"Yes, that works." With her head bent over the calendar Lucy thought of how Negar had her teaching profession, Bermudadas with her travel agency, Saffron with her art career, and Rebecca the full-time mom. All these women seemed so accomplished, it was daunting. *I could never be like them* she thought.

"So, tell us about your art show Saffron," asked George who was acutely aware her inner spark had recently been fading.

Hesitantly she answered, "Well the show is next Thanksgiving, so I have almost a year. It's all in line with the provincial centennial celebrations."

"Yes, I heard Queen Elizabeth and Princess Anne will be here in May for a visit," said George.

"Yes, and there is a big event planned at Empire Stadium on July 20, a new stamp is being released, and there are province-wide events being organized to illustrate the character of the province, it's going to be a lot of fun," continued Saffron. "And the art show here is one of Riverville's community events."

"That sounds great Saffron," said Negar.

"My canvases have arrived, I've been sketching, and now I'm ready to transfer them onto the canvas. My intent is to somehow convey the universal in the human condition. I want to touch people's hearts, whether they're open or not I don't know. But I want to trigger awareness, not so unlike Warhol who believes that we need to be more conscious of how blind we are as we consume more and more of this world without thinking and recognize that love is more important than all that. I'm not sure if that makes sense, I'm still churning it around."

"It does," said George.

"As I see it, artists find a sight that no one else sees. We see the world in a way no else does, then we move towards it, and then we create or choose a medium to express it. I always ask myself, 'How am I going to express it?' I embody art, this is how I see the world, and this is my life. Vincent van Gogh painted for love, for joy, his work was an expression of him, there was no motive. I get that, I feel the same."

"Where is the venue?" asked Negar, eager to support her.

"It's going to be in the entrance foyer to city hall, there will be two other local artists and we all have a different style and medium so hopefully something will appeal to everyone. I'm a little uncomfortable with all the extra attention I'm getting because of Daisley being the mayor. I've become careful of other people's compliments. I'm getting a lot of extra perks through all his media contacts and I'm not so comfortable with it all."

"Oh relax woman," said Bermudadas. "Just be happy you're getting the added attention and suck it up."

"Well, that may be how you operate Bermudadas. But I don't want any special treatment. I choose to earn my place among my peers because of my talent, not because I'm the mayor's wife. And as for all those people who want to help out, I have to wonder do they really want to help me and the show or are they just trying to score points with the mayor?"

Round one thought George as their row bounced back and forth, "Well, I'm sure it's something you need to be aware of Saffron. And I'm sure you'll figure out how you want to respond to them. Okay Rebecca, you're done. Next ..." looking around the room he continued, "... that would be you Bermudadas."

"Well Saffron," said Negar, "I'll be there to support you and let me know if I can help you with anything. I can be your personal assistant! Okay, I'm going to head out."

"Thanks Negar. I'm heading out too, I'll walk with you," added Saffron standing up and walking to the reception desk. "Lucy, don't forget that I also have to pay you for the hairpiece."

"Right, okay let me add that up for you."

"My check is right there beside the phone Lucy," indicated Negar.

"Yes, I got it, thanks."

Saffron paid her bill, the two ladies got all bundled up, and headed outside into the cold winter air.

"Okay, see you all soon," said Negar holding the door open for Saffron.

"Cheerio," answered George. "Go get inspired Saffron!" teasing her.

"Sure George," she smiled back at him.

After they left Lucy asked George if it was okay to take a break and grab an early lunch, to which he complied; that left Rebecca sitting in the reception area and Bermudadas in George's chair.

"So how are the twins and Elizabeth?" Bermudadas asked Rebecca. Happy to have Saffron gone, she felt she could relax a little more. The sooner she ended it with Daisley the better. Well, she had survived worse things than this and she knew she'd figure it out.

"They're busy, as I know your daughter is too. They're looking forward to the Christmas break of course. Lance and I are thinking of sending all three of them to stay with family in Saskatchewan next summer.

We would like them get to know their relatives more and experience life on a farm. We've taken them out to visit over the years, but it would be good for them to spend a long period of time there. I don't want my kids growing up with just a city lifestyle, we feel they need to discover where food comes from and experience prairie life."

"That makes sense," agreed George. "We'll probably head back for visit next spring, it's time to take the baby back to meet the clan."

"Oh good for you, both you and Marthina must be ready for a holiday," said Rebecca.

"Yes, time to get back to the farm – but only for a short time. Hard to believe this is the baby's first Christmas."

"I remember those days," mused Bermudadas. "The kid is with Richard this Christmas. I don't like being alone, but I have to fulfil my end of the bargain. We may all get together for turkey dinner, let's see. It would be nice for the kid."

I really don't want to be alone she thought to herself, the pharmacist was going to be with his parents; he didn't seem interested in taking her with him on Christmas Day.

"I'm sure that must be tough Bermudadas," said Rebecca from a place of sincere compassion. "As it is with every holiday season I'm so busy between the thrift shop and canvassing for Christmas hampers. Plus, fundraising has already started for next year's lacrosse league. I'm the head fund raiser you know."

"Why do you do it all?" asked Bermudadas who was just so weary of Rebecca's perpetual Mother Theresa image. "I mean, really, are you going for the Citizen of the Year award? Are you trying to show the world how indispensable you are to humanity?"

Feeling embarrassed because Bermudadas had just revealed her truth; she did want to win Riverville's Citizen of the Year award. She was horrified Bermudadas had guessed her truth, hiding her reaction as best she could she answered, "I have nothing but the purest intentions at heart Bermudadas."

"Well, knock yourself out. Just don't whine and get bitter like you always do when people aren't always expressing their thanks. You always sing the same old song, 'Look what I did for them and not even a thank you'."

Recognizing what Bermudadas was saying as true, she was speechless, "Well, I just wish people would express a little more gratitude for what I do for them, that's all." Then, changing the subject, "How are things at the agency?"

"Busy, this is always a hectic time of year for us. So many people flying here and there, we're hopping busy. I'm not complaining, January is traditionally slow, so may hay while the sun shines! Isn't that what you prairie folk say?!"

"Yes, we do!" answered George.

Rebecca sat and thought to herself; despite their obvious moral differences she did have to admit she would miss Bermudadas' constant chatter, spontaneity, and crazy antics if she wasn't around, "Well Bermudadas, perhaps as we learn more about each other the more we'll understand why we both do the things we do."

"Agreed," their eyes met in the mirror.

"And perhaps you'll end up discovering just how much you're both the same," teased George.

"Well, I wouldn't go that far George! Okay, I'm off, next stop is the church. I'll leave my check on the desk George."

"Okay, thanks Rebecca. And don't forget you're coming in early next week for your perm."

"I'll remember," she answered as she reached for her coat and scarf. Moments later as she was pulling on her gloves she added, "Lucy's family is getting another hamper this year. I know her father must have been devastated when Pearl died, but that's a few years now and he's become nothing but an old drunk. I mean, he drank before Pearl died, but he needs help. I worry about those two girls. Considering what Lucy has to cope with she's doing quite well don't you think?"

Cautious to talk about Lucy he answered, "Yes, she is. From my understanding her father takes his working buddies home to drink quite often."

"Yes, I always see a couple of cars parked in their drive way. I go by their house on my way to the church. Does Lucy ever say anything to you George?"

Not wishing to engage in gossiping about Lucy, even though he knew Rebecca's intentions may be good, he guardedly answered, "A little bit, but not much. You know Lucy, she's like a clam."

"Well," pulling her gloves on, "Pearl would be devastated if she knew those old bastards were drinking in her home."

"Rebecca," said a flabbergasted Bermudadas, "I think that's the first time I've ever heard you swear. I like it!"

"Well, it's true. Sometimes I just want to stop and give that man a piece of my mind. The yard looks like a dump, Pearl's rose garden has gone wild, every spring I just want to get in there and maintain it. You'd think that old fool would be more than that, but he's just getting worse. I don't know how those young girls live there, it must be a nightmare."

"Well, they could always come and live with me and the kid. We've got plenty of room. I wonder if I should suggest that to her. What do you think George?"

"It would be a sensitive matter, though it couldn't hurt to ask her. I just advise caution, despite how her father seems to be, she's incredibly loyal to him. And who knows how he would react."

"That's true. That's a very Christian thing to do Bermudadas."

"It's not a Christian thing to do Becs, it's a human thing to do."

"Oh, but of course it is ... " rolling her eyes, "Well before we get going at each other again, I'm off. See you both next week." And she was gone.

"It's so quiet in here George, it's not often you have just one client in the salon," she suddenly felt a little anxious with the silence.

"Very true Bermudadas. So, how are you ... really?"

Not knowing whether to confide in George or not she answered, "I'm fine, but what do you mean by adding *really*?"

"Well, *How are you?* seems to be a question we're asked all the time and we automatically say, *I'm fine*. I'm asking are you *really* okay? From my viewpoint it seems you are walking on egg shells around Saffron."

"It's that obvious is it?"

"Yes, it is. Saffron is what, ten years younger than you?"

"Yes, ten or twelve, something like that."

"And she's only been married for two or three years. Perhaps you need to understand she has a basic fear of being defective, and that spills over into a fear of not fitting in, and with her husband being the mayor she has her challenges."

"I know that George. She's young, an artist, and married to Daisley. It seems to me that she has it all."

"Well, what about you? You're dating the pharmacist right?"

"Yes, it's going okay," then, deciding to confide in George she blurted it out, "Daisley and I have been having an affair George."

Completely un-reactive, he nodded and continued to unroll the big oversize rollers out of her long back hair, "I thought so."

Shocked by his reply she asked, "Do you think everyone else knows too? I don't want to hurt anyone. I don't know how it happened. I got sloppy. Initially it was an impulse, we were so drunk, after the first time that was going to be it, but then … "

"Come on Bermudadas, you're an adult, it was a choice. Perhaps this is an opportunity for you to ask yourself why you've created the situation."

"We were drunk."

"Don't blame the booze. You're both adults with responsibilities and other people are involved."

"Well George, it's not easy being a single and honestly I don't like being alone. It's like my married friends pity me. They never come out and say it, but I feel it. Society sells the notion that life without a partner is incomplete. Women are forced to look for someone; as though we're not strong enough to be alone. It seems to me the general consensus that being single in this world isn't okay. Society has created and successfully maintained the belief that it's impossible to be single and be happy. It's like I'm a loser if I'm single."

"Don't define yourself through the eyes of society; actually, I'm surprised you care so much about the so-called social order."

"Well, I don't, but I do ... of course I care. Society is made up of my family, my friends. I live in society, I'm not anti-society, I just don't want to conform to society and allow it to define me."

"That makes sense because society needs your cooperation to evolve."

"True, though fitting in has never been a big concern of mine," she answered.

"That's very clear!" laughed George. "But are you truly happy? It seems to me, because you are constantly active, shopping, running here for a weekend, running there for a weekend that you never stop to really look at yourself and reflect. From what I've witnessed your life is an accumulation of experiences and acquiring things; you're like a tornado. You stay busy to keep yourself stimulated. It's as though you are feeling deprived when actually you are not; everything is actually inside of you. What about slowing down for a while to see things on a deeper level? Perhaps then you'll quit escaping and acting impulsively. It's as though your appetite for life takes over and you don't think of the consequences."

"I am thinking now George. I'm going to end it with Daisley. The kid would be devastated if it ever got out. I can't imagine how life would be for her. It's for her that I'm going to end it. And every time I see Saffron the guilt just takes over."

"Yes, I can see that. Well, good. That's a start Bermudadas; however, as I see it don't fall back. Really use this situation as an opportunity to study yourself and reflect. Examine your life, or as Socrates taught, *Know thyself*. The world doesn't exist just for your gratification."

"I know you're right George. Thanks for listening. You won't tell anyone will you George?"

"Of course not. Okay, you're done."

George then held up the mirror for her to see the whole of her head and for a moment their eyes met in the mirror, "Take a good look at yourself Bermudadas and perhaps ask yourself, *Is this how I want to exist?*"

"No George, it isn't."

"Well, it's up to you to get your world in order. Eventually the truth will reveal itself. I'm not going to coddle you, you created this situation, and you accept responsibility for it, take ownership."

"I know and I will. Thanks for listening George."

"Sure," as he was unclipping the apron from around her neck the door opened and in walked Lucy.

"Sorry I took a little longer than I thought George."

"That's okay Lucy," he answered, "That's okay."

07

Three weeks later Bermudadas was sitting under the dryer, eyes closed, the heat warm on her neck. She didn't want to talk to anyone. The hum of the dryer was perfect; it took her away from engaging with the buzz of the salon. The Christmas holidays came and went. She didn't get excited about them. The kid was with her father on Christmas Day and she spent it at the old people's home pouring wine and listening to the old timers tell their stories. One of her favourites was an old postman whose mail route used to be downtown Vancouver on Robson Street during the 1930's and 40's. She asked herself, *I wonder if life was simpler then?* She enjoyed spending time with them, she always left feeling she received more than she gave. She always took her dog Maggie, they loved to pet her and the old Scotty-lab loved the attention. Other than the staff, no one in her outer world knew she went there on a regular basis; she certainly wasn't going to go around bragging like Rebecca. In fact, since she had moved to town she had been a volunteer and she started taking the kid shortly after she was born. All the old grannies had loved to hold and play with her, and the kid enjoyed it too. The old people's home had become a huge part of their lives.

Right now she was tired. This morning in a rush to get the kid to school she got another speeding ticket. Reflecting, she wondered if that was a metaphor for her life; always in fifth gear. *What am I doing with my life?* She had never really thought about anything but having fun.

She had broken up with the pharmacist just after New Year's; he seemed disappointed, but not devastated. She had told him that she wanted to spend more time with the kid before she graduated and left home forever. It wasn't completely true, but he bought it and she was able to end it amicably.

And then there was Daisley. After confiding in George she really did it; she had followed through and ended it. They arranged to meet one last time at the Swinging Lantern to talk. She stayed for a few drinks and as soon as she finished the last one they both slipped outside to the parking lot to discuss their situation in private.

"It's over Daisley," she told him.

"Yes, I know. I'm racked with guilt. I want to tell her."

"Why would you tell her?" she was getting freaked out. The panic was causing her breath to stagger. The consequences of their affair suddenly appeared right before her, "How could we have been so stupid?"

"I don't know Bermudadas, calm down," he answered. "We really weren't thinking about anyone but ourselves. We fell back to an old habit." Taking a deep breath he just felt sick and out of anger he threw his cigarette into a puddle.

"Don't tell Saffron," begged Bermudadas. "This will be devastating for her. Plus, I don't want my daughter finding out. Can you imagine what she would face at high school if it got out that her mother was having an affair with the mayor? She may choose to go live with her father, he's a great father, but I don't want her to leave and she might just to get away from the shame."

"Well, I can't live without telling her. She's stopped asking me what is wrong. We aren't communicating at all. When I get home, she's withdrawn, and I feel her anger. I'm afraid to talk to her; it's like she's a time bomb. And I don't blame her; I haven't been easy to be around. We have our third wedding anniversary coming up in a few weeks. She was the most beautiful bride. I fell in love with her because of her love for humanity; she just seems to bring out the best in me. I don't want to lose her."

"Well then don't tell her. We were only together a few times and it's over, just leave it be. What good is telling her going to do? Bloody society morals, she doesn't have to know, no one has to know. You still want to be with her, so put it aside and work at getting things right with her again."

"Maybe that's the best," he just stood there shaking his head looking at the ground wondering how he could have been so stupid. He loved Saffron. Bermudadas was just naughty and fun, but he didn't want to have a relationship with her. It was strictly sex.

"Look at the people in our lives and the mess we'll create if they find out. And what about your political career? You'll be fucked. Leave it be." Stubbing her cigarette out on the ground, she said, "Okay, I'm leaving. I'm going home."

Neither one of them noticed the person standing in the shadows with a camera, not close enough to hear everything, but close enough to get some photographs. With the intent to give each other a gentle peck on the cheek their embrace once again turned into a heated passionate kiss. Suddenly, Daisley backed off and opened the car door; she got in, fired up her Mustang and drove home feeling completely distorted. She knew she shouldn't be driving. She wasn't hammered, but she was always driving under the influence, sometimes she woke up totally ashamed of her bad habit. Each time it happened she told herself it was the last, but it never was. Meanwhile, Daisley walked back inside the Swinging Lantern for one more beer determined to somehow get back on track with Saffron.

That evening, when she arrived home, she had actually called George at home to tell him what had transpired. He didn't say much, other than to suggest that perhaps she try being single for a while to get some clarity on her life. She told him she was trying to, but it was painful. On the inside she was filled with self-hatred, emptiness, she was lonely and feeling so depressed. Her demons were in her face everyday. On the outside she was maintaining her lie, a chameleon act, carrying on as if all was well - and it was draining.

She recognized that her life was an accumulation of experiences, she drove fast cars, ate fast, partied hard, always in pursuit of life's many pleasures which she justified coming from poverty – and she did love her lifestyle. There was no denying that. George had said she was like a tornado. Richard had said the same thing and hearing it again really jolted her back to thinking about her marriage. Richard was a kind man. He had told her that if leaving him would make her happy then she had to go. He didn't make anything about him; he just wanted her to be happy. He deserved better she thought. He was dating someone, the kid said she was a sweetie, so good for him.

The dryer clicked off, bringing her back to the present moment. Opening her eyes and looking around she saw George taking the rollers out of Rebecca's hair; Lucy talking on the phone; Negar sitting next to her under the dryer reading a book about tennis; and Saffron was just coming through the door. *We all have our shit* she mused.

Saffron and Bermudadas' eyes met. She didn't know what Saffron's eyes were saying. Looking away Saffron removed her winter coat, scarf, and gloves. Underneath she was wearing her paint-spattered clothes; obviously she was taking a break from her work thought Bermudadas. *I wonder how things are going?*

She and Daisley hadn't spoken since then and it was killing her not to know what was going on, but she was determined to butt out and get her own life in order.

Tilting the cone back she reached for her cigarettes. Noticing the ashtray was full she picked it up, walked to the back of the shop and emptied it into the trashcan. Sitting back down, lighting a cigarette, she offered one to Negar, who accepted and nodded thanks.

Flipping her cone back Negar said, "I need to quit smoking, but I just really enjoy it. I'm thinking about taking up tennis and I doubt smoking is in-line with the philosophy of fitness!"

"Tennis, why the hell would you want to start playing tennis?" asked Bermudadas.

"I have to start doing something physical, I have to start taking better care of my health and there's a new tennis club that just opened up on the north side of town. Karim is interested too, it could be something for us to learn together."

"Have you tried it?"

"No, but for some reason it seems appealing. I don't really know, I'm just thinking about it!"

"Good for you," Bermudadas answered. Her heart not really into talking.

"Are you okay?"

"Oh, sure, I'm just tired," she said trying to deflect the attention. "Things have been busy at the agency and I've been running the kid around here and there. I got another speeding ticket this morning. I have to admit it, I do get tired! Hey Becs, how are your kids?"

"Well, as I was just telling George, I nominated Rachel for May Queen and she got so mad at me."

"Does she want to be May Queen?" asked Bermudadas.

"Bermudadas, why wouldn't any young lady want to be May Queen? You get lots of attention, you get to be in the May Day Parade, your picture is in the paper, and there are all kinds of other reasons. Plus, it would be good for her to get out of her jeans and into a dress."

"Okay, but I'm asking does she want to be May Queen?"

Answering hesitantly she said, "No, but she's young and she doesn't understand that it will be good for her. Every young lady in Riverville wants to be May Queen."

"Really? Let's test your theory." Lucy was off the phone so Bermudadas called to her, "Lucy, would you want to be May Queen?"

"May Queen? I wouldn't ever want to be May Queen," she answered. "I wouldn't want all the attention. Plus it's the snooty girls who always win, they think they're really special."

"Okay, you're wrong Becs. I know the kid would be horrified if I demanded she enter the contest."

"Well, I just think it would be good for her, she's such a tomboy."

"Do you let your kids make any of their own decisions? Or are they living out your idea of how they should be?" asked Bermudadas.

"Of course they make their own decisions, but I know best and it's only for her own good."

Rolling her eyes Bermudadas asked, "Do you really believe encouraging your daughter to participate in a beauty contest is a good life experience?"

"She's such a tomboy, she's a young lady now and needs to dress and act like one."

"And you think that becoming the May Queen will change all that? Too many women are trying to be Barbie dolls.

Do you have any idea of the jealousy and the nonsense those contests create? Women get so depressed from beauty pageants, do you really want your daughter to grow up thinking that's okay?"

"It's not a beauty contest."

"It sure as hell is! Is the contest a celebration of beauty or does the contest celebrate the only beautiful thing to offer? She won't be winning for her brains. What are you teaching her? All those contests do is create divisiveness between women. In the madness of competition women can be so cruel, they cripple each other. As I see it it's teaching women to be so self-serving. Sometimes women can only relate with other women through jealousy, it's a competition; who has the best car, the best boyfriend, they become their own worst enemies. I would never subject the kid to such nonsense."

Rebecca sat speechless; internally she had to admit that Bermudadas did have a point. She had never looked at it that way, but she wasn't about to admit it.

"Next you'll be wanting her to become a trophy wife and get married. Perhaps what you are training her for isn't necessarily her soul's choice," said Bermudadas. "Women are selling their looks and men are buying it. Men end up loving their looks and not them."

"Now you're an expert in that department."

"Let me make one thing perfectly clear Becs, as I see it, you're teaching your daughter the belief that beauty is the only criteria for a man to be with a woman. As for myself, I'm not here to live out your idea or society's idea, I'm here to live out my idea."

Bermudadas then gave up on the conversation and settled back into her chair, she didn't even have the energy to banter with Rebecca. She decided to put forth an effort with Saffron, "So, looks like you're painting Saffron, how is it going?"

From his position George saw Saffron's body language react with indifference, so he opted to help Bermudadas along, "When exactly is your art show Saffron?"

"It's in ten months, Thanksgiving weekend," she had no problem answering George. She wasn't going to cosy up to Bermudadas and although she didn't have any proof, she just felt so sure Bermudadas and Daisley were having an affair. But to his credit, he had been trying to communicate and he had quit going to the Swinging Lantern. He was spending a lot more time at home in the evenings, so something had shifted in him, but was it guilt? Or did he really want to spend time with her again?

Not really interested in Saffron's art show in that moment Rebecca announced, "Did you hear Manjira's husband wants to get into politics?"

"Yes, I did," said Saffron. "Daisley mentioned it, he wants to run for councillor in this fall's election."

"That's right," said Rebecca. "I saw Manjira at the dry cleaners and she was rambling on about it."

"How's their business?" asked Bermudadas.

"She didn't really say," said Rebecca.

"I sent a potential client to her last week, I hope things are going okay for them. They generally have a good run over the holidays," said Bermudadas.

"Yes, they do. It's just unfortunate she doesn't come here anymore," said Negar. "I do miss her."

"I have to admit it, so do I," laughed Bermudadas. Every one else agreed in unison.

"I have a feeling she'll be back," said Negar.

"Of course she will, she'll want to know all the gossip," retorted Rebecca. "Hey, what do you guys think of the funeral home? I don't know how they stay in business, people aren't dying on a regular basis and they re-paved the parking lot last summer. I think there's something fishy going on there."

"Listen to yourself Becs - and you label Manjira as the one who likes to gossip! But go on, I've got to hear this, what possible theory do you have to share with us?" asked a sarcastic Bermudadas.

"Who knows? Drugs probably, money laundering."

"There you go again, gossiping away with out knowing any facts. You do excel in gossiping Becs, you get an A+," laughed Bermudadas.

"Well, it just doesn't make sense to me."

"Nothing outside of your little bubble makes sense to you Becs." Wanting another cigarette she turned to Negar, "Do you have a light?"

"Sure," handing over her lighter.

Eyeing Lucy at the desk Bermudadas said, "Cool tie dye T-shirt Lucy." She had wanted Lucy to know she had a place to stay if she ever wanted to move out, but the opportunity had never come up. She had so much going on in her own world right now that she hadn't put forth the effort, but she felt she needed to let her know as soon as possible. She had talked it over with the kid and she was in full agreement. George is right, that girl is like a clam. She had seen Lucy's father at the Swinging Lantern many, many times; he was a pig, always hitting on the waitresses and getting behind the wheel and driving home drunk, but then who was she to talk.

"Thanks, I got it at K-Mart."

"You flower child! How are things? Are you losing weight? You look so skinny."

Never comfortable about talking about herself, she answered, "Maybe a little, no big deal." Then switching the subject, "Negar do you have Ned's check ready? He'll be in later this afternoon."

"Yes, George has signed it and it's in the drawer, on the left."

"Okay," opening the drawer she found it, "Thanks." George had asked her the same question about her weight when she arrived that morning. She thought about all the discussions that took place in the salon and at first it was the part of the job she hated. She didn't want to hear all the gossip; she was on autopilot just moving around behind the scenes doing her job, she liked to feel invisible. She was grateful for the work and that George was so patient and understanding. He had given her so many chances; she was starting to get a little freaked out about losing her position. She knew she drank too much, but it numbed her from the pain. Recently she had started smoking dope with her friend Sherry, and last weekend they had dropped some acid. Everyone thought her issues were from the loss of her mother, it was true, life had bottomed out when her mother got sick and died, but it wasn't the only reason. Her father had contributed to it too, he was never a loving father, and she despised how he treated all of them when her mother was alive; now it was worse. How many times growing up had they all heard him say, *Why couldn't one of you been a boy?*

She missed her mom. She was a proper mom, a proper lady. She made life fun; baking raisin cookies, playing dress-up with all her clothes. One of her fondest memories was the three of them driving to Lions Park to collect chestnuts in the fall and then going home and making long necklaces out of them. She still had one necklace in her trunk. Her mom called her Snookums, it was her special name and she called Karen Muffin because she loved her homemade blueberry muffins. They had a home; until her mom got sick. At that time she was 12 years old, her sister seven. After her death they entered another world. A horrible world created by their father.

Their house had become the party spot for all his friends to hangout. They were wanna-be musicians, always jamming and attempting to play the latest hits. Nobody grocery shopped on a regular basis; there was rarely any food in the house. We scrounged for dinner, she remembered bitterly. It was usually leftovers from a pizza order or Chinese take out. Her father taught her to roll joints for him and his friends. Her small fingers did a great job; they all thought it was funny. Her household chores had switched from helping her mom in the kitchen to keeping beers in the fridge and plastic baggies filled with rolled joints. Her and her sister Karen were left to fend for themselves amongst these adults: who were always wired on something. They were supposed to go to school, and they did, but their father was indifferent if they went or not. He had no problem writing notes to excuse them. After a couple of years her sister had taken up with a good crowd; her best friend's mother really took her under her wing. Karen even went on summer holidays to Penticton with them, but not Lucy, she became a loner from the shame. After a while, once she got older, she just starting stealing drugs and booze from her father. She remembered when he caught her; he beat the crap out of her, just like he did their mother when he'd get pissed off at her for something. He was a violent man. Her mother would always make excuses for him, *Oh, your father is having a bad day, his job at the railway yard is very stressful* ... he had beaten the crap out of their mother more than once and now she was the chosen target. The best thing about his friends hanging around was he never did it in front of them.

Her thoughts were suddenly interrupted when the door swung open and a cold draft made her shiver; standing before her was Ned.

"Hi Lucy, hi everyone!" he bellowed.

A unison of *Hellos* was returned to him. Everyone continued on with their friendly chitchat as Ned strolled through the shop carrying two boxes of product to the back. On his return he stopped and sat in the chair next to George.

After contributing to the friendly bantering he said, "Well, I must say, coming into this shop is one of my favourites."

"Why?" asked Saffron.

"Well, it just seems different for some reason. I can't seem to put my finger on it, but when I walk in here the atmosphere seems ... seems, friendly." Looking directly at Saffron, "No, it's more than that, you all seem to be such good friends who care about each other."

The salon went silent for a moment. Ned felt the place shift, so he smiled and said, "Okay, have a great weekend everyone. See you in two weeks." He smiled at Lucy on his way out the door; he still hadn't asked George about her. He didn't want to cross the boundary between business and personal, but he'd had his eye on her for a long time now.

After he left a silence fell over the room. Lucy, standing at the desk, stared out the window, but wasn't seeing. Saffron, sitting in the reception area, stared down at her magazine, but wasn't reading. Negar, sitting under a dryer, stared at her tennis book, but she too wasn't reading. Bermudadas, sitting under a dryer, stared at her cigarette burning, but wasn't smoking. And Rebecca, sitting in George's chair, stared at herself in the mirror, but didn't see.

George reached over to grab the can of hair spray and repeated Ned's words out loud, "You all seem quite good friends who care about each other ... interesting, isn't it?" No one spoke.

08

Riverville's Daisley Michael caught cheating on wife – is it time for the mayor to step down?

Exactly one week later a stunned George sat in the reception area of his salon reading the headline of Riverville's Friday morning paper. Beneath the headline was a slightly blurred photo of Bermudadas and Daisley embracing and kissing in a parking lot. George took a deep breath in and his eyebrows came together in deep concern, *What happened?*

George had gotten into a daily routine of arriving early for time to sit, smoke, and drink a coffee before his day began. Sometimes he would even go for a stroll along the river dike to enjoy the peace and quiet. Staring out the window; he was completely flabbergasted. He tossed the paper on the table, leaned back in his chair, closed his eyes, and tried to figure it out. Bermudadas had told him she ended it and he believed her. *Who took the photo?* Things were going to erupt.

The door opened, he opened his eyes, it was Lucy.

"George," she said in obvious shock, "Have you seen the paper?"

"Yes," nodding towards the table.

"Can it be true?"

"Yes, Lucy. It's true."

Slumping into the chair next to George, Lucy was speechless. Finally she spoke, "Do you think Bermudadas or Saffron will still come in today?"

"I don't know Lucy, let's see."

An hour later Negar was sitting in George's chair getting the finishing touches on her Mary Tyler Moore hairdo, Rebecca was sitting next to her, and Lucy sat on one of the footstools.

"I don't know how Saffron is going to survive this George. I don't think she has the inner strength. I'm really worried about her. I called their house, but there's no answer," said Rebecca. "Maybe I should drive by and stop in, but maybe not, I just don't want to go unannounced in case they're talking."

"She hasn't called to cancel," offered Lucy. "Maybe she'll still show up. Her appointment is for 9:30. That's in about twenty minutes."

"Yes, but she always comes in early and she's not here," answered Rebecca.

"And what about Bermudadas?" asked Negar. "What time is her appointment?"

"Ten o'clock," said Lucy.

"You don't think that cow is going to show up do you? She wouldn't dare!" snapped Rebecca.

"Now Rebecca ..." started Negar.

"Don't you go defending her like you always do!"

"I was going to say – before you interrupted me - that they are both our friends and we need to find out the truth before we start reacting. It's not fair to start name calling and it's not going to help the situation," she reasoned.

"I agree with Negar," said George. "Let's see what they both have to say."

At that moment dishevelled, teary-eyed Saffron pushed open the door with great effort.

"Saffron!" exclaimed Rebecca. The older woman jumped out of the chair, hurried over to her and threw her arms around her. "Sit down and tell us exactly what is going on. Take your coat off."

Rebecca helped remove her coat and handed it to Lucy to hang up while she got Saffron settled in a chair. Negar was done, but she didn't move from George's chair. The four of them; George, Lucy, Negar and Rebecca all waited patiently for Saffron to speak.

Finally she choked out, "Daisley told me two nights ago, Wednesday I guess it was, when he came home from work. Apparently, Tom, you know Tom, from the paper? We went to high school together, well, sometime recently he was at the Swinging Lantern and he saw them leave the bar together, so he followed them with his camera. He said they've been pretty cosy for a while and he wanted to see if the rumours going round were true. He took the picture, developed it and then met with Daisley in his office. Tom told Daisley he had one week to tell me. Tom has always been like a big brother to me and he was pissed, but he wanted to give Daisley time to think it through because he knows he's a solid person and so far he's been a great mayor. He also told Daisley he better tell me or he would do it himself." Saffron took a deep breath and then continued, "Daisley promised Tom he would tell me and he did. Then, yesterday Tom called the house and asked if he could see me. Of course I said *Yes*. He wanted to tell his side of the story. He said he was sorry, but he wanted me to know the truth. He was always a good friend to me in high school; we worked on the school annual together. Anyway, he said its been obvious to everyone at the Swinging Lantern that something was going on between them. He told me how torn he was to show his editor the photos, but he felt he had to, it's his job and that was that. Now it's today's front-page news. He wanted me to know it was going to be in the paper."

11

"He sounds like a good friend," said Negar.

Saffron nodded and slumped over into Rebecca's arms.

"My parents … I just came from their place. They don't know what to think, they love Daisley."

"Where is he now?" asked George.

"He went to work to face the music," she answered. "I don't know what will happen, if he'll be asked to resign or what … I'm sure his opponents will love this."

"That's not important," soothed Rebecca. "You're what is important. Not Daisley."

"I knew it, I just knew it," sobbed Saffron.

"That Bermudadas, she's just so predictable. And to think all this time she's coming in here and carrying on the way she does and all the while she's having an affair with your husband. How long has it been going on?" demanded Rebecca.

"Daisley said not that long, that she means nothing to him, that they were both at the Swinging Lantern one night, they were both really drunk and they went to her place. He said it only happened a couple of times; he's begging me not to leave him. His parents are horrified - their prodigal son."

Suddenly the door swung open and in charged Manjira, "Where is that hussy? Is she here? I'm going to give that woman a piece of my mind!"

"Now settle down Manjira," said George. "Your support for Saffron is great, but give it some time before you start reacting."

Manjira sat next to Saffron without taking her coat off and said, "I told you so. That woman pounces on anyone she feels fit."

"Let me remind you Manjira, it does take two," stated Negar.

Ignoring her, Manjira asked Saffron, "What are you going to do?"

"I don't know, I just don't know. How can I walk around town? Everyone will be gossiping about me, I just want to hide."

"Of course you do," comforted Rebecca reaching for some fresh tissues for her.

"My mother told me not to defend him. She told me to look at the facts and not make any decisions or talk to the media until the shock has worn off. She said right now I don't want to see the truth and it's all so fresh and the wound is deep."

"What she says makes a lot of sense," said Negar. "She's a wise woman."

Lucy sat frozen, not knowing what to do. She remembered when her father had an affair while her mother was sick. She recalled the argument between her parents when her father blamed her beautiful mother for the affair. She overheard her father yelling, *You're sick, but I'm still a man, so shut up woman, you have no right to get angry.* Lucy didn't know how her mother found out or who the other woman was, but she did know her mother didn't have the energy to argue. As always, she hid her pain and carried on like everything was fine for her daughters' sake.

Silence fell on the room. Finally Manjira spoke, "Well dear, I agree with your mother, take time to process everything. I always liked Daisley; he's a fine young man. He's been a stellar mayor and I'm sure he must be feeling like a fool right now."

Saffron nodded in agreement, "I love him. I don't want to lose him. I'm numb; I don't know what to feel. I'm angry, I'm sad, I don't know how he could do this to me."

"Well," said George. "It takes courage to look at the facts Saffron. Be conscious of your suffering, but give it some time, and if you can; detach from your broken heart, don't follow the pain, go opposite from it and you will rise from this."

"This is going to sound crazy, but now that I know the truth I do feel better. Since the Chamber dinner I've kept wondering and it was eating away at me. Now that I know, I feel relieved. It's out now."

"Your brain is resting into the truth," said George. "That's good, that's a start."

"I have to give myself time. I have to reconcile with the truth. I won't defend him. The fairy tale is over," she sobbed.

Manjira said, "Saffron, you're right the fairy tale is over, but perhaps this is an opportunity for you to see that your idea of love is an illusion. Let this truth liberate you and perhaps this experience will bring you both closer together. I don't know, but as I see it, if you decide not to leave him, you can both move forward in more awareness of just how much you mean to each other. One way or another, with or without him, you will survive this."

"He said he doesn't want me to leave him, he doesn't want to be with Bermudadas."

"Of course he wants to be with you," Manjira agreed. "As for Bermudadas, I don't think any man would expect or want a commitment from her. That woman has such a history." Looking at everyone in the room, "Remember the story she told all of us, you probably haven't heard it George. It was in Toronto, before she met Richard. She was engaged to some family friend. Anyway, he left her standing at the alter! Have you heard that story George?"

"No," replied a cautious George.

"Please, let's not bash Bermudadas," begged Negar.

"I'm just telling the truth, well, she had been dating this guy for a while, I guess in high school. I'm not exactly sure. They had been dating and they got engaged, it was to be the wedding of the century, everything was lavish, the invitations, everything. Her parents spent so much money. Apparently, there she was on her wedding day, sitting in her designer gown in the limousine parked outside the church and the groom never showed up!"

"How devastating for her, I've never heard that story either, poor thing," said Negar.

"Why do you always defend her?" asked Rebecca.

"Because she has so many lovely qualities and I don't feel it's right to toss all the blame on her."

"Fair enough, but the fact is Saffron is her friend and friends don't do that to each other," argued Rebecca.

"True," agreed Negar. "I'm not going to defend what she did. And I'm sure right now she is feeling absolutely sick about the whole situation, but Daisley made a choice as well. I can't imagine how she's going to face the day, starting with her daughter."

Negar's prophecy was absolutely right. Sitting at her kitchen table, with the paper spread out in front of her, Bermudadas sat with Constanze seated across the table. Early this morning, her chest caved in as she picked up the paper from her doorstep and read the headline. She knew her nightmare was long from over.

Daisley had unravelled late Wednesday afternoon; he was in panic mode. He had called her at the travel agency to tell her what transpired with Tom. She had sat paralyzed at her desk. Daisley told her he was now forced to tell Saffron the truth and for her to expect everything to come out in Friday's paper. He didn't know how Saffron would react; his parents, her parents, or how it would affect his political career. He was a mess. He had confided in Paul Ross, one of his councillors who had become a good friend. Paul advised him to hold an emergency meeting on Thursday with his staff so everyone would know before the news broke out in the media, to which he had agreed. Daisley then advised Bermudadas to tell her staff, Constanze, and Richard too; to spare them the shock of finding out from a third party.

She had left work immediately, went home, poured a gin and tonic and called Richard. Thankfully he was at home. He had sighed and scolded her for thinking only of herself and not their daughter. He offered to drive out that evening to be there when she told Constanze, to which she agreed, *Who was she to argue with anything at this point?* She poured another gin, she'd just have one more, one more before Richard arrived and the kid got home from school.

The kid showed up first and immediately detected something was horribly wrong by the devastated look on her mother's face.

"What's wrong mom?" she asked.

Not waiting for Richard to arrive, she told Constanze the whole story. Then she said, "Your father is on his way over now. He knows too. I'm not going to make excuses for myself Constanze. What we did was terribly wrong. I'm not going to blame the booze or Daisley, it just happened and now we both have to pay the piper. In our selfishness we've hurt people. I don't blame you if you hate me."

"Mom, I could never hate you!"

Tears rushed down Bermudadas' face as the kid comforted her, This isn't how it's supposed to be, thought Bermudadas, I'm supposed to be the one taking care of her.

Richard showed up and the three of them had the family talk. "Your parents don't need to know all this," he consoled Bermudadas. "My parents will most likely hear about it through the media and they're going to be embarrassed. As you know, for them, it's all about *What will the neighbours think?* But their reaction is not my problem. Constanze, you're 17 years old and graduating in five months. You have a choice. I won't make it for you. Either you stay here with your mother and weather the storm, or you switch schools and come and live with me in Richmond. It's your choice."

Bermudadas had agreed that the choice was hers. At this point she felt she had no right to influence her daughter's decision. She sat silently, saying nothing, waiting for the kid to speak.

"I'm not going to leave mom alone," she finally said.

Bermudadas, in shame, held her head in her hands unable to speak.

"Mom, you've always lived on the wild side, but that's what I love about you. My friends are always in awe that I have such a funky mom who is young at heart and out there living life; not confined to doing what everyone thinks you should be doing." Turning to her father she said, "Dad, I love you too. But I can't leave mom right now, if I leave she'll be all alone. Besides, I really don't want to deal with changing schools, my life is here and I'm on the grad committee. I can't let my friends down."

Richard had agreed. He stayed for dinner and it was nice for the three of them to spend time together. The evening had, for a short time, taken her away from her fears of what was yet to come. What was going to happen between Saffron and Daisley? Their families? His career? Her business? So much was at stake.

After Richard left and the kid went to bed Bermudadas poured herself another gin, sat down at her kitchen table, and started thinking about how to manage the next few days. She panicked, poured another gin, and lit up another cigarette. She knew she had led a recklessly extravagant life, and now she was going to have to face her demons. Feeling so relieved and overwhelmed that the kid wasn't going to leave, her mind now moved on to what she had to face next. Men were always casual accessories. *My life is a nothing more than a casual affair.* How was she ever going to face Saffron again? Let alone walk into George's. She wanted to call George. *No*, she said, as she rolled the ice around in her glass, *I've had too much to drink. Society and its fucking morals, all those high and mighty judgemental do-gooders … I've hurt people, I've hurt people I love.*

Pouring another gin, she didn't care that she was getting bombed alone. *Damn*, she was out of ice, *Oh well, what the fuck, I want to go to the Swinging Lantern.* She grabbed her purse, looked at the clock, it was almost 11:30pm. She started to look for her car keys, *Where the fuck are my keys?* Losing her balance she tripped and fell over the coffee table. The loud crash woke up the kid who ran downstairs to her mother's side to help her up onto the couch.

"Mom, what are you doing?"

"I'm going to the Swinging Lantern."

"No, you're drunk mom. You're going to bed."

Bermudadas in her disgrace just started to cry her eyes out. Eventually her sobs became deep and she was border-lining hyperventilating.

"Mom, get a grip. Things are going to be okay, come on, let me put you to bed."

Bermudadas woke up the next morning with a bruised elbow and her head pounding massively.

I'm so fucked up, she said to herself. Getting out of bed she showered and realized she had one day to do some damage control before the world knew. She dropped the kid off at school and went to work to tell her staff. She was floored by their response. They told her not to worry; they said they would be there for her, that her personal life was her personal life, for as they saw it, she was a wonderful boss. She was so taken back by their kindness. She thanked them quietly and stopped at the liquor store before driving home and taking the rest of the day off.

Now, 24 hours later it was Friday morning and she was sitting at her kitchen table staring at the paper with the kid sitting across from her.

"Rachel is picking me up this morning mom, so you don't need to drive me to school."

"Okay," she answered. Rachel, Bec's daughter, and the kid had become good friends in their senior year when they started working on the grad committee. The Barnicot's had an old Ford that they let Rachel drive to school and she would pick up some of the other girls along the way. Becs was going to have a heyday with this one she thought.

After the kid left she wanted to call George's, but she just couldn't bring herself to pick up the phone. It was now 9:30am, *I need a drink before I call,* and poured a gin.

Back at George's Rebecca was now at the sink with Lucy shampooing her hair, Negar and Manjira were sitting in the reception area with Saffron between them and George was sitting in his chair.

The phone rang. Intuitively George knew it was Bermudadas. He walked to the reception desk and picked up the phone, "George's Salon, Good Morning."

"George ..." it was Bermudadas.

Not wanting to give her away he didn't say her name, "Hi."

"This is awful, I don't know what to do ..."

Eyeing George Manjira asked, "Is that Bermudadas?"

George nodded a reluctant *Yes* to her and said into the phone, "Bermudadas ..." but before he knew it Manjira had jumped up, grabbed the phone and bellowed, "Bermudadas, this is Manjira. What were you thinking? I'm coming over to your place right now."

Everyone was shocked, silence radiated throughout the salon and on the other end of the phone.

Bermudadas held the phone and didn't utter a word.

"Did you hear me? I'm coming over right now."

Still nothing but silence from Bermudadas' end of the phone.

"I'm going with you," said Negar. She was worried about what may happen and wanted to be there.

"Are you there woman? I'm coming over and Negar is coming too."

Having no energy to argue, Bermudadas mumbled, "Okay," and put the phone down on its cradle.

"Come on Negar," grabbing her purse, "Let's not waste any time. I'm going to give that woman the scolding of a lifetime."

Looking at Manjira Rebecca smiled and said, "It's so nice to have you back Manjira!"

Her remark elicited a few giggles even from Saffron.

"I'm staying with Saffron," said Rebecca. "We'll be here for a while."

Watching the scene George said, "Let me know how she is doing ladies."

"Of course George," said Negar and the two women were out the door.

They arrived at Bermudadas within a few minutes; they let themselves in and found her sitting at her kitchen table with a glass of gin and an almost empty bottle. Through her tears she looked up at them and Manjira's anger turned instantly to compassion and Negar gave her a hug.

"I'm so fucked up," she said.

"Yes, yes you are Bermudadas," agreed Manjira. "Saffron is sitting back at George's completely devastated."

Negar said, "I'm making some coffee," dumping the gin from her glass and the remaining amount in the bottle down the sink. "Alcohol isn't going to help, come on Bermudadas, you're more than this." Trying to get a smile out of her she asked, "Where is the strong dynamic woman we all know and love?!"

"You look terrible," commented Manjira as she sat down. "Now, tell us what the hell is going on?"

Bermudadas didn't hold back. She was grateful they had come over and she began to tell the truth about everything – starting with the Chamber dinner. "I've ruined their marriage. What is Saffron going to do? Did she say anything?"

"No, she's still in shock and doesn't know what to do," said Manjira.

Meanwhile, back at the salon, Saffron had decided to stay at George's and get her hair done. She was undecided until Lucy had suggested, "You know, my mother always said when I'm feeling sad to go get my hair done because it will make me feel better, it has always worked for me, maybe it will work for you too Saffron."

"Thanks Lucy, your mom was an acquaintance, I never really knew her that well, but she was a gentle, sweet lady. I'll take her advice."

"I wonder what is going on at Bermudadas'?" said Rebecca.

"Well, it's good they went over," said George. "Regardless of their different beliefs, it's good that Bermudadas won't be alone right now."

"Rachel picked up Constanze this morning. She called me when they got to school and said that Constanze wasn't going anywhere, she loves her mother and she was going to stay by her mother's side. That girl loves her mother."

Surprising everyone Saffron quietly commented, "That's so beautiful, I'm happy for Bermudadas that her daughter loves her so much and is so strong right now. That tells us something doesn't it?"

"Yes, I agree," said George. "And you can bet Bermudadas is feeling absolutely horrible right now Saffron."

"I know. I've thought about that George. This will sound crazy, but I've always loved her individuality and her spirit. It wasn't until the Chamber dinner did I see that flirty side of her and I just got so jealous. It was like a switch that went off in my brain. My mind went crazy and I just didn't know what to do. I was consumed with worry that Daisley would leave me. I don't want to be cruel to Bermudadas. My mother said not to be cruel to those who have been cruel to you and I agree. Jealousy leads to hate and I never want to hate anyone."

"Good for you Saffron," said George. "From where you're sitting right now, that's an act of kindness."

"Well, I think it's being too kind," said Rebecca. "Will that woman ever change?"

"If she changed she wouldn't be the Bermudadas we all love and know," replied Saffron. "I don't want to be angry with her. It's just that I'm so hurt right now."

"Of course you are," said Rebecca.

"Perhaps this is an opportunity for you to really see your beliefs about relationship and love Saffron," suggested George. "Just take it one day at a time for now. Don't think too much."

Drawing in a deep breath, Saffron looked at herself in the mirror and thought of her husband. "I wonder how things are going for Daisley right now. When he left this morning he was going to tell his council that he was willing to step down if that was what they wanted. The election is in the fall, he was hoping they would allow him to finish his term." Pursing her lips together she said, "I just want to get through this day."

"And you will, you will get through this Saffron," said Rebecca.

"Can I get you a coffee?" asked Lucy.

"Sure, thanks Lucy."

Lucy got up and headed to the back of the salon and while she was pouring coffee Saffron quietly said to George and Rebecca, "That girl lost her mother, what I'm going through is minor in comparison."

"Well, my grandmother used to say, 'We all have our crosses to bear'," said Rebecca.

A little over an hour later Manjira and Negar returned. Everyone turned to face them, waiting to hear what they had to report on Bermudadas.

"She's devastated. She's a mess right now," said Negar.

"Yes, we found her sitting there at her kitchen table drinking gin," stated Manjira.

"What, drinking at this time of the day?" asked a startled Rebecca.

"Yes, but we made her some coffee and got her to eat some toast. I'm going back, I just came to get my car," said Negar.

"Good," said George.

"She feels so much shame Saffron," Negar quietly offered.

Silence took over the salon. Regardless of what had happened and all the mixed emotions everyone was going through, the overall question in everyone's minds was, *Could everyone ever be friends again?*

"I know things are so fragile right now and this probably isn't a fair question, but do you think its possible that you could eventually forgive her? Forgive Daisley?" asked Negar.

"You can't ask her that!" exclaimed Rebecca. "Its all just happened."

"No, that's okay Rebecca. I've had a couple of days to process all this. I have always compared myself to others, like George said; I've always felt that I'm missing something. I thought once I got married that that would change. I've always been concerned what others think and I've always admired Bermudadas because she has always disregarded what others think. Maybe this is a chance for me to not worry about others and learn to trust myself. Have the courage to be myself. Trust that I have the capacity to make the right choice."

"Take your time Saffron," suggested George. "Perhaps because you're the mayor's wife you feel you have to live up to some role. You're human. You don't have to prove anything. Maybe ask yourself, *What am I ready for?* Look at the situation with your heart. Have faith. Faith in your intuition. Through exercising the courage to be you, you will discover your capacity to survive, that's your first responsibility. Figure out your beliefs in regards to your relationship with Daisley and your friendship with Bermudadas and then decide what to do. You just may be surprised when you discover that you have far more courage that you ever fathomed."

"Okay, that makes sense. I wonder how Daisley is doing? I'm so worried about him. I think I'll go home now. Thanks everyone," and she stood up to get her coat.

"I'll walk you to your car," offered Rebecca.

"I'll walk with you," said Manjira.

"Thanks," she replied.

"I'm heading back to Bermudadas'," said Negar.

"Okay, ladies take care," said George.

"Lucy, can you book me for next Friday?" smiled Manjira.

Smiling back Lucy said, "Sure, Manjira. It's nice to see you again."

After they left Lucy headed out for her break and when all was silent George picked up the phone and called Bermudadas.

A shaky hello answered her phone. Relieved to hear George's voice, she asked, "How is Saffron?"

"She's looking at it all Bermudadas."

"What is she going to do?"

"I don't know, she doesn't know."

"I really fucked up George."

"Well, you can rise up from this Bermudadas."

"How?"

"You are more than this, you have an idea of who you are, you create your own limitations, it is your fear and your resistance to change that stops you from any personal transformation. You have a choice, either to rise or to fall, I've told you that before. The truth was bound to come out sooner or later."

"I know. I don't know if I can survive this George, I've hurt so many people. I crossed the line this time."

"It's all up to you Bermudadas, as I said, you created the situation now you have to walk this path and figure it out. If you can look upon this situation as the benchmark to reveal you to you, your healing will be found in self-acceptance. What you are now, is not what you might be in the future, it's up to you."

"I know George," she answered, pausing to take a sip of gin, "I know."

09

"Read it out loud woman," demanded Manjira from George's chair.

One week later, all the ladies minus Bermudadas were back at George's and Rebecca was wide-eyed as she sat next to Saffron reading Riverville's paper.

"Okay, sure ..." answered Rebecca, "You're back and in your true form aren't you Manjira?" Not giving her a moment to reply she continued, "Lucy would you mind turning off the radio please?"

Standing at the reception desk, Lucy reached behind her and flipped off the switch while everyone waited to hear the latest headlines.

"*Mayor's affair stuns Riverville,*" she began, "*On Monday February 1st, Riverville Mayor Michael issued a statement confirming that the rumours were true. 'I had a brief relationship with Ms. Beppolini and I take full responsibility for my actions. It is now over. I hope everyone will respect my desire to maintain my privacy at this time. I'm deeply sorry. My wife and I are working our way through this and I'm not going to comment on it any further'.*"

Ms. Beppolini has been unavailable for comment.

His image of a family man is damaged; however, it appears that there won't be a political fallout. Since news of the affair broke out last Friday residents interviewed although unhappy with his conduct, stated he is a popular mayor and his record at city hall has been admirable.

Not everyone feels the same, Councillor Peter Jones stated, 'He owes it to the citizens of Riverville to step down. How can his judgement be trusted now?'

Where as Councillor Paul Ross stated, 'I consider the case closed. He did nothing criminally wrong and if anything, look at his work ethic and commitment to our community.'

Michael has been on council since 1967, first as a Councillor and then he was voted in as Mayor in 1969. His intent has been to run again for re-election this fall."

"Well, there you have it," she said shaking her head and folding up the paper. Sitting next to Saffron in the reception area she patted the younger woman's knee.

"Have you decided what you're going to do Saffron?" asked Negar cautiously from the dryer.

Contemplating aloud, not intending to ignore Negar's question she said, "I've always felt as a person I'm missing something and that Bermudadas seems to have it all."

"Don't compare Saffron," said George. "The world needs a bamboo tree as much as it needs a fir tree. We're all unique. Comparing doesn't serve any good. You're allowing your emotions to overwhelm you. You are not your feelings, they are telling you something about yourself in this moment, examine them, but you are not the feeling. Instead of being stuck thinking that you are missing something, perhaps turn in and see what is there. Get connected to your real feelings instead of abandoning yourself and looking for fulfilment from an outside source and comparing yourself to Bermudadas. You're not missing anything. Don't allow your emotions to determine you. Act from your beliefs not from your emotions. If you continue with this comparison, you will be creating your own self-fulfilling prophecy and you will suffer the consequences – and it will be all your creation. Right now you're allowing the negative in you to out weigh the good."

Nodding she agreed, "I get what you're saying George. It's tough not to compare though. She's so chic and debonair ... at the beginning of all this I just felt like such a failure. I haven't accomplished anything worthwhile and I hold doubts I ever will. It's like all my hopes and dreams vanished. I was drained. Paralyzed. I couldn't hold my easel. I wanted to stay in bed all day. For the first few days I couldn't stand being in the same room with Daisley. I held myself back from showing any reaction. I was so depressed. Everything seemed to be futile. I've made mistakes, wasted time. I haven't contributed anything to this world. I felt like I was slipping into a black hole. My art was mocking me, I'd go to my studio and my unfinished work is a reminder that I'm a failure, it cut me deeply. Everything just looked bleak. Then, I started to walk down by the river a lot and I really started to examine the whole situation. I really love him. He gives me the freedom to be myself. He's always filled my heart. In all the time we've been together, it's the first time I've lived in fear of another woman."

"Has he offered any explanation? What is he saying?" asked Manjira.

"He said I've always given him everything he wants with devotion and commitment. He's begging me not to leave him. He does feel terrible and it seems he won't have to resign, although he said he would if I wanted him too. I would never ask him to do that, I believe I've been a good wife, I've always supported his desire to be in politics. I've always believed that genuine love wants what is best for the other. I truly believe that love outlives mistakes, if I can't forgive him, then maybe it wasn't ever really love in the first place? I don't know. My head has been going around and around and I keep seeing that my heart is still devoted to him. I'm in conflict between my heart and my head."

"Well, that's understandable," said Negar.

Saffron continued, "Most people don't seem to get loved for who they really are, it wasn't like that with Daisley and I. I see how love, being the greatest treasure can transform into the greatest poison; I must be careful now. Is there love in the world? I don't know, but I know I love and that's that."

"Perhaps you need to be conscious of both your head and your heart and truly decide what is right for you," suggested George as he was finishing up with Manjira.

Saffron nodded and continued, "My mother showed me something that she had read years ago by Khalil Gibran … "

"Who was he?" interrupted Lucy

"A Lebanese American artist, poet, and writer," she said.

"Ohhh," said Lucy.

"He says, 'Be like two pillars that support the same roof, but don't start possessing the other, leave the other independent. Support the same roof – that roof is love'."

"Wow, that's profound. Your mother sounds like a wise woman Saffron," said Negar.

"Yes, she is, she's had her journey too. My parents don't want us to split up, but they said they would support any decision I make. Daisley went on his own to talk to them."

"I'm sure that wasn't easy, that took courage," said Negar, "Good for him."

"Yes, and they told him that they hope we survive this, they love him, but at the same time they will support what ever I decide."

"And his parents? What the hell have they said?" asked Manjira.

"They scolded him and told him he has embarrassed the whole family with his flippant actions, that response was to be expected though, they are all about the collective and society nonsense. I feel for me, there is nowhere to hide. My intuition tells me to stay with Daisley. I know I'm not perfect, I have my flaws too. I have to be true to me. I love the scene in Hamlet, 'This above all: to thine own self be true, and it must follow, as the night the day, Thou canst not be false to any man'."

"Well, Daisley clearly hasn't lived that has he?" stated Manjira. "And I have to wonder, would he have told you if someone else hadn't forced him into a corner? Or would have this whole affair remained a secret? That's what I want to know."

"I asked him that same question Manjira, and he said he wanted to tell me, but Bermudadas talked him out of it."

"Of course that hussy would. As I see it, you have to do what is right for you," said Manjira.

No one spoke.

Then thoughtfully Saffron said, "I have to be true to me. I know love won't grow out of fear and I've been living in fear. So, if I do stay I have to trust him again and drop my fears."

"Can you do that?" asked George.

"I'm not sure George. I was just so content, we both were, or I thought we both were. I see how jealousy and love can become so mixed up. If I become a jealous person, how can I be loving? I don't want to be a jealous person."

"Of course you don't," said Negar.

"Perhaps my test is to love when it seems impossible, as I see it, being a jealous person is totally destructible, I'm not going to be mean to Bermudadas, but ..." she paused, "Having said that, I do know I'm not going to justify their actions."

Silence again.

"That's very admirable of you Saffron," said Rebecca.

"I've always loved how sassy and alive she is, really, I mean that. We live by different beliefs, but we've had so many laughs over the years in this salon, how could I possibly wipe her out of my life?"

"But she crossed the boundary," argued Manjira.

"True, but look at how they both feel now, I have to recognize that. I don't believe either one of them ever had an intent to hurt me, I just don't believe that."

"I agree," said Negar quietly.

"I have to remain open, maybe there is some good in all of this. I mean, since we've been together Daisley has really loved me. He's always told me, 'What ever makes you happy, makes me happy'. And he's still saying that and he's told me again and again that no one can replace me. I'm starting to see that in our relationship if I know there is nothing to replace me, if I can understand and hold onto that, then there is no room for jealousy."

"Well, good for you," said George. "Jealousy is so destructive. Jealousy arises from the absence of oneness and that energy can lead to hate."

"I don't want to hate anyone. If I can accept that all my hurt is a part of inner growth, perhaps on some crazy level we will become closer as a couple. I don't know, it's just how I feel. I want to forgive both of them."

Everyone sat surprised by Saffron's insight and willingness to absolve both Daisley and Bermudadas.

"Well, I think I'm going to go for a walk down by the river. Do you mind if I cancel today's appointment George?"

"Of course not, you do what you need to do."

"Do you want me to come with you?" offered Rebecca.

"No, I would just prefer to go alone, but thanks for asking." Putting her coat back on she said her good-byes and was out the door.

"Well, I have to give the girl credit, just walking down the street alone right now must be tough," said Manjira. "Perhaps she knows more about relationships than I have given her credit for."

"Don't be hard on yourself Manjira," said George, "I think she's surprised us all this morning. Okay, you're done." Looking around the room he asked, "Who's next?"

"I think just me George," said Negar.

"Yes, I'm off," said Rebecca as she stood up and got out her wallet to pay Lucy.

"Okay, Negar, to the chair, I'll comb you out and you'll be ready to go in a jiffy," said George.

"Thanks George," said Manjira as she got up from his chair and went over to the coat rack. "I'll have to put this on my account. I'll pay you next week."

"Sure, that's fine Manjira, see you next week," he replied cheerfully as the door closed behind her.

"George, I have to agree with Rebecca, you really shouldn't allow her to get away with running up an account," said Negar.

"Well, let's see ..." answered George.

Concurrently, as the ladies were all heading out from George's, once again Bermudadas was sitting at her kitchen table reading the paper. She hadn't gone out all week long. She isolated herself at home, she left her staff to run the business and she just wanted all the drama to go away. Thankfully the kid's friends weren't all that interested in the town's gossip, they were much more interested in getting ready for their graduation.

Negar had been encouraging Bermudadas to get out of the house and go for a daily walk along the riverbank - rain or shine. She would just show up, tell Bermudadas to get dressed and with Maggie happily wagging her tail they would be off. Concurrently, all week long Manjira had her staff leaving full course meals on the doorstep; she wanted to make sure the two of them were eating well.

Despite the positive intent of both her friends, Bermudadas continued to drink and she was drinking hard. The more she drank the more Bermudadas knew she was avoiding facing her truths. She knew she was teetering between crashing and surviving right now. Drinking numbed her pain, it put her life on hold and if she was high she didn't have to figure out what to do next.

She knew the kid was worried about her, but for the moment she still couldn't manage without her gin. She had even called the liquor store and asked them to deliver so she didn't have to go out and risk running into anyone. She told herself she'd quit drinking when it all blew over. When she was alone she kept both the TV and radio on at the same time, she detested the silence.

In the past she had bounced back from all the hard knocks, but this was different. She usually didn't have the patience to listen to people tell her what to do; however, this time she was grateful that Manjira was leaving food and Negar was getting her outside in the fresh air - even if it meant she had to listen to advice she didn't want to hear. She had never been a goody, goody. She was becoming bitter and negative with life, something she had never felt before.

She knew she must be a nightmare to live with right now. When the kid came home she did her best to be upbeat, it was all she could do right now and she just didn't have it in her to truly change. She didn't know how. She knew her life of self-indulgence meant nothing now; she was empty, lonely, and filled with self-hatred. Why should she expect Saffron to have anything to do with her in the future? She was anxious and insecure, and drinking numbed everything.

She had never been afraid of dying and due to her chosen lifestyle she had had her will and last wishes all documented. Richard had seen to that, he insisted with Constanze that they both had to have all their paperwork in order.

Yesterday on their walk Negar told her from the outside looking in it seemed she was stuck in a vicious circle of experiences, and if she could, this was an opportunity for her to step out of that circle and truly look at what is important to her.

Recently Bermudadas knew all the fun times she created were starting to feel like an anchor around her neck, her years of hard living were weighing her down. During the last few months it had been an effort to maintain the projection, whereas before she loved to party hard and experience all the crazy things life had to offer. It wasn't satisfying any longer and it scared the shit out of her. She was terrified and didn't know what to do. She wasn't gratified instantly anymore, like a drug, it took more and more to keep her up. She always needed a bigger fix to be happy.

She had bottomed out and she knew it. She felt panic like never before and the gin was the only thing that helped. She knew life was to be revered and respected. Life could change in day. Life was a gift, but she couldn't bring her self to the state where she could do something about it. Perhaps she needed to see that she would never be deprived, that actually life couldn't be exhausted and to rest into that – but how?

She always saw herself as happy and enthusiastic. She knew people liked being around her; she was fun, the life of the party. She was always positive. Everyone always loved her parties, she was a great hostess. She never censored herself; she always said exactly what she felt. Once the newness of any relationship wore off she would end it. Richard had once told her she was hyperactive because even on holidays she couldn't sit still. Relaxing on the beach drove her crazy, whereas Richard had no problem listening to the waves roll in and out. He had grown weary of her constant relentless need to be active and she didn't blame him.

She was materialistic and she knew it, she loved excess shopping trips, another thing that drove Richard crazy. He had told her she was insensitive to others; that she could be so self-centred and just be a hardcore bitch. She knew he was right. Her gratification always came first. She had become emotionally hardened and increasingly unsatisfied and that was why he left. Her habitual excess was too much and he was always concerned that the kid would get influenced, but having said that he knew she was a loving mother who adored and took great care of their daughter.

After he left she had abused tranquilizers and uppers, something to dull the pain to keep her from feeling anxious and uppers to enjoy herself. No wonder Richard couldn't stand to be around her. She knew she could be obnoxious, belligerent, hostile, and unpredictable.

Right now the booze and dangerous uses of prescription drugs helped her to maintain her feelings of elation. She was deteriorating. She had nothing to hold onto. She didn't know how to help herself. She felt as though a dark pit was swallowing her up. The panic terrified her. She had nowhere to hide. She was paralyzed with fear, trapped, and no way out. She told herself again and again, *This isn't how I want to exist.*

She needed emotional stability. How to find the way out, the way up? Suicide? No, she always thought that was selfish, but she was starting to understand why some people choose it. It was an escape from a dark reality. She had spent her whole life depending on the environment to make her happy.

This morning, before she started drinking, she was looking at the group photo Ned had taken of them all at George's. Looking at all their smiling faces she wondered if they'd ever all be smiling together at George's again. *What have I done?* She asked herself again and again. Suddenly she remembered George had talked about gratitude. She grabbed a piece of paper and started to write all the things she was grateful for. She contemplated her list ... the kid, my health, my family, my friends, my home, fresh air to breath ...

She suddenly realized that her fear of being deprived of the happiness she sought was perhaps because she didn't trust life enough. She had lived for gratification through experiences, but did it really bring her true happiness? Had she ruined herself in her quest for happiness? It came to her like a 2X4. The very thing she had been in pursuit of was destroying her. All this time she believed that happiness was to be found in something outside of her instead recognizing that happiness is an inner state; it's her choice to be happy or sad. Something clicked and she realized that how she reacts to a situation determines if she's happy or sad.

In that moment of clarity she knew in order to survive she had to concentrate on her beliefs. It was alchemy. Things could change. But could she do it? And how could she turn this nightmare into a positive? Suddenly she knew she had to stop; she was creating so much destruction and ignoring those who loved her. Negar had told her, *You don't have to drink.* Alcohol was controlling her and she was allowing it.

She knew she had pushed things too far; it was a wake up call for her to be sensitive to others. But now what? She knew eventually she could get back to work and get out again, but what about Saffron?

With that thought she decided to put on her coat and leave the house by herself. Negar would probably stop by sometime, but she wanted to get out of the house now. Scribbling a note for Negar, she stood on her veranda, took in a deep breath, looked at the overcast sky, and with Maggie headed for the river.

By then everyone had left the salon and George asked, "Lucy, I'm going to head out for a while, are you okay on your own?"

"Sure George," teasing him, "If anyone comes in, I'll just cut their hair!"

"You do that Lucy!" he replied with a smile and headed out the door.

The river was only a couple of blocks north of Riverville's downtown area, it ran parallel to High Street so it didn't take George long to reach the trail.

Moments before, on the same trail, Bermudadas and Saffron had almost run into each other. They were so absorbed in their own thoughts that they didn't notice the other's presence until they were standing several feet apart.

Their eyes met.

"Saffron ..." Bermudadas managed to choke out; she just wanted to hug the younger woman.

Saffron stood completely frozen. She almost didn't recognize Bermudadas, she looked like she had aged ten years.

Bermudadas' body began to shake. She knew she had to sit down, she couldn't control her shaking, she felt so weak.

Saffron's shock wore off and recognizing Bermudadas' condition she ran to her and helped her to sit down on a rock. In that moment Bermudadas completely lost control of her emotions and started to heave and weep, words came out of her mouth, but Saffron couldn't decipher them.

"Bermudadas, breathe, breathe ..." she was on her knees with her arm around Bermudadas' shoulders.

"It's okay, we're okay ... breathe ..." although scared of Bermudadas' condition, Saffron felt instant pity for her. In that moment she got her answer, she knew she could be compassionate to the woman who had slept with her husband. All her anger and jealousy dissolved. She suddenly saw Bermudadas as another human; just like her, with her own issues and in that moment to come from a place of compassion was the only way she could be. She couldn't be angry. She also knew that perhaps her and Daisley could survive this, that maybe they all could.

A few seconds later; George appeared beside them.

"She just started shaking George, I'm not sure what is wrong."

"I'm okay," Bermudadas whispered hoarsely.

For a few minutes no one spoke as Bermudadas gained control over her emotions and started to breathe regularly, "You must hate me Saffron."

"I don't hate you Bermudadas. I don't hate anyone."

Bermudadas looked at Saffron in awe.

"I just don't know if I can survive this," sniffled Bermudadas. "I know this is all my own making, I can't blame anyone."

Saffron was silent while George said, "You can overcome anything Bermudadas, and in fact both of you can." George suggested they walk for a while to which they both nodded in agreement.

Several yards further along the path, Bermudadas stated, "This time I went too far, I know I did."

"Well, move forward, just like you are doing right now, one step at a time," advised George.

"I've spent the last week looking at all this, I'm not defending, I'm just looking and I fucked up."

George stopped and sternly said to her, "Can you see this as an opportunity to learn? Can you internally be resolved with this, burn the bridge behind you, be done with it and rise to your ascended state? If you can do that, you can move forward, but it will take courage Bermudadas."

"I don't know if I can."

"The loss of courage is the loss of living," he informed her. "The moment you are with the facts, when you can live with what is, you become courageous and the brain rests. The fact is you had an affair with Daisley and people have been hurt. That's your truth. Now encounter it, look at it square in the eye, don't run from the facts."

"I know …"

"Don't deny the facts."

"I'm not George," she argued. "I take full responsibility, I know it was selfish and stupid."

"Right now all of this is like gravity, pulling you down lower and lower. You're caught there. It seems to me you're stuck in the belief that you can't rise and that isn't going to serve you. You need to detach from that belief and see that you are beyond the destruction and that you can't be destroyed by all this."

"I just feel like all my energy has been sucked from me," she said in a defeated tone.

The whole time Saffron was listening in silence, not offering anything, just listening.

George started walking again and continued, "Get your power back and by seeing your truth, your mind will rest and your power will come back to you."

"I'm so afraid to go out of my house and run into people, the longer I stay inside the harder it's getting to leave."

"Well, you're out now and look who you ran into - Saffron. Don't you think if you can survive running into Saffron, you can survive running into anyone?"

Bermudadas stopped walking and the two women stared at each other. Saffron had never seen Bermudadas looking so terrible. The stylish woman she always knew stood before her in old, navy, baggy track pants and an old Hudson Bay blanket coat, no make-up, and her hair tied back into a pony tail.

"Bermudadas," said Saffron, "This has wiped me out, that's true, but if I can move on certainly you can. I'm not going to allow this to break my spirit, what happens to me now depends on me. We both have to transcend this, if we don't we will be giving the situation more power and we will never grow. I'm know I'm not living my life that way.

I'm starting to see that it is through difficult experiences that we become more comfortable with our identity which ultimately is a stepping stone to augmenting the courage it takes for me to be me."

"She's right Bermudadas. As I see it, look at this as a wake up call to make some changes in your life."

"I just don't know if I can."

"Well, I see it as being choiceless Bermudadas," said Saffron.

"I don't love him Saffron, he loves you. Please give him a chance. I know it's not my business, but what are you going to do?"

Everyone had been asking her that same question and she was finally clear on her answer. "I'm not going to leave him, I'm going to suggest we get some counselling and see how we can move forward. When we got married, I never dreamed of splitting up, I thought we would be happy forever. Manjira was right when she told me I had a romantic idea about love and my perfect husband. I still can't imagine my life without him. Will we stay together? I don't know. I can't think that far ahead. I can only think about right now and right now I want to see if we can recover. Right now it's one day at a time and I'm okay with that. I have to be."

Bermudadas felt so much relief. She took a deep breath and then asked, "Can you forgive me?" Her eyes began to tear up again and her nose was running.

"Forgiveness is a powerful tool. I want to forgive both of you Bermudadas. Right now it's all still so fresh, I believe I will. I believe that I have to in order to truly move forward. I don't want to harbour any negative feelings about either one of you.

That's where I want to move towards, I may not be able to do it right away, but I'm clear that's where I want to go. I want to learn from this nightmare by not betraying myself. Having said that, I want to be in a way that others will discover love and trust through me."

As soon as she said that, Saffron somehow felt liberated, she had spoken her truth to the woman who had deeply hurt her. She sounded confident, but she knew they were words and the moment of truth would happen in the days to come, the test, could she actualize all this?

A slow drizzle began to fall, George looked up at the sky and suggested, "Let us walk you home Bermudadas, it's not too far from here is it?"

"No, it's not."

The three of them and Maggie continued down the path, three abreast with George in the middle. Nothing more needs to be said he thought.

"How was it you were out for a walk and found us George?" Saffron suddenly asked.

"Oh, I walk down this path every now again. Once it warms up, I'm going to start bringing my fishing rod and try my luck!"

A gentle laughter rose from both women and it felt like a healing as they continued to walk in the gentle rain.

They got to the fork in the path where Bermudadas and Maggie were to head down and not knowing what to say to each other, Saffron finally teased, "You look terrible Bermudadas, you need to get your hair done!"

Smiling Bermudadas replied, "I know. I'll come in sometime soon."

"Sure, just pop by or give us a call," added George.

"Thanks George," as she leaned into him for a hug. The two women stood awkwardly apart. Bermudadas wanting to hug Saffron, but not knowing if she wanted a hug; finally, it was Saffron who stepped forward and embraced Bermudadas.

The older woman regressed to heaving and crying, "I don't deserve your kindness Saffron."

"Bermudadas, I don't want to be unkind to you." She released her grasp and put her hands on Bermudadas' shoulders, "We've know each other for a lot of years and I believe we can move on, it's just going to take some time."

Nodding Bermudadas was speechless, all she could say was, "Thank you …"

With that she turned and headed on down the path with Maggie while Saffron and George turned around and headed back towards town.

Nothing more was said until they arrived at the next fork in the path.

"I'm going to keep going for a while George."

"Sure Saffron, I do believe you're teaching the meaning of love."

"I don't know George, but I do know that I don't want to live my life in anger or jealousy. I know Daisley and I have a journey ahead of us. Perhaps now I have a more realistic idea of what it means to relate to another, especially for the long term. I'm just trying to be human. I know love means different things to different people. I love him and like I said before, I believe that love outlives mistakes, no matter who is at fault or who hurt who. If I can't forgive him then perhaps love was never there, maybe our relationship has all been an illusion. I need to find out if I can I love again. I believe it never stopped, its just changed, I'm defining it differently. As you always say George … let's see."

"Good for you Saffron, now give me a hug. I have to get back to the shop before Lucy starts talking people into allowing her to cut their hair!"

10

Three weeks later spring was springing and Mother Nature's rebirth seemed to be an omen for the change happening between Saffron and Daisley. She had agreed to stay together and they were attending regular counselling sessions. Although Saffron knew she didn't want to lose having Daisley or Bermudadas in her life, she knew she had to get through a lot of work to arrive there.

Daisley offered to step down from his position as mayor, but the majority of his Councillors asked him to stay. They pointed out that the next election was only seven months away and to allow the results to decide his political future; besides, it could derail some of their projects and cost the taxpayers a lot of money. Grateful for the second chance everyone was giving him, he was determined to work harder and get his world in order. He quit partying at the Swinging Lantern, he had truly discovered what was important to him, and he was determined to prove it to Saffron.

Bermudadas was slowly stepping out of her shell. It took everything inside of her to walk around town: she knew it was choiceless, she had to get out and face people. The frostiness she felt from several people was obvious, to survive she held her head high and projected that she was okay. She started going back to work and was considering taking a holiday herself, but she reconsidered for she knew it would be running away. She had to give life time to unfold and although she wasn't religious, she prayed that things would eventually settle down. She didn't want to quit drinking, she enjoyed it, but she knew she had to change her habits. She decided to stop drinking during the week, only on the weekends would she allow herself a few gin and tonics. So far, although it had only been a couple of weeks, she was disciplined and sticking to it. The kid was great. She kept encouraging her mom that they'd all survive. Grateful that everyone who mattered to her seemed to be giving her a second chance, she was determined not to let anyone down like that ever again. She hadn't spoken to Daisley - and she didn't want to, she was relieved he wasn't stepping down. She knew she had her own internal work to do, she didn't know if she could do it, but she knew she didn't want to live the life she had been living.

Recently she was hit with a massive realization; she didn't feel as frightened to face her demons. It was a roller coaster ride, to stay up was a challenge, but she knew she may never get another chance like this. She was truly surprised that partying just didn't have the same fun and allure for her anymore; sometimes it took so much energy to be social. It wasn't natural anymore, she was actually happy staying at home. She had returned to George's on Fridays, but she made sure her timing wasn't co-insiding with Saffron's appointment. At first she was going to change her day, but Negar had insisted she stick to Fridays. Bermudadas agreed, but she was adamant that her appointment be scheduled for later in the afternoon.

Negar consented for the first couple of weeks, then she insisted Bermudadas get back to her regular morning schedule and face everyone. She pointed out the longer she waited the tougher it would be. Besides, Saffron had made it clear that she didn't want Bermudadas out of her life and the others all knew that, so why continue to hide?

Bermudadas finally agreed. Negar picked her up one Friday morning and they went together. It was ten o'clock; Bermudadas pulled the door open and walked in with Negar behind her. Lucy was shampooing Rebecca and Manjira was in George's chair.

An awkward silence filled the room as they entered the shop.

"Bermudadas!" smiled George, "Hang up your coat and stay a while!"

Manjira spoke up, "I know Saffron has absolved the two of you, but I haven't. I'm not going to sit here and pretend that what you did was okay."

The old Bermudadas seemed to surface as she was taking off her coat, "I don't expect you to absolve me Manjira and quite frankly - I don't need you to. I know I'm responsible; I'm not denying or defending anything. And I'm grateful Saffron is giving me a second chance. As for you, you don't have to like me; I'm fine with that, it's Saffron who I'm concerned with. I came here to get my hair done and that subject isn't up for discussion, especially with you."

Before Manjira could respond George suggested, "Well ladies, as I see it, it's for Saffron and Bermudadas to figure out how they move on and for us to support them in any way we can."

"I agree George," said Negar as she hung up her coat, "Give me your coat Bermudadas."

"Thanks Negar," handing it to her, "And just so you know Manjira, I'm grateful for all the food you left on my doorstep these past few weeks."

"I know you are. I just wanted to make sure Constanze was getting fed, it was her I was worried about not you."

George and Negar's eyes met and George winked; everyone knew Manjira was just as concerned about Bermudadas.

From the sink Rebecca looked at Bermudadas and stated, "I agree with Manjira, I'm not going to pretend what you did was okay. But I'm happy to see you're up and about, I hope you've learnt something from all this."

"Don't start preaching to me Becs, I don't need your input either." As humbled as Bermudadas felt, she wasn't going to roll over and allow everyone to start telling her what to do. She sat down next to Negar and waited for the next comment that she assumed would be forth coming.

Suddenly the door swung open and in walked Saffron. Everyone froze. It was the first time the two women had seen each other since that day by the river, and the first time everyone was seeing them together.

Bermudadas was silent; she didn't know what to say. Everyone watched them.

Saffron, in her grace, looked at Bermudadas then leaned over and gave her a hug. Mixed emotions floated around the room.

Finally it was Manjira who spoke up, "You're being too kind to her Saffron, she doesn't deserve your forgiveness."

Reaching for a hanger and eager not to be the highlight of conversation, she said, "Well, I just can't live in the past Manjira. I have to move on, for myself. I'm not perfect either and if it were me, I would hope to receive compassion, so I have to extend it now. As I see it, we have to evolve with life's challenges, they're an opportunity to wake up."

"So, you're just going to forgive and forget?" asked Manjira.

"I'm forgiving for forgivings sake. I'm not going to close my heart."

"Haven't you become the wise one, maybe you're not as naïve as I thought you were," said Manjira.

"I don't want to speak about it anymore, the story telling is over and I have to be settled in the past to move forward, can we not talk about it? Please?"

"Of course Saffron," said Negar.

Bermudadas breathed a sigh of relief; the initial encounter was over.

If not for the radio playing in the background, the room would have been dead quiet. Slowly conversations resumed and the awkwardness, although still felt, was losing its power as everyone seemed to be relieved that their Friday mornings may be getting back to normal.

As Saffron sat down next to her in the reception area Negar asked about her art show. She answered, "Well, you won't believe it, but yesterday I painted our piano!"

"Your piano?!" repeated Rebecca.

"Yes, I painted our piano a bright red colour, it seemed crazy at the time, I just felt compelled to add some new colour to our living room! Lately I've been going down to the river to sketch and then I go home to my studio. Sometimes creativity is difficult to sustain, but not lately. I draw inspiration from my experiences; I want my work to have some resonance and meaning. I don't know where the creativity comes from. It's spontaneous. It's like … as I renew myself, my art gets renewed. I take refuge in my art. From my art I have figured out that I'm a creative individual who is an artist. I constantly aspire to recreate my art and myself. My life experiences augment my art. For me art is a way of communicating to the world what I have discovered, something in me gets resolved when I paint. It's like I harness my emotions and something happens in me that comes out when I hold the paintbrush. I get a feeling of liberation when it's completed. I want to know why I feel different from other people. I withdraw into my art; it seems to give me answers. It feels so amazing at the end of the day to be tired from creating endeavours of the heart. As I see it, passion is transforming my being into something I love to do, which is my art. For me, my work is the only way to show my love."

"Perhaps," said George, "your motives for painting are to communicate and to also conceal yourself from other people. You paint for love, for joy, it's the expression of you. You have found your self-discipline and you are contributing to this world. For those of us that don't have any artistic talent, we appreciate those of you who do! If your creation is beautiful - you must be beautiful. It seems to me that you're combining your intuition with insight and I have no doubt your work will be stunning!"

"Well, thanks George. I have a lot of work to do before the show, but I feel I'll be fine. Everything is really flowing now, when I wake up in the morning I can't wait to start. I'm just so excited about my work again."

"Good for you Saffron," said Negar. It was so nice to see the younger woman enthused about life again.

Bermudadas just sat and listened; she took a deep breath and felt so relieved that Saffron's life was getting back on track. *I'll get my own shit together too* she told herself, *slowly, slowly.*

"So, how is business Manjira?" asked Bermudadas, happy the attention was taken off of her. "What have I missed around here?"

"Didn't you hear?"

"Hear what?"

"Last Saturday evening we had the contract for the Wilson wedding, 75 people. Some damn fool didn't close the back door of the catering truck properly; it didn't get 20 yards before all the food was dumped out on the parking lot, it was an absolute disaster."

"Oh my goodness," gasped Bermudadas, "What did you do?"

"Well, I wanted to fire the fool, but my husband told me to keep my trap shut. He's never spoken to me like that before. In front of everyone he told me I'm not a good team player and that I use fear to motivate people. I was shocked. Then he took charge! He saved what food he could; he had someone check what supplies we had in stock; called in two extra staff members; called the Wilsons and told them there was a delay; and then everyone ran around madly recreating the menu. The wedding party wasn't too stressed out because they arrived at the reception so late themselves. They had taken forever to get their photos taken. So, the delay wasn't as disastrous as it could have been. We lost a lot of money on that job. I was so angry. Everything was a frenzy. I just went home, my husband told me to stay away. He even said that no one should have to be around me. My husband is a damn fool too. And he's determined to run for council, I keep reminding him we have a business to run and why would he want to get into politics when we have to make money?"

"There is more to life than money Manjira," said Negar.

"I know."

"You always have to be in control don't you?" added Bermudadas.

"I like control," *I like using my power*, she said to herself. "And my staff needs to fall in line. I expect total obedience. I will not be taken advantage of."

"Oh, but it's okay for you to take advantage of them?" piped up Rebecca who was thinking of her neighbour Joy.

"Those people need to be grateful, I've employed them. There is nothing wrong with me."

"That's delusional Manjira. We all have something wrong with ourselves," said Saffron. "No one is perfect."

Ignoring Saffron she said, "When my husband got home we had a terrible row. He told me I intimidate people until I get what I want. That I'm not flexible or willing to listen, 'What I say must be the only way it goes', he said. And, listen to this, apparently after the job they sat around drinking wine! He's the boss and he sat with our staff drinking wine! What kind of leadership is that? After a few drinks they all confided to him that they didn't want to work for me any more, they want to work for him, but not for me. He said I make enemies out of the very people we depend on. Apparently they all resent me. He said I demean others and I better change or I won't be welcome to participate in the business. He said he's had enough of watching how I treat people and he's had enough of working with me too. He said I use anyone with a weakness, that I see weaknesses as an invitation to take advantage of them. He said I should be inspiring them, not exploiting them. He said I'm always overbearing and intimidating to get my way. He actually called me a bully and that my staff call me the barracuda."

No one spoke.

Taking a deep breath she let it all out, "He actually said, I'm a mean son of a bitch. He's never spoken to me like that in all our married life."

"So, what is happening now?" asked George.

"I'm only in charge of the finances, he's ordered me to stay away from the office and he's taking over the logistics. He admitted that I'm a sharp businesswoman and that I do have a head for figures, but he said if he doesn't act everyone will probably quit and he's not going to allow that to happen. He reminded me that they all have families and depend on us for employment."

"How do you define success Manjira?" asked George.

"I want to have money, I don't want to fail. I have a family to take care of."

"Yes and it's very honourable that you take on that responsibility. You're doing what you have to do. Manjira, I see success as giving the best of you. Look at Saffron, she's giving the best of her to her art, she's creating and she's working on not comparing herself to others. She's not out to compete with Monet or Picasso. It's coming from her heart, her being. She has accepted exactly who she is …"

"Hold on George," Saffron interrupted, "I still have a long way to go, but it's true, I am finally seeing that to compare is silly. For years I have compared myself in so many ways to others, and as a result, I have struggled. Finally, I feel I'm dropping that idea and I'm starting to understand that I just have to rest into being me, and the more grounded I become in that belief, the more effortless it seems for me to paint. It's happening now, but I still have a long way to go."

"Good for you," said George, "You're moving there. Self-acceptance is a healing and as I see it, from that point success is born from within."

"And what about money George? No offence Saffron, but because of Daisley you are in a position where you can stay at home and paint. Your husband financially supports you. That's a luxury from where I'm sitting."

"True, you're right Manjira. I am fortunate. I have made money over the years, but not a lot of money. I'm hoping that this next show will launch me into my next step and my art will start to generate an income for us."

"And you have a gift," added Manjira, "Not everyone has a gift like that."

"Yes, that's true," said George, "Her gift is that she can paint, but you have gifts too Manjira. Obviously you have what it takes to run a business. We all have gifts and when more and more people discover their gifts and celebrate their gifts I believe people will be happier."

"Well, I have to make money. Our business can't fail, we have responsibilities."

"You are financially successful," stated George. "You have worked hard and your business is a success. You're dependable, reliable, and honest. But you are always complaining about your staff, you certainly don't seem to be happy about your work. A boss should be a guide."

"That's true Manjira, rarely do we hear you say anything positive about the people who work for you," agreed Rebecca.

"Perhaps you need to look at your idea of failure," said George. "Think about it, if in your work, you're giving the best of you and you're rested into it, how can you fail? Perhaps you need to heal from your idea of failure. Are you happy Manjira? Have you lost you in the process? Have you lived? Or are you working and living out of a fear of failing? It seems to me that you don't trust yourself, you're not trusting life. As I see it when you are truly being you, at your best, celebrating you as how you are, success flowers. When you are being you, it's natural. Extend the best of you to others. People trust you don't they?"

"Yes," an obviously shaken Manjira answered "Well, I think so, but after the Wilson wedding I'm not sure about anything anymore."

"Well, give the best of you, spend some time recognizing you and then extend that to another. Inspire others, inspire your staff instead of always putting them down and putting the fear of God into them. Then you are living and that living is your success."

"But," she confided to everyone twisting her hands on her lap, "To be honest, sometimes I panic, I get stressed out,"

Everyone was surprised by Manjira's confession; she had rarely, if in fact ever revealed anything of her private self.

"Sometimes I just don't think we're going to make it," she said with a few tears swelling up in her eyes.

"That's where trust comes in Manjira. When I bought this shop from Huxtable I had to trust. I learned to trust that being me was the right way to be, and from resting into that, the business is a success and I'm not living in panic. If something fails, it's a beautiful opportunity to see what is being revealed to me. What did the Wilson wedding reveal to you?"

"Well, I did panic. My husband was a cool cucumber and although we lost money on that job, we held onto our reputation and it's looking like we're getting a couple of more clients from some of the wedding guests."

"See, so look at that. There was no reason to panic."

"I guess not ..."

"If your success is where you grow, you live, you flower, and if your success inspires others to do the same then I see that as real success. Then life is fun."

"I've never thought about inspiring others, I've never looked at my staff that way."

"You silly woman," said Rebecca. "Of course you could inspire them, you're their boss. Right now when they go to work they're living in fear, you're not inspiring them at all." She didn't want to reveal what her neighbour Joy had told her, but at the same time she hoped their working conditions would improve if Manjira could only listen to what her own husband was saying and what George was advising - it was actually making a lot of sense.

George added, "For me, living in success means to live in it. Saffron is an artist, for her - everything is art. Look, she just painted her piano red!"

Everyone started to laugh.

He continued, "Maybe next month it will be blue! Who knows? Everything she does is art. Whatever you are, it is you, and your reality. Don't die trying to be successful Manjira. Just be you. Allow others to see the highest of you and inspire them to do the same."

Manjira was quiet, so Saffron piped up, "For me, something so meaningful happens when I create, it's like I'm giving birth to something. It's like a meditation, I sit and my senses open up. Yesterday it was so warm, I opened the windows in my studio, the birds were singing, they were sharing their songs, the trees were giving shelter to all the robins and birds who have returned for the summer, the freshly cut grass smelt heavenly, and the sun rays were so golden; it was like every thing was celebrating being alive, everything was a mystery. I want to welcome that mystery into my art and share it; perhaps it will trigger others to see the beauty we live in. My parents always encouraged us kids to see the beauty in nature."

"I grew up watching my parents work and struggle so hard to create a better life for us here in Canada ..."

"I'm sure you did Manjira," said George. "And I'm sure they worked hard. But you don't have to accept life as a struggle. In fairness to them, that's all they knew, and their intent was from a place of love. Bless them. Perhaps for you it's about trusting yourself and having some fun! Live in abundance. An abundance of friends, laughter, success, love ... right now your idea of success is created from a defeated mind, see what you have been, transform to live from an able mind, create from an able mind. Have the strength to be that which you want to be: rise to be the best you can be, share, inspire!"

"Well," Manjira said, taking a deep breath, "I have to agree, what you say makes a lot of sense. I guess I've never really looked at life like that. My whole life the thought of poverty and of not having enough money has always scared me. That's been the consciousness I've lived in."

"Don't be hard on yourself, it's all you've known. Maybe see this as an opportunity to really look and let's see what you come up with."

"George," said Negar as she was standing behind the reception desk getting all the receipts out of the box kept in the drawer, "From how you define success I would have to say Karim is very successful. He really loves what he does, he shares and he's so happy in his work. I think that's why I used to get resentful sometimes - because he'd be having so much fun and I'd be at home alone and miserable. Now I know my misery has been my own creation and I love to teach, and so, I think I'm starting to recognize my own success."

"Good for you Negar, what a lesson, something we can all learn from. Okay, Manjira, you're done," as he held the mirror for her to see. "Rebecca, you're next. Lucy can you shampoo Bermudadas? Saffron you'll have to wait a while."

"No problem," she smiled, "I came in early to hang out."

An hour or so later Manjira had left; Negar was finishing up with February's accounts; Lucy was sorting through the old and new magazines on the trolley; Saffron was in George's chair getting the finishing touches; Rebecca was sitting in the reception waiting for Saffron; and Bermudadas was under the dryer.

A few moments later the dryer clicked off and Bermudadas titled the cone back, reaching for her cigarettes she offered one to Negar, "Smoke?"

"No, thank you, I've decided to quit!"

"What, really? Why?"

"I've definitely decided to take up tennis, the new tennis club is offering a spring package so I've signed up for some lessons. Karim is going to join me when he can. Anyway, I've decided it is time to quit and start taking better care of my health."

"Good for you Negar," offered Lucy. She had tried smoking a couple of times, but she got so nauseous she didn't quite understand how people enjoyed it. Plus, she didn't want to spend money on the habit. She had stolen some of her father's packages a few months back; he had caught her and beat the crap out of her, so she wasn't about to try that again.

"Thanks Lucy, well, let's see how well I do. I've been smoking for over ten years and its been tough, the withdrawal has been brutal. I woke up one morning and suddenly didn't want to be a slave to a cigarette anymore. I just made up my mind that I have to do this. Food tastes better, but I'm gaining weight; I'm trying to chew gum whenever I feel the need for a cigarette. I'm seeing how habitual it became, when the phone rings I want to light up, or when I sit reading the paper with my morning coffee I want to light up. I'm breaking my habits; it's really tough. I had no idea how habitual it had become. I've had nasty headaches, and my doctor said I just have to go through it."

"I can't imagine, I love to smoke, but good for you." Bermudaas then said to Rebecca, "Our girls seem to be quite busy getting ready for grad."

"Yes," she answered hesitantly.

"Is something wrong?" asked Bermudadas pulling a long drag off her cigarette.

"Rachel and I have been arguing day in and day out about the May Queen contest. She doesn't want to co-operate at all. She just doesn't see how good it would be for her, I keep telling her she'll love it once she's in it."

Bermudadas shook her head. "You can't possess your children Becs. She probably feels like a prisoner." Bermudadas knew everything going on between mother and daughter because the kid had been coming home with stories of how miserable Rachel was these days. "You're so serious. You're burdening her, you're constantly telling her what to do. As I see it you're destroying her personality."

"I am not!"

"Sure you are. You have imposed your ideas on her her whole life. She's not in this world to live out your idea or your opinions. You're crippling her. You don't give her the freedom to explore this world. They're 17 years old Becs! They'll be going off to university in the fall. I want the kid to have confidence in herself, to know that she can choose for herself."

"Not all children are the same," retorted Rebecca.

"They aren't children any more. They're young ladies, capable of making their own choices. I have raised the kid to have her own power of choice and to know she's always loved. Respect Rachel, love her. Give her a clean slate to create her own life, you just may be amazed at her maturity and capacity to … as George's says … be successful and live in abundance."

"I've made so many sacrifices for her."

"Then that's duty, that's not love."

"She could have said *No.*"

"She has and you haven't heard, you keep poisoning her with your beliefs, she'll end up confused. You haven't allowed her to investigate life for herself. This is going to sound harsh, but as I see it you've polluted her with your prejudices. You want her to be an obedient daughter who lives out your idea of how she should be."

"That's not true!"

"Let me ask you this, when have you allowed her to make a decision on her own? And if you have, have you respected her choice?"

"I'm sure I have."

"Well, she's your daughter, it's not for me to interfere, but I can't sit by and be a witness to something and not say anything." She didn't want to reveal what the kid had told her about how much Rachel dislikes her mother, it would be breaking her confidence, but she hoped by provoking Rebecca she would wake up before something disastrous happened.

"Its been a bad week, my arthritis is acting up, and my doctor said I have to watch my high blood pressure, and I didn't win the citizen of the year award. I was passed over again. Everything I do for this town and no one recognizes me, I'm not appreciated," complained Rebecca.

"Well, maybe you should forget about winning some social climbing award and just do for doings sake," said Bermudadas. "Why do you care about all that society nonsense anyway? It doesn't seem to bring you much happiness."

"I want to set an example for my children."

"No, you want the ego trip."

"That's not true, I have nothing but the best intentions at heart."

"Well, whatever. From the outside it's as though you want to be indispensible, then if people don't tell you how wonderful you are, you get resentful. You overvalue what you do for others and undervalue what others do for you."

Rebecca didn't say anything for a few moments, then she surprised everyone with a soft laugh, "Isn't it great? We're all back at George's, bickering like we always do!"

"Yes, and the fact is all of you probably wouldn't have never met if you hadn't started coming here to get your hair done," said George.

"I guess that's true isn't it?" said Bermudadas.

"So, he's the one I have to thank for all these headaches!" laughed Rebecca.

"Well, I don't know, but it is nice to have everyone back again," said Lucy. She had been trying her best to get to work on time and do her best for George. She knew she probably would have been fired if she had been working anywhere else. Every time George asked her if things were okay, she just said *Yes*. She was so embarrassed of her family life. She wanted to leave the house, but she had her younger sister and how would her father feel? When he was sober he was a kind man. He always felt remorseful and he would try to make up for things. It was just so tough sometimes. She was planning to leave home after Karen graduated. She had started spending her paycheck on groceries and every week she gave her sister spending money, Lucy didn't want her going without anything. So, she couldn't lose her job with George, she had to pull up her socks and she was trying.

Interrupting her thoughts she heard George say, "Okay, Saffron, you're done."

"Thanks George," as she got up from the chair, "Let me give you some money Lucy."

"Sure," said Lucy.

"Okay," George continued, "Bermudadas to the chair and Negar are you ready to be shampooed?"

"Yes, I'm done George. February is all in order," she answered. "As we are … hopefully!"

Everyone laughed and as Rebecca and Saffron headed out the door Bermudadas said, "Good-bye ladies."

In unison they both looked at her and Saffron said, "Good-bye Bermudadas, see you next week."

"See you next week," Bermudadas answered.

Rebecca nodded in agreement and the ladies were out the door.

"Well done Bermudadas," said Negar. "You did it, now everything else is baby food, when ever you run into someone around town just remember this morning and how you survived this, now you can survive anything else."

Not feeling as confident she answered, "Let's see Negar, let's see."

11

Six weeks passed, it was now mid-April and the province was gearing up to celebrate British Columbia's 100th anniversary into confederation and next month's royal visit of Queen Elizabeth II, Prince Philip, and Princess Anne. Communities around the province were hosting parades, pageants and a wide variety of events to illustrate the character of the province and Riverville was getting caught up in the enthusiasm too. Schools had been getting involved, adding more local history to their curriculums and Riverville's high school was planning celebrations to run in synchronicity with their grad ceremony. Rachel and Constanze had been working hard with the student body committee and they were getting so excited about their plans.

One sunny spring evening as Bermudadas was parking in the driveway, she hadn't even turned the engine off before Constanze was out the door and running down the steps towards her.

Getting out of the car, Bermudadas asked, "What is it? What's wrong?"

"It's Rachel. She ran away from home, she's gone to Vancouver."

"What are you talking about? Why?"

"She told me she is completely fed up with her mother."

"Well, we all saw that coming, but is it bad enough to run away?"

"Yes, you have to do something mom …"

"Of course, let's go inside and tell me the facts."

The two hurried up the steps and sat down at the kitchen table.

"Okay, Constanze, from the beginning …"

"Well, this morning when she picked me up to go to school she was so angry. Her mother was going on about how she's a young lady now and needs to stop being such a tomboy and how disappointed she is that she didn't want to be May Queen."

"Not all that again, I thought the May Queen issue was over."

"No, her mother keeps bringing it up. In the car Rachel said she was going to run away to Vancouver to be a go-go dancer just to piss her mother off, apparently there are lots of jobs downtown."

"What?! How would she get a go-go dancing job?"

"She said she would."

"And where does she plan to live?"

"At a youth hostel."

"She has thought everything through, hasn't she?"

"Yes, she has. I told her to stay at home, to hang in there until after grad and then she's free. To quit school when she's so close to graduating is crazy. But she said she couldn't do it. At lunch time she went home because she knew her mother would be at church; she left the car, packed a bag, and caught the bus downtown."

"Were you with her?"

"Yes, and I tried to talk her out of it. I told her to come and stay here with us. But she said *No*, that she'd still be too close to her mother. I sat on the bench and cried when the bus pulled away."

"Do her parents know where she is?"

"Yes, well no, she just left a note to say that she's going to Vancouver and to leave her alone."

"Okay, do you know where she is staying tonight?"

"Yes, at a hostel. She got the address out of the telephone book."

"Okay, go get it, then we're going to talk to her right now."

"She won't move back home mom."

"I understand, but perhaps she'll move in with us."

"She already said *No*."

"She said *No* to you, she hasn't said *No* to me. Now go, find the telephone book and I'm going to call her mother."

"Don't mom, no!"

"I have to, I'm a parent too and don't worry I won't allow her mother to come with us. Now go, find the telephone book."

Bermudadas picked up the phone, dialled Rebecca's number and a panicked voice answered the phone.

"Rachel!!"

"No, Rebecca, it's me Bermudadas. I just heard what happened."

"She's run away Bermudadas. Lance is on his way home and we're going to call the police."

"The kid knows where she is, we're leaving right now."

"I'm coming with you!"

"No, you're not, you're the reason she ran away. You silly woman if you come it will only make things worse."

"Where is she?"

Ignoring the question Bermudadas said, "I will call you from downtown, I have to go."

Hanging up the phone, she grabbed an extra pack of smokes from a drawer in the kitchen and called to the kid, "Constanze, are you ready?"

"Yes mom, I have the address."

"Okay, let's go."

With that they were in the car and speeding down the highway. Just outside of Riverville's city limits Bermudadas looked in her rear view mirror and saw the flashing lights, it was a police car, *Not another fucking speeding ticket, not now.*

She pulled over to the side of the highway and asked Constanze, "Get the insurance papers out please."

"I know the drill mom, how many tickets have you had with this car?! My mother the race demon!"

"Enough from you young lady or I'll leave you downtown!" both enjoyed the friendly banter and affection for one another.

It seemed to take forever for the policeman to get out of his car and stroll over to her door.

"Good evening Mam, may I see your driver's licence and insurance papers please?"

She didn't recognize him, she thought he must be new in town, "Certainly Officer, I was speeding for a good reason."

"Everyone has a good reason Mam."

"But I really do, my daughter's friend had a falling out with her mother and she has run away to Vancouver, we're going to find and her and drag her skinny little ass back here."

Looking at Constanze the officer recognized true concern, "Is that true young lady?"

"Yes," nodded Constanze.

The officer started to fill in the details of her speeding ticket while Bermudadas glanced at her watch, over at Constanze, back at her watch … when finally he handed her paperwork and ticket to her.

"Okay ladies, good luck, I hope you find your friend and don't hesitate to call the us if you need help."

"I believe her parents are in the process of doing that right now, thank you for your concern Officer," smiled Bermudadas, suddenly seeing how handsome he was.

"You're welcome Mam," he tipped his hat and said good-bye.

Bermudadas stuffed the ticket and her licence in her purse, handed the insurance papers back to the kid and was once again roaring down the highway.

An hour later they parked on Granville Street and quickly found the hostel where Rachel said she would be staying.

Constanze wasn't comfortable being downtown in the evening, she had spent time here during the day, but the evening had a different feel and she didn't like it. She was happy her mother was with her; nothing seemed to rattle her. They walked up to the shabby front desk where an overweight, unshaved, unsavoury character was leaning back in his chair reading a porn magazine. Bermudadas asked if a Rachel Bannister had checked in.

"Who's asking?"

"I am, and if you don't tell me in this instant I'm going to come behind there and re-arrange your anatomy!" demanded Bermudadas. Constanze stood behind her mother in awe at the authority she oozed; she had never seen this side of her.

"Okay, okay, settle down lady. Yes, she's in room 202, at the top of the stairs."

"Thank you," came the curt reply.

The two went quickly up the stairs and Constanze began earnestly knocking on the door, "Rachel, it's me, Constanze, open up!"

The door opened and a devastated, scared Rachel opened the door. The girls embraced and they all went into the dingy room to talk.

"You are not living here young lady, this is a dump, I don't even want to sit on the furniture," stated Bermudadas. "You are coming home to live with us, you are welcome to stay as long as you want, I will talk to your mother."

Offering no argument, Rachel nodded, "Okay, I didn't think this place would be so bad. And I was so scared when I went out to get something to eat, I don't know where I am and the man downstairs is so creepy."

"Get your things together, we're leaving now," stated Bermudadas.

The two girls got up from the bed and were ready to go within moments.

Downstairs Bermudadas asked to borrow the phone, to which she received no argument and called Rachel's parents.

"Rebecca, I have Rachel, she's coming home to live with me."

"What?!!"

"You and Lance can meet us at my place to talk about all this. But she's only willing to come back if she lives with us, she will not live with you. That's the deal, you have to accept her decision and you can talk about it with her. I don't want to talk about this anymore on the phone. I will call you when we get back home."

The three of them were soon blazing down the highway headed east back to Riverville.

"Thank you Mrs. Beppolini," Rachel said from the backseat.

Turning around in her seat, Constanze reached for her friend's hand and gave it a squeeze.

"You know, my father told me the highest honour is to be there for another," Rachel reflected, "I want to thank you both for being there for me this evening, I was so, so scared."

"Your father is a wise man and I'm sure you were scared young lady, but perhaps you had to experience that to recognize what a crazy idea it was. I admire your spunk! But with independence comes responsibility, here's one for you, the word independence can mean *In me I depend* ... Now, think about it, what are you going to say to your parents?"

For the rest of the drive Rachel revealed her misery to Bermudadas while in turn she tried to explain that her mother meant well, it was just that she came from a different generation and it wasn't easy for her to let go. By the time they got back to Riverville the healing had begun, but Rachel still wasn't going to move back home.

Pulling into the driveway Lance and Rebecca were already there sitting on the veranda chairs with Maggie between them. They ran down to Rachel and a mild hysteria took over Rebecca. Her words didn't make any sense.

"Let's all go inside," suggested Bermudadas.

"Yes," agreed Lance who was eyeing up Bermudadas. He was intrigued to meet the woman who had had an affair with the mayor.

Once they were all settled in the living room it was Rachel who finally spoke, "Mom you never allow me to do what I choose, I can't make any of my own decisions, you just don't listen to me. I'm staying here."

The conversation went back and forth with Rebecca and Lance finally agreeing to the living arrangements. In the meantime Constanze had put her friend's belongings in the upstairs guest room next to hers and was secretly looking forward to having her friend live with them.

Chapter Eleven

The evening was getting late, after everyone had emotionally settled down the Bannistors left, the girls retreated into Rachel's new room and Bermudadas started to prepare a late supper for them. Suddenly, she remembered her speeding ticket and as she reached into her purse to read it she noticed some scribbling on the bottom. Puzzled, she read in very neat handwriting a phone number and a note, *Perhaps we could have dinner sometime! Sebastian Kitchen.* She was absolutely shocked, a potential suitor! Laughing to herself, she recalled that he was extremely handsome. *Well, why not? I'll give him a call tomorrow.*

Tomorrow arrived; by chance it was Friday. Bermudadas dropped the girls off at school, went to her office for a couple of hours and by the time she got to George's everyone already knew what had happened.

Negar was under the dryer, chewing gum to help curb her tobacco addiction and reading her book on tennis. She smiled at Bermudadas, tipped the cone back and shut of the dryer; she wanted to hear what was going on with Rachel. Manjira was in George's chair getting the finishing touches and Rebecca and Saffron were sitting in the reception area. This time it was Saffron comforting Rebecca.

"Hi Bermudadas," said George.

"Hi George, hi everyone," she replied. She felt everyone looking at her with a different energy, she wasn't sure how to label it, but something was different.

"I hear you're a hero!" he added.

"I'm not a hero, I just did what anyone would do."

"Not anyone," said Manjira.

"How was she this morning Bermudadas?" asked a clearly fraught Rebecca.

"She's fine, I dropped them off at school and they seem quite excited to be living together, they were talking about being roommates out at UBC if they both get into the classes they want. She's perfectly fine."

Not sure how to react, Rebecca's face tightened up and tears swelled up in her eyes.

"Relax woman. She's safe. She's not downtown, she's at school and you need to back off, give her some space and she can stay with us for as long as she needs."

"We're very grateful for what you did last night," she said.

"Yeah, that was so good of you Bermudadas," added Saffron.

"Thanks," she said smiling at Saffron, "You don't have to say thanks Becs. Just chill out and try to see things from Rachel's point of view. You have managed and controlled her entire life. Can you imagine what a nightmare that would be? You have taken her power away; she's always doing things to please you, not what she wants to do. I always tell the kid not to do anything against her life force. When are you going to wake up and just allow her to be herself and quit managing her life? You can be so narrow-minded. Try to see it from her side of things."

"Well, I guess I have been like that, but my intent has only been from a place of love."

"Of course its been," said Negar.

"I know and she knows, but lighten up woman," said Bermudadas. "Everyone has to be their own person, let her meet her own challenges and let her figure things out. I don't expect people to be how I want them to be. Figure it out Becs, you need to stop saying what you think is right for her, she just may surprise you."

"I'm going to try Bermudadas, I'm really going to try. Lance has been hinting the same thing for years. I promise I will try to be more open-minded. Do you think she'll want to see me?"

"I'm sure she will. I'll give her a nudge to call you this evening."

Reaching for her purse Rebecca offered, "Let me give you some money for rent and groceries."

"Nonsense, I don't want your money. And she's going to have to do chores around the house just like the kid does, so she'll contribute in her own way."

"You're sure …?"

"Yes, put your wallet away … and I just might have a date from it all too!"

"What?" asked George. He was concerned that Bermudadas may fall back to her old comfort zone and forget about the past several months.

"Last night I was pulled over for a speeding ticket just outside of town. I explained the situation to the handsome officer and he wrote his phone number down on the ticket and suggested we have dinner sometime, I didn't even notice it until I read the ticket when I got home! Isn't that fabulous?!"

"Trust you Bermudadas," said a disapproving Manjira. "Haven't you learnt anything?"

Ignoring her Bermudadas asked, "Hey, where is Lucy?"

"Once again, missing in action," retorted Manjira.

"Now Manjira," said George, "This hasn't happened for a long time. I'm sure I'll hear from her soon, she's been working really hard and has been trying to get her world in order."

The phone rang.

George put down the can of hair spray and quickly found his way to the reception desk.

"Good Morning, George's Salon."

"George ..."

"Lucy?" he could barely recognize the voice. A hush took over the room as everyone turned towards the reception desk.

"No, it's Karen, Lucy's sister," came a barely audible voice.

"Oh, hi Karen, what is happening?" asked a cautious George.

"It's ... it's ... Lucy," said a scared voice.

"Karen, take a deep breath, tell me what happened."

"Our father beat her up again, this time it was really bad."

Holy shit thought George. He had had his suspicions, but she always clammed up.

"Where are you?"

"We're at the doctor's office, this time it's bad ..."

"Okay, stay there, I'm on my way."

"Okay ..." and she hung up the phone.

Turning towards the five women staring at him he said, "Lucy's father has beaten her up, apparently it's not the first time. Both girls are at the clinic. Ladies, can you hold the fort while I go over there?"

"Of course," came a unison reply.

"I'm coming with you," said Bermudadas. "Those girls aren't moving back with that jack ass, they're moving to my house." Not waiting for an answer she put her coat back on and was out the door with George right behind her.

As the clinic was directly behind George's, they were in the reception area within a couple of minutes. Catching their breath they walked in, they went immediately to the front desk and were immediately directed to one of the examination rooms in the hallway. Once inside George and Bermudadas were horrified at the sight both girls. They looked absolutely devastated, shocked, and defeated. Lucy's face was badly swollen and reddened from the beating, her right eye was purple and pinched nearly shut.

Lucy was shaking. Bermudadas immediately hugged her, then she leaned over to embrace Karen too. George stood aside and took a deep breath, now everything seemed to make sense, the drinking, the pot, the coming in late.

"When you're ready, tell us what happened," urged George quietly.

Lucy was unable to speak, so Karen piped up. "Our father came home drunk this morning around six o'clock, he wanted his breakfast made and so he started ranting like he always does, but this time it was different, he was meaner. I ignored him and tried to go back sleep. He went into Lucy's room and started ordering her to get her fucking ass out of bed and into the kitchen. She didn't move fast enough for him, the next thing I heard him hitting her and she was screaming ... it was horrible. I got out of bed and ran into her room, he never hits me, it's always her that gets it, she's always protected me, and I tried to get him to stop, there was so much screaming, he was vicious ..." she couldn't continue.

Before either George or Bermudadas could comment the door opened softly and in walked the doctor and two police officers. Bermudadas immediately recognized Officer Kitchen from the night before. They nodded in recognition.

Quiet and quick introductions were made. Dr. Petersen was a well-known family physician in town, he was near retirement and known to be a kind man to all. Pearl and the girls had been his patients for years. The older RCMP officer, Calvin Smith, had been with the Riverville detachment for several years. Riverville was a small town and both Dr. Petersen and Officer Smith knew Dan Cassidy and the facts of his seedy reputation.

Bermudadas stood up to allow the doctor to sit next to Lucy; he quietly explained Lucy's injuries to the officers. "She has a black eye, bruised ribs and right now she needs total rest."

"You girls are coming home to stay with me, you're not going back there," Bermudadas stated matter of factly.

Turning towards George and Bermudadas Officer Kitchen asked, "And how do you know the girls?"

"I'm George, I own George's Salon, Lucy works for me."

"My name is Bermudadas Beppolini, I own the travel agency." All the men did their best to hide their knowledge of the recent scandal as the girls' welfare was much more important. She felt their attempts to hide their reactions and determinedly continued, "I suggest both girls come and live with me. I have a huge house and as soon as you're finished talking with them, I want to take them to their house to get their things and get them out of there."

Officer Kitchen nodded and asked, "Was this the young lady you went to Vancouver to help last night?"

"No, Officer, that was another young lady."

"Oh," intrigued he looked at the girls, "Is that what you both would like to do?"

"Yes, I don't want to live with him anymore, he's a mean bastard. I don't think he's ever been a kind man, I can't stand it anymore," said an unwavering 13-year-old Karen.

Lucy nodded in agreement.

"Okay, that's fine. Can you tell us what happened?" he said.

The girls repeated the events while George and Bermudadas stood back and listened to the details.

"Do you know where your father is now?" asked Officer Smith.

"After he beat Lucy up, he started yelling how it was her fault he was late for work and he stormed out the door. He was drunk and shouldn't have been driving, but that certainly never stops him, so I guess he's at the yard," said Karen.

"The yard?" asked Officer Kitchen.

"He works for the railway, he'll be at the yard on the north side of town."

"Okay, we are going now to arrest your father."

"Do you have to arrest him?" asked Lucy.

Surprised the older officer stated, "That is the procedure. We are going to arrest him and take him in for questioning, as this appears to be his first assault, we may release him on conditions, most likely he will be held for court until Monday. Then a judge will decide if he is a danger to you or anyone else."

"It's not his first assault, he used to beat up our mother," said Karen, happy now to finally tell the truth. "She always made excuses for him."

Bermudadas' body froze, her brain jammed, *He beat up Pearl?*

"Yes," agreed Dr. Petersen, "She's telling the truth, once Pearl came to see me after he had beaten her up, she needed sutures, if she hadn't I'm sure she wouldn't have come in. I wanted to call the police, but she wouldn't allow me to and I'm sure it wasn't the first time."

"What will happen to him?" Lucy asked.

Officer Smith compassionately explained again, "The judge will decide if he is a danger to the public and or to his family."

"He'll have to stay in jail?" gasped Lucy.

"Why are you so loyal to him?" asked Karen, she was now getting angry with Lucy.

"He's still our father," argued Lucy.

"Well, I don't care what happens to him," said Karen.

Silence took over the room as everyone was caught off guard by Lucy's allegiance to the man who had been so cruel to her and obviously had been for a long, long time.

Officer Kitchen broke the silence, "Yes, Lucy, we have to arrest him and he may be held for court until Monday. If we do release him before that, I'll be sure to let you know. Otherwise, the judge will decide if he is a danger to your safety and won't allow him to come within 500 metres of you. You're aware what he did to you is wrong?"

"Yes," she answered quietly.

"Okay, so we're going to go now and do our job. Are you both in agreement to go live with Ms. Beppolini?"

"Yes," they both answered.

"Okay," said Officer Kitchen, "Doctor, if you're done then we'll escort the girls and Ms. Beppolini to their home while they get their things together."

"That's fine. Lucy, you need some rest and keep icing your bruises. You're young and healthy, so you'll heal fast, but keep icing and just rest. Come and see me again in a few days."

"I'll make sure she does Doctor," said Bermudadas.

With that they all left, Bermudadas piled the girls into her car and the officers said they would meet them at the Cassidy home.

George went back to the shop to inform the ladies of what happened.

"Those poor girls," said Negar.

"That miserable old bastard," said Rebecca. "You mean he beat up Pearl?"

"Yes, that's what the girls said and the doctor concurred," said George.

"We had no idea," said Manjira shaking her head.

Everyone sat in a shocked stillness as the truth of Pearl's life was revealed.

"Now we know why Lucy is the way she is," said George. He had sat down in his chair.

"And they're moving in with Bermudadas?" repeated Manjira.

"Yes," said George.

"That woman has a huge heart," said Negar.

"Yes, she certainly does," said George.

"What will happen when their father finds out they've moved in with her?" asked Saffron.

"I've been wondering the same thing Saffron. The officers are going with them to the house, they're going to wait while they pack, and then they are going to the rail yard to arrest him."

"I don't know why Pearl married that miserable man in the first place," said Rebecca. "I don't think he's ever been kind to her."

"Well, we never know why some people get together, but right now we have to do everything we can to support them," said Negar. "Where are their grandparents? Don't the girls have any other family here?"

"Both families are from Revelstoke," said Rebecca. "I believe Pearl and Dan were high school sweethearts. Her parents must be quite elderly by now and she has a sister. I doubt they really ever knew how unhappy Pearl was, we sure didn't and we saw her every week. I remember Pearl saying that Dan always wanted to live on the coast, he was working for the railway in Revelstoke, so he put in for a transfer and eventually got it; that's how they ended up here. They were already married when they moved to town. I know Pearl always tired to cultivate a relationship with his family, but I don't think her efforts were reciprocated, so I doubt they really care about the girls."

Manjira stood up and walked over to the phone, "I'm going to call my husband and have dinner dropped off for them. How many are there now? Rachel, Constanez, Lucy, Karen and Bermudadas … that's five."

"I can help you with the shop if you like George. I used to help out in my auntie's salon in Iran when I was a teenager. I know my way around," suggested Negar.

"Thanks Negar, that would be great until Lucy heals and feels up to coming back."

"Dan Cassidy is a nasty man," said Rebecca. "He's always at the Riverville Pub or at the Swinging Lantern. He has always been a partier and after Pearl died he just got worse. I just never knew what to do to help those girls; I did the best I could. I'm really worried about what will happen when he finds out they've moved in with Bermudadas."

"We all are," said George, "We all are."

Within a couple of hours both girls were settled at Bermudadas'. *Thankfully I have a big house. The kid and Rachel have the upstairs, I'm on the main floor and the Cassidy girls can have the basement.*

Bermudadas showed them to their rooms, it was a half basement that Bermudadas had made bright and cheery years ago. While the girls were down stairs unpacking she called the school to have the kid paged to explain the situation so she wouldn't be surprised when she got home with Rachel. Thankfully she had a great staff and they could pretty much run the agency without her. She knew she also had to call Richard to let him know what was going on. Plus, she needed to call Karen's school principal. The past 24 hours had been full on, well, that's what you do, you help when you can.

Both girls were soon comfortable and upstairs watching Bermudadas making lunch. Lucy was horizontal on the couch, covered in a quilt, eyes closed and almost dozing off with a bag of frozen peas wrapped in a T-towel over her right eye. Karen was sitting at the kitchen table enjoying the presence of the older woman.

The phone rang, Bermudadas answered, "Hello."

"Ms. Beppolini, it's Officer Kitchen."

"Yes Officer,"

"We have arrested Dan Cassidy and we will hold him for court and the judge will decide his fate on Monday."

"Okay, he'll be there all weekend?"

"Yes," he answered.

"How's our father?" came Lucy's cracked voice from the couch.

"How is he Officer?" asked Bermudadas glancing over Lucy.

"He's angry and he's very volatile. I'm sure he never thought the girls would have the courage to call the police."

"Yes, I agree," she answered.

"He went ballistic when we told him they've moved in with you. He went as far as to say he's going to beat the crap out of you. We have it documented for the judge, but he's a scary man and you need to be fully aware of the situation. Call us if anything comes up."

"I'm aware Officer," doing her best not to alarm the girls. "I've known Dan as an acquaintance for several years."

"He's angry, but he does look a little remorseful, he obviously has a history of this so the judge will look at all the facts. That's all I can tell you at this time."

"I will let them know, thank you for calling Officer."

"We'll call and keep you apprised of the situation," he promised.

"Great. I won't be going to work tomorrow, we'll all be here."

"Okay, we'll be in touch," then he hesitated as the timing didn't seem appropriate, but he did continue, "And if you're up to it, we'll have to go out for dinner when things settle down."

"I'd like that Officer," she said, smiling to herself, happy he had mentioned it.

Bermudadas hung up the phone and relayed the news to the girls, "Lucy, right now it's time for you to rest, and Rachel, what would you like to do?"

"I need to do my homework."

"Of course, Constanze and Rachel will be home soon, so we'll all have dinner together. I hope you like Italian!"

Both girls were more than happy to have Bermudadas take complete charge of the situation. And although the circumstances were dire, they confided to each other that they were so happy to be out of their house. They felt safe and for the first time in a long time someone seemed to truly care about them.

As her younger sister went downstairs to get her schoolbooks and Bermudadas started to bake cookies, Lucy laid on the couch in deep thought. Her emotional pain far surpassed her physical pain. Thinking of her father brought on a level of anxiety she had never felt before. She was oscillating from the relief that she was away from him and guilt from allowing her sister to take her to the doctor and call the police. The mass of contradictions went around and around, her mind was taking her to places of doom as she envisioned and feared what would happen next.

Chapter Eleven

I love my father, what is going to happen to him? She asked herself again and again.

She had spent her young life trying to please him, always wanting his approval yet never receiving any. Now, here she was, laying on the couch, beat up, and disgusted with herself because she couldn't stand on her own two feet. *I'm a coward* she thought and with that she finally drifted off to sleep.

12

Monday arrived and based on the fact that this was Dan Cassidy's first filed offense the judge released him.

Dan Cassidy wanted to see his girls. Finally, after a few phone calls, it was agreed that the officers would escort him to Bermudadas' house.

Bermudadas timed the visit when the kid and Rachel were at school. She didn't want them being around to aggravate him or witness Dan Cassidy's potential explosive temper. The doorbell rang; Lucy and Karen sat side by side on the couch. Bermudadas answered the door and welcomed the officers and Dan inside with an air of authority.

She is as cool as a cucumber thought Officer Kitchen as she led them into the living room where the girls sat patiently. Bermudadas knew she had to project confidence and not allow Cassidy to take her power away.

Cassidy was a shrewd man. He knew for the time being that he had to be on his best behaviour, but he certainly wasn't going to allow anyone to take his daughters away. *Who would keep the house clean?* For now, he'd dance their dance as he certainly didn't want to get arrested again. The weekend was a nightmare, he'd never spent any time in the slammer and he wasn't interested in going back. The judge laid out the consequences and if he didn't behave he would be going back to those four walls. *Those little bitches, calling the cops, wait until I get them back home, they'll soon learn not to mess with their father ever again.* He walked in the room and saw his girls sitting together, seeing Lucy's face he could barely remember hitting her. All his anger and thoughts dissolved as he looked at his girls and wondered what had happened for things to get this bad.

Lucy's body began to shake. She couldn't control it. Everyone noticed. Cell memory thought Bermudadas, she's seeing the man who has hurt her so often and her body is reacting.

The officers strategically stood to the side while Dan Cassidy sat down opposite his girls. His head dropped and one hand went to his temple. Bermudadas thought for a moment that he may actually be feeling some remorse, but she wasn't sure if it was authentic or not.

No one spoke.

Finally, "We hate you," lashed out Karen.

"No we don't, hate is a terrible word," argued Lucy.

Cassidy spat out at Karen, "Don't talk to me like that young lady!"

"I'll talk to you any way I please," she wanted to hurt him.

"Since your mother died I have given you a home and taken care of you, and this is how you repay me? You call the cops over a little disagreement?"

"A little disagreement? We should have called the cops years ago when you were beating up mom," said Karen, clearly showing her distain for her father and finally able to speak her true feelings with the protection in the room.

The senior officer sat down next to Dan and said, "This is a very stressful time for all of you." He suggested, "Do you have anything to say Mr. Cassidy?"

Looking at the swelling and bruises on Lucy's face he wanted to tell her he was sorry, but then he thought of the beatings he got as a kid and they certainly didn't hurt him much. His psychology switched, *Fuck it, a little beating never hurt anyone.* He didn't think it was such a big deal, he had survived and lots of parents hit their kids.

"Yes, I do. You're both moving back home, I'm your father and the only family you have in this town." Then, pulling the guilt card he added, "What would your mother think?"

"What would our mother think?!" said Lucy, finally finding her voice. "After what you put her through, she would be happy we were out of there." As much as she loved her father, she was afraid of him, she didn't ever want to get beaten up again.

She had never spoken to him like that, but with Bermudadas and the police present she felt she could finally speak her truth. "You haven't been a father to us. We are not moving back in with you. That's what our mother would want, for us to be safe."

Taken back by her assertiveness he bellowed, "Well, I don't care what you both do. Stay here and live with this hussy, let's see how that goes and let's see exactly what she teaches you."

Bermudadas stood aside completely unreacitng. *I want to throttle the bastard*, she thought to herself, *but I have to remain cool.* She told herself, *It's not about me, it's about the girls, don't react, don't react …*

"Now Mr. Cassidy," said the older officer, "This is an opportunity for you to try and move forward with your daughters. Mrs. Beppolini has been extremely kind to them."

Bellowing at Bermudadas, "You hussy, taking my daughters away from me? What the hell have you been saying to them?" His anger started to percolate, "Get your things, you're both coming home with me right now!"

"No we're not, I hate you," said Karen.

Cassidy wanted to slap her but good, but he couldn't. *Wait until you get back home you little bitch.*

"I believe this visit is over," said Officer Kitchen. "Things are still quite fresh, let's take you home Dan."

Until then Bermudadas had been silent, "The girls are welcome to stay for as long as they choose. They're lovely young ladies and I hope you come to see that someday Dan. Children are precious, you can all heal from this."

"I don't need you to tell me anything," glowering at her. With that comment the officers were between him and the girls. Bermudadas remained cool, she wasn't going to react and allow Dan Cassidy to determine her.

"It's time to leave," said Officer Smith.

Standing up he laughed, "I'm happy to get out of this whore house, that's all my girls are good for anyway."

The pain on their young faces superseded any physical blow.

"Stay here, I don't want you back. You're both useless and good for nothing except cleaning the house."

The girls remained on the couch while Bermudadas led the way to the front door, opened it, and stood on the veranda as Dan and the officers walked past.

Cassidy stopped and pointed his finger at her, "You just wait you bitch, you better be careful where you walk in this town."

She wasn't going to allow him to intimidate her, "Do you want to hit me too? That's really cool, beating women, you're not a man, you're a bully."

"You bitch!" and he took a lunge at her; however, both officers had him pinned in seconds.

"That's enough Mr. Cassidy," said Officer Smith.

"Good-bye Dan," she said coolly. Nodding to the officers, "Thank you gentlemen."

Nudging him down the stairs, Officer Kitchen added, "Remember what the judge said Dan? He told you to be on your best behaviour or you'll end up in a tougher situation."

The older officer escorted Cassidy to the patrol car while Officer Kitchen said in a low voice, "Call us if you're nervous about anything Mrs. Beppolini. We'll be circling the neighbourhood."

"I will, thank you ... and you can call me Bermudadas."

With a cautious smile he added, "And you can call me Sebastian."

Bermudadas watched the patrol car pull out of her driveway. Dan Cassidy was an evil, spiteful man. How have those girls lived with him? Poor Pearl, none of us knew. Walking back inside the house she put a smile on her face and thought about getting some counselling for the girls.

Although the interaction was brutal, Bermudadas was convinced it was good for the girls to encounter the truth of their father so they couldn't sugar coat his personality any longer. She was gravely concerned about Lucy's loyalty to her father, in time she worried that that bastard just may talk her into moving back home.

Both girls sat on the couch looking weak and exhausted. Bermudadas sat down,

"Well girls, let's just take everything one day at a time. Your father has had a lot to think about and right now he's an angry man."

"He's always angry," said Karen, "Unless he's partying with his buddies."

"Well, sometimes adults don't make the best choices and perhaps somewhere inside he's feeling remorse. We don't know, we never really know another person really. For now, you're here and this is your home too.

I love having you around and let's hope for him that in time he sees the wrong he's done. If I've learned anything in life, I'd say never conclude anyone. Maybe he'll get some counselling."

"He'd never go for counselling," said Lucy.

"Well, let's just allow things to settle. I think it would be good for you two to talk to a counsellor, what do you think?"

"Sure, I'll go," agreed Lucy.

"Me too," added Karen.

"Okay, I'll look into it and for now let's think about the rest of our day," she said in an upbeat voice.

"I'd like to see my friends after school," asked Karen.

"Of course, and Lucy?"

"I'm going to call George, I know it's Monday and the salon is closed, but I'll call him at home. I'd like to get back to work soon, maybe tomorrow."

"I'm sure he'd like to hear from you and getting back to work sounds like a good idea, but give yourself some time to heal."

"Will our father come here and hurt us?" asked Karen.

"No sweetheart he won't," said Bermudadas, not sure of who she was convincing herself or Karen.

"When will we see him again?" asked Lucy.

"Well, let's give him some time to cool down and see what the police advise, does that sound okay?"

"Yes."

"I don't care if I ever see him again," said Karen. "I like living here and he's an evil, nasty man who has never cared for us anyway."

"He's still our father," replied Lucy.

"He's not a father," argued Karen. "He's a bastard!"

Surprised by Karen's language Bermudadas said, "Lucy, you're right he's still your father and your concern is kind.

And Karen it's your right to feel the way you do. You're both right. Everything is so raw and fresh. He has hurt you, see the truth, feel the pain, don't push it away, just be with it, don't bury how you feel."

Silence.

"Bermudadas, I'd love a beer, do you have any?" asked Lucy. She just wanted to get high.

"No, I haven't Lucy. As I'm sure you're aware I've drank my share of booze and let me tell you, it's not the answer. Alcohol destroys families Lucy. Now is not the time for a beer."

Disappointed Lucy sighed and agreed. Although to herself she didn't think it was such a big deal to have a couple of beers given everything that had happened.

"Shall we go for a walk by the river?" Bermudadas suggested, "Come on, the fresh air will do us all good."

A few days later Lucy was back at work and Karen was back at school. The girls had met with a counsellor, their father had stayed away, emotions had settled down and everyone at Bermudadas' home had settled into a new rhythm. She called Richard and although he was deeply concerned about Dan Cassidy's potential revenge, he was fine with the living arrangements. He drove out to meet the girls and Bermudadas could see their surprised faces when they witnessed the love and kindness between Constanze and her father.

Good ... they need to see how a father can be.

Lucy's eye was still bruised, the colouring had transformed slightly and although it was awkward at first, the ladies were happy to see Lucy back at work. One by one they expressed their concern, and everyone was determined to do whatever they could for Pearl's daughters.

Rinsing out Rebecca's hair Lucy was somewhat happy to be back into her routine, her work took her away from worrying about the future. She was meeting Sherry down by the river for a couple of beers after work.

"I have to wonder," said Manjira from George's chair, "How did the male and female psyches evolve the way they did? From birth, instead of just being human, divisions are created and boys and girls are branded. How has society's conditioning, since childbirth created these roles?"

"Well," said Negar from the dryer with all the receipts spread out on the footstool, "All around the world women are the primary caretakers of children. If not the mother, it's the grandmother, the sister, the aunt. Therefore, women are the most influential adult figures in moulding their children's character and identity."

"It seems to me that so many men ooze their importance and superiority over their wife's role," said Saffron seated on a chair in the reception area.

"Let me ask you this ladies," injected George, "If women accept to be born a man is luckier than being born a woman, what does this do to women?"

"Well," said Bermudadas sitting in the stylist chair next to George, her hair was done but she decided to stick around for awhile and see how Lucy was doing her first day back, "This consciousness will prevail for as long as women allow it to happen. Women need to have the intelligence to be aware of the damage that has been done. Women need to have the intelligence to know the wrong that was done – then the right can be chosen."

Lucy looked up at Bermudadas, "The right has to be chosen? I don't understand."

Choosing her words carefully she said, "What your father did to your mother all those years ago was wrong. She knew that, she must have been so frightened and so scared, I'm sure she just didn't know what to do. But I bet in her heart she knew things weren't right and she just didn't have the energy to cope, to call the police, to leave him. Who knows? We will never know."

"Lucy," said George, "Your recovery will start when you can acknowledge *I'm not what my father made me to be*. You need to have the self-respect and the self-esteem to carry through with what you need to do for yourself. The capacity to act starts with being attentive to our life situations."

Wrapping up Rebecca's hair in a towel she nodded in agreement.

"I think men expect women to be pure," said Saffron.

"What is purity? What does that mean to a woman?" asked George. "Does purity have to mean being a virgin?"

"Where did that logic come from?" asked Bermudadas.

"I'm just asking," said George. "Provoking you to think. Let me ask you this, why isn't society concerned about a man's virginity?"

"Good question George," said Negar. "Virginity isn't a tool to measure a woman. Men say women have *Lost it* meaning they're defiled, impure. Don't women *Lose it* with a partner? Was the moment not shared?"

"In the East," added Manjira, "Many women go mad if they've lost their virginity before they're married, but it's globally acceptable for a man to brag he's had sex. The woman is labelled a slut and she will judge herself on this value too."

"That's so true Manjira," said Negar. "What I'm angry about is how men, in many cultures, expect or demand their brides to be virgins. Ironically it's perfectly okay for them to sleep around and brag about the number of women they have slept with before they announce their nuptials. Is that not a double standard? What right does a man have to demand his wife is pure when he is not?"

"Can purity mean purity of heart, purity of compassion, or purity of values?" asked George.

"Of course it can," said Saffron. "Purity is in the heart. The purist thing to measure is love and I believe women need to hold on to this belief like fire in their eyes. Women must take that stand and firmly state, 'Don't touch me unless there is love'. When there is love there cannot be violence. If you love, whatever you do is right. You can not do wrong, it's not possible."

Lucy sighed. She knew what the ladies were saying was true.

George said, "Lucy, you were frightened as a child, but remember you were only a child. There was nothing you could have done. Now the past is the past, it's not you."

"I know George," and with that she sat down and started sorting out the old and new magazines on the trolley.

Manjira then stated, "Is it any wonder the women's liberation movement was created? I believe the movement was created due to ages of suppression and the pain of being labelled the weaker sex. It was a reaction of oppressed women. Everything inhuman that has been done to humanity has been done to women. Women are not secondary species to men. The rights of boys and men do not supersede the rights of girls and women. This may sound harsh right now Lucy, but women need to know their rights and they need to act with dignity to enforce and protect themselves. Gender based violence against women must stop. It must end. Every day women are raped, killed, assaulted. Violence against women is worldwide. It happens in the so-called safety of their own homes, their work environments, prisons, every where."

Negar added, "Shouldn't human life hold the same value everywhere? Let's hope one day that the United Nations writes a declaration on violence against women, perhaps that will legally bind nations to end discrimination and obligate nations to enforce equality of rights and benefits between men and women."

"Do you really think government systems are going to be perfected and actually implement what the UN tells them to do? Now that's a romantic idea," chided Rebecca.

"I'm just looking at it all Rebecca, and no, I don't blindly believe that government systems to protect women will be perfected," said Negar. "But if they can be improved, significant benefits will arise for women. It is vital for everyone's survival; both men and women. To help us all attain freedom, to cultivate mutual respect, significance, dignity, love. It's about integrity, honouring one's self. It is true life. It's non-negotiable if we're ever going to evolve as a species."

"I believe women can only be truly free and equal when they cease to speak of it as a fulfilment," said Saffron. "Women need to support women and together create a new awareness, a new universal energy. Women need to take responsibility and be a part of the solution."

"You all have the intelligence to say 'It's not okay'. Why can't women be women?" asked George.

"I don't know George," sighed Manjira.

"Perhaps this is the beginning of living rightly," he suggested. "Meaning, having right relationships and living rightly."

"Do you mean like my father not being right with us?" asked Lucy.

"Yes, Lucy. I do. But let's not conclude him, we don't know how he's feeling and we don't know how he was raised, there is so much we don't know. When I say living rightly I mean getting in touch with the real of your life. Don't do anything you feel is wrong, don't override your instinct and don't do anything unless it's from your heart. Look at the beliefs you have chosen to carry, don't agree with stupid beliefs. People may leave you because you got yourself right, but right attracts right."

"As I see it," mused Saffron eyeballing Bermudadas, "Our souls have cycles and we need to be aware of them. We need to look at the link between the past and the present. We must be brave enough to allow chapters of our lives to die and meet the challenges to embrace the new."

"I agree Saffron," said Bermudadas. Nothing more needed to be said between them, the storytelling had stopped. They had both moved on and with everything going on this past week Bermudadas hadn't thought about the town gossiping about her. On some level she was back to her old self, but not back to her old habits and she planned to keep it that way.

Gathering up all the receipts Negar said, "I don't think human problems everywhere aren't all that different. I know women in Iran who have the same challenges as women here, and I firmly believe that if we want out outer world to change, we must first take a deep look inside ourselves."

"Agreed," said George, "Through encountering that which we are not, we are able to define who we are. There is always an element of risk and consequences come with the territory, but it makes life memorable!

As I see it, it is through challenges that we must live in truth, each and everyone of us has to discover our own position in reference to our values for it is how we define ourselves."

"Pearl was made to feel she had nothing," said Manjira. "I'm sorry to say this Lucy, but I think your mother spent her life with your father nurturing his manhood."

"Are you going to be able to forgive your father for deliberately hurting you, your sister, your mother?" asked George.

Silence. Lucy looked up and said, "I don't know, I'm trying. Right now, I can't even entertain the thought. I just want a break from life. But thankfully I do have some memories of when he was kind to us. Karen doesn't though; I think he wanted her to be a boy. I remember him yelling at my mom and blaming her because she didn't give him a son, only girls. I want to forgive; I'm just not there yet. I don't think Karen will, not now anyway."

Happy she was at last finally talking George added, "One day at a time Lucy, be kind to yourself, take care of yourself first."

After a few moments of silence Rebecca said, "As I see it, a gentleman is someone who will act from love, from respect, from strength."

"Why do women, or men too, stay in damaging relationships?" asked George. "Is it because they feel inadequate? Are they serving an idea? *It's as good as it gets*; fear? I think guys want to be macho, 'I can deal with it, I've been taught to take the knocks, be strong' … I believe men don't want to look like a wimp to anybody and that's why they can be so aggressive. One of my friends believes that once a woman has a child, she loves their child more than her husband; and that that creates a lot of angst in the relationship."

"Nonsense," said Rebecca.

"Well, think about it Becs, things do change when we have kids. We don't have the time or the energy to pfaff over our husbands when we're changing diapers and chasing after a toddler. I wouldn't dismiss that belief so fast," said Bermudadas.

"Sadly, many men see their wives as a burden," said George.

"It is sad, I agree," said Manjira, privately wondering if that was how her husband was feeling about her. He still wasn't allowing her to return to the business. "And women are on the constant hunt for a man, look at you Bermudadas."

"I don't hunt men, that's nasty Manjira," she retorted.

Rolling her eyes she snorted, "Right!"

In a second Negar's peacekeeping genetics kicked in, "I think women compromise just to have a man in their life."

"Both men and women compromise to have someone in their lives Negar," said Saffron. "We all live in fear of being alone."

"We are born alone, we die alone. Relationships are not about escaping loneliness," said George.

"True," Negar said, "It's a tragic belief that everyone always wants to fit in, to conform, to feel normal, whatever normal is, but to have a partner means to fit in. Eastern and Western traditions do differ; however, it seems to me that glamour and having a man encompasses all borders. Woman globally identify themselves through comparing their looks and their marital status with those around them."

"I agree Negar, and as I see it," said George, "One should never allow their soul to become the possession of another, it is not to be reduced to a thing."

"Due to a lack of will and courage women have allowed themselves to be dominated," said Manjira. "Women have sanctioned the damage."

"I believe ..." said Saffron, "that the soul's adventure is to experience every emotion in life. Otherwise, how is one able to love wholly when one hasn't felt the pain of rejection, or the bliss of love? It's my belief we must experience the lows and the highs of life, if not, how can we feel for another in exercising compassion?"

"Well, I'm sure it's damn tough being a man too, isn't it George? A family man has so many responsibilities. We need to stop crippling each other," said Bermudadas.

"Sure, being a man is tough too. Let me ask all of you this, what do you want to live for?" queried George.

"Lucy," he repeated himself, "What do you want to live for?"

She took a deep breath, "I don't know George, I don't know."

"Well, let's take it slowly, you will figure it out and you have lots of people here to support you. As I've told you before, don't conclude yourself. The past is the past. Don't create your own limitations Lucy. Believe in yourself. The greatest tragedy is when you never followed what you could have been."

"I'm not adequate enough," she said, looking down at her hands.

"That's a belief you carry. Feel where you want to be, if you aren't happy with your life situation; choose to walk out of it. You don't live in anyone's shadow. Remember yourself at your best, not your worst. You will survive this. Don't reduce yourself to your past. The day you are totally you, it's not an achievement, it's a realization, a discovery, an awakening. Your father completely dismissed you, your sister, your mother. He made your mom into nothing. Violent people need people they can dismiss so they can exist. It's all about ego. Love is absent the moment a woman allows a man to make her absent."

"Men must respect women and women must earn that respect," said Bermudadas.

"I don't know if men are really better off than women, perhaps once we take the time to truly get to know each other a mutual respect will be activated."

"I feel so ashamed, it's just all so sad," said Lucy with tears swelling up in her eyes. Saffron jumped up, pulled a footstool next to her and gave her a hug.

An uncomfortable silence took over the salon as everyone wondered if Lucy would ever be able to recover from the years of abuse.

Finally George spoke, "There are men who love to reduce women to shame. As a result, women have allowed shame to become deeply rooted to their self, it becomes their identification. Shame is an insult to your senses. Shame is when your self-respect is broken. Lucy, if you allow shame to get to you that means you're allowing the outside to make you what you aren't."

"People commit suicide because of shame," said Manjira in her blunt matter of fact voice.

"Manjira!" scolded Negar.

"Well, it's true," she argued.

George continued, "She's right, people do commit suicide because of shame. You are not what someone else made you Lucy. Remember, you have to say, 'I'm not what you made me out to be. I'm not that'."

"If anyone should feel shame it's your father, he's the criminal. He deliberately broke your mother down," said Rebecca.

Bermudadas added, "Men must realize that they too have lost, women have been so unkind to men as well." Reflecting on how she treated Richard from time to time she said, "I know that from personal experience. I've been nasty to some men. We live our lives day to day carrying on like we have all the time in the world. We don't have all the time in the world. Some people seem to be completely absent minded, living in an aimless state. Sometimes I think it borders on delusion. Our state of mind shouldn't be wandering about. I think we need to participate in life, I've discovered that I need to commit myself to learning how to best manage my life situations. As I see it, learning is limitless, it's a life long process."

"Well said Bermudadas," said George. "We are designed to act and I think we are accountable to humanity to rise to our best."

"Why did my mother put up with all that pain for so many years?" asked Lucy.

"Well," said George, "Your mother relied on your father economically, I think he felt a great joy in knowing he made her feel powerless and he did the same thing to you and Karen. Lucy there is no shame. Heal first. Take your time. When your fears disappear, rise to the point where you can act. Don't rely on someone else for strength. With the right spirit, your own spirit, you can find your own way. Learn to express yourself exactly as you are, without any reservations. This is not a hair cut change, this is a soul change, it's going to take time."

"That's a rather fitting quote coming from a hair stylist!" smiled Saffron, giving Lucy another hug.

"You have to accept the fact that each of us must find our own way. No one can act but you. Yes, we will receive help and we will help others, it's a perpetual process, but ultimately, as Buddha said, *Be a light unto yourself.* I stand by you, we all do

Lucy, but eventually you'll need to develop the tools to figure it out on your own. For now, you need to stop self-sabotaging yourself, your life. Struggle is when you hope against the facts. Contact with truth becomes creation, everything unfolds."

"I was such a fool to allow the same thing to happen to me," muttered Lucy.

"Don't beat yourself up," advised George. "We haven't been taught to act. Take your time, let it percolate, instinctively you'll know when it's time. Your dignity will be restored and you will feel composure and learn to act when life demands it. Find your place in this world. Teach your father who you are. Maintain strength and self-reliance within you. Get pro-active with your life. See your truths and choose to walk out of the ones that are negating your existence. In time, start to look at what facts in your life need attention: your living situation, your health, your relationships. Just take it slowly, slowly. Don't wish, don't hope from an unable state, take responsibility and participate, you have to make the effort. Right now the world may be an ugly place, but really, the world is okay. You have people who love you, a place to live, a job, so see the good that exists on this planet."

Negar got up and handed Lucy the tissue box while George continued, "Right now you're operating from the defeated mind, and you believe all this is more than you, something beyond you. And that is completely understandable; this is all so fresh. You're so overwhelmed; perhaps you don't have the inner strength to act right now. And for years you have created a personality to protect yourself out of fear, and you have become a victim. Do you understand?"

"I think so, but how do I shift from the defeated mind to a thriving mind?"

"You need to see your own power. Your power was robbed; your father robbed your power. Your defeated mind believes you don't have any power. You need to reclaim your own power. Right now you feel paralysed and that is perfectly understandable, that's all you've known, but you can free yourself from this state by first recognizing your own power and your right to choose a new belief and your right to participate in your life. You can look upon your past as a tragedy or you can look at it as an opportunity to learn and move forward having mastery over your life. Go beyond the doubt you carry."

After being around George for almost two years Lucy had started to understand some of the insights she had learnt, but in that moment she just didn't know if she could really do the work and rise, she thought … *I'm just so tired.*

He broke her thoughts and said, "Don't you have an urge to live? To be alive? To celebrate? Start with remembering that you exist and you have the right to act from your belief system. Allow the grace for the new to be born, the birth of the mystery, the unknown. As I've told you many times Lucy, it's your choice, you have to choose."

Nodding in agreement, she knew George was right.

At that moment the door opened and in walked Ned. The smile on his normally cheery face fell away as he stared at Lucy's battered eye.

Tossing his box of product on the reception desk, not looking at anyone, he strided quickly over to Lucy, bent down and gave her a hug.

"Oh Lucy, what happened?"

Lucy was so shocked by Ned's sudden affection, everyone was, well, not everyone, for months George was wondering when Ned was going to muster the courage to ask her out.

Everyone politely allowed them their moment as Lucy wasn't rejecting Ned's attention.

"Okay," George said quietly. "Manjira, you're done. Rebecca to my chair and Saffron to the sink."

13

Friday of the May long weekend arrived; Riverville was buzzing with anticipation of the town's celebrations, everyone was excited and smiling, and the weather forecast was favourable for the parade and the fair.

"So, Becs," asked Bermudadas from the dryer, "I'm trying to understand … please explain, why does May Day mean so much to you?"

"Well, sure," she replied hesitantly from George's chair. "Just to explain a little local history, it's a British tradition that a school teacher started here in Riverville after World War One. It's Riverville's biggest annual event, and it's so much fun, the entire community gets involved one way or another. In the old days they had an afternoon tea, races for the younger children, a baseball game for the older children, and pole dancing! It's about celebrating our community, everyone works so hard year round and May Day is a time when everyone stops and takes time to be with family and have a good time together."

"Okay, I get that, now please explain to me why it was so important to you that Rachel be this year's May Queen?"

"Well, like I said before, it's such an honour for any young woman to be chosen. There was a time when the May Queen had to be born in Riverville, but that's no longer the case today."

"Thank goodness that bias has been dropped," retorted Bemudadas.

Ignoring the slight Rebecca continued, "One of the May Queen's duties is to officially start the May Day celebrations with a speech, she wears a white dress and gets crowned. She also receives two gifts; a gold locket and a silver bracelet. Along with her five attendees, she rides on the royal float in the parade; she is the highlight of the day; and, at one time the dance was the social event of the year, everyone got dressed up, but that's changed. And since last year the royal party was invited to go to other community events as well. Did you know that last year Riverville entered a float in the New Westminster parade? And did you know that New Westminster hosts the longest running May Day celebrations in the British Commonwealth? I just thought it would be something Rachel would enjoy, especially as it's our 100th anniversary as a province and with Queen Elizabeth visiting. I know you're not a royalist Bermudadas, but I respect the royal family and I sincerely thought Rachel would enjoy it. It's her last chance as she graduates this year."

"Were you ever the May Queen?" asked George.

"Me? No, never."

"Did you ever want to be?" asked Negar from the dryer next to Bermudadas.

"Oh, of course," Rebecca's eyes lit up, "When I was in school every young lady dreamed of being chosen."

"Is that why you wanted Rachel to be May Queen?" asked George.

"I've never thought about it, maybe …" she mused. Internally she had started to understand the importance of everyone being themselves. She wanted to be close to her daughter again. She missed Rachel's presence around the house so much and she hated to accept how much happier she seemed to be living with Bermudadas.

Last night she admitted to Lance that perhaps she has suffocated her and looking at their younger daughter Elizabeth she didn't want to make the same mistake. She wanted Rachel to move back home, but she had backed off. Lance had taken Rachel to Ken's barbershop last Saturday and he had reported that she was firm about living with Bermudadas until after grad; and she wasn't making any commitments until after that. At first Rebecca was horrified with Rachel living with Bermudadas, *What would everyone be thinking?* But after a month she had to admit that Bermudadas had surprised her. She had taken in Karen and Lucy without any hesitation; she just acted from a place of kindness. Perhaps one day she would be able to talk to Bermudadas about everything, but not yet.

"Well," said Negar looking out the window at the sunshine, "It's looking like the weather will be perfect for tomorrow's parade."

"Yes, my staff are all fired up and into decorating my Mustang with flags from around the world. They're going to walk beside the car dressed up in clothes from other cultures," informed Bermudadas. "They made a big paper mache globe of the world that they're going to mount on the roof, they're totally into it, they want to celebrate Riverville's diversity and encourage people to travel and see the world. If I'm honest, especially as the organizing committee is very strict about not using the parade to advertise, it's actually good marketing."

"I know, it's good for us too," said Manjira from the sink. "Otherwise I wouldn't allow so much money to be wasted on a parade. If it wasn't for the free exposure and the fact that kids want to be in the parade, there's no way I would allow it to happen. And did you know one of your staff is coming over tomorrow morning to get dressed up in one of my saris?"

"Yes, and that's very kind of you to help out Manjira," answered Bermudadas. "Another is borrowing a kilt from the jeweller, it's going to be a lot of fun. I'm going to take lots of pictures of them from the sidelines." In the past she never really got excited about May Day, but this year with the four girls living with her and seeing their excitement it created an awareness in her of how fragile life can be from one moment to the next. It was just great to see them all truly happy and having fun, she was redefining happiness herself. She hadn't told anyone she had been out on a couple of dates with Sebastian; she wanted to keep it quiet for now. It was casual, they were enjoying each other's company and although he knew all about her history with Daisley; he didn't seem to be judging her.

Breaking her thoughts she heard George say, "Lucy, the parade will be going right by our front door!" said George. "I love parades, Marthina is coming in with the baby, and we'll move the chairs outside and enjoy the festivities."

"You should be in it George," said Rebecca.

"I know, next year I'll get all of you ladies on a float wearing rollers in your hair!"

Laughter erupted as Saffron came through the door, "What is all the laughter about?" she asked with a beaming smile.

"Didn't you know?" said George, "Tomorrow all of you are going in the parade dressed up with aprons around your necks and rollers in your hair!"

"Sure George ... I'm in, I'll do it! Just think, the mayor's wife in the parade with rollers in her hair, I like that!"

After the laughter settled Lucy said, "My mother always took us to the parade when we were little. I used to love the clowns, they always gave out candy!"

Lucy and Karen had been going for counselling once a week, although it had been only for a few weeks, from the outside it seemed to be helping. Bermudadas knew Lucy had been drinking; she couldn't hide that from an old partier like herself. For the moment she wasn't saying much, she was just watching her very carefully. She was just so happy they were open to getting counselling; talking to someone neutral will do them good thought Bermudadas. Dan Cassidy had kept his distance, things had settled, but she was still on guard and the police were keeping an eye on him too. She didn't trust him and she had heard through the grapevine that he was boasting at the Swinging Lantern how happy he was that he didn't have to feed his girls anymore, it was more beer money for him.

"Tomorrow we'll keep an eye out for the clowns and get you some candy Lucy!" said George.

"We'll all come down and join you George," suggested Bermudadas.

"Sure," he answered.

"Bermudadas, if you're going to be here with Rachel, do you think it would be okay if Lance and I came with Elizabeth and Keith? We've always watched it as a family," asked Rebecca

"Of course, it's perfectly fine with me. Why don't you call her later this evening and discuss it with her? I'm not the one you have to ask."

"Okay, I'll call this evening, I'll make some banana bread and some of her favourite oatmeal chocolate chip cookies," she said smiling hopefully.

"I'll come too George," added Saffron. "Daisley will be in the parade, he'll be on the municipal float and my parents have rented a convertible for my father's company, so I'll come and hang out with everyone too. I'll bring some snacks or something to drink."

"Sure, that sounds great," agreed George.

"Yes, I will bring something too," added Negar. "I'll bring some refreshments, Karim said he wants to watch it too. We want to take photos to send home to Iran. We'll bring some lawn chairs, it will be so much fun to watch it all together."

"Great, the more the merrier," said George looking forward to seeing everyone with their spouses and children.

"And after the parade Karim and I are going for a tennis lesson!" announced Negar.

"Good for you," said Bermudadas. "Let me know how it goes, maybe I'll drag my butt out one day."

"That would be great Bermudadas, we'd have so much fun! I'm really enjoying getting some exercise and meeting new people. I'm becoming more aware of my body and smacking that ball let's out all my frustrations!"

"I'd like that part, but let's see. I'm not making any promises woman. I won't be quitting smoking to play tennis, no way."

"That's fine," smiled Negar, happy to see her friend get enthused about something other than a party.

"So, Lucy," asked Saffron, "How is your love life? Ned sure seems smitten with you?!"

Everyone looked in her direction and Lucy started to blush, "Last weekend he took me to see the new James Bond movie, *Diamonds are Forever.*"

"And ..." Saffron pushed her for a little more information. "Are you interested?"

"He's sweet, I'm not used to getting that kind of attention," she answered as she wrapped up Manjira's hair in a towel.

Surprising everyone she continued openly, "The psychologist said that when my father gave me attention I felt that I existed, even when he was mean to me. She said I was just happy to get some attention. Since my mother died, I see how I have allowed my father to control everything I do.

I wanted to please him, to gain acceptance from him and to feel I belonged. I gave my power away. I get what you mean now George. I hid behind my attempts to smile, my pain was silent, my anger buried. I was locked. I have lived like that for so long. Now I'm working to have the courage to face my confusion, the shame, the pain, everything that has been fighting inside of me for so long."

"Good for you Lucy," said Saffron.

"Well, I have a long way to go. I know I have to take responsibility for myself, I'm trying, I have to," she stated quietly.

"And how is Karen?" asked Negar.

"She's mad as hell. She said he's a brute. She has nothing good to say about him. Since he got out of jail he hasn't called us or tried to get together - nothing. It's like he's completely dropped us from his life, but I'm going to call him, I want to see him, just to talk. She doesn't want anything to do with him and when I suggest that we call him, she gets angry with me; calls me a fool. I told her not to be cruel to those who are cruel to us, I remember when you said that Saffron. It's because of my mother that I'm loyal to him. I remember her telling us she could never leave him because we were his children and she couldn't take us away from him."

"Well," offered Negar, "I'm sure your mom did the best she could with the tools she had, and perhaps in time Karen will be able to process her anger and see things differently. As cheesy at it sounds, time will help with the healing."

"I hope so," then changing the subject she smiled nervously, "I enjoy spending time with Ned, it's fun. I've never met someone who actually wants to spend time with me."

"Good for you Lucy, you should be out having some fun, that's great," said Saffron. "Follow your heart, women need to follow their heart. There are good men out there and we need to appeal to that. Men need women too."

"Yes, and Lucy …" added Bermudadas thinking of Sebastian, "Don't rely on another for strength, you're slowly finding your own strength now and hold on to that. A strong man will strengthen a woman."

"And never, never, ever, apologize for being a woman," said Manjira getting up from the sink to sit next to Rebecca in one of the empty stylist chairs.

"I don't want to end up like my mother," said Lucy, sitting down on one of the footstools. "I think that's my greatest fear. Sometimes I'm so angry with her."

"Your mother was a lovely woman Lucy," stated Negar. "And you embody the good in her."

"Your mother's life became a misery because she didn't act," said George. "Her fears prevented her from acting. And don't be angry with her, like Negar said, she didn't have the tools."

"I suppose," said Lucy.

"I'm sure I've said this before, but I'll say it again anyway, bravery is when you are courageous enough to be you," continued George. "Anything that is done where your will is violated is rape. Be brave, you don't live in anyone's shadow. Be strong to know you're strong."

"I'm learning George."

"I know you are Lucy and whatever life teaches you, take it with great humbleness. And don't forget with freedom comes responsibility."

Lucy nodded, as she looked him square in the eye. "Yes, I get that now, I am responsible for my own life and the psychologist said that I need to be aware that I'm moving from deconstruct to construct. Pessimistic to optimistic."

"And you're doing it Lucy, and it's great that you're having some fun with Ned, he seems like a terrific guy. He'd never make you a beggar. As I see it …" said Bermudadas lighting up a cigarette, "Women have to drop the beggar's mentality. Women beg for love."

"Look who's talking!" chided Manjira slamming her hands on the arms of the chair.

"I may be many things Manjira, but I'm not a beggar. Men love how women look, they don't necessarily love the woman. A man can't resist a woman wanting him; men are actually the insecure ones. Well, not all men of course. Ned has had his eye on Lucy for ages, he sees her inner beauty. So many women are selling their looks, Lucy doesn't do that and Ned realizes Lucy is much more than her body. How did something so obvious get so mixed up?"

"You're the expert aren't you?" said Manjira. "You, who was left at the alter from one relationship, divorced from another, several men in between and then there's your most recent history."

Manjira's words stung and everyone in the room held their breath, but Bermudadas chose not to react, "No, I'm not an expert. I'm just sharing from my life experiences and as I see it women don't need men to protect them, those days ended long ago. Like George once said, a woman should be a man's joy, not his burden. And there are so many women out there who need constant reassurance that their man loves them. It's pathetic."

"I agree," said Saffron who once again was enjoying Bermudadas' insights. "So many women define themselves through their husbands, I've had to face that one by being labelled the *Mayor's wife* day in and day out."

"Well," said Negar. "I've fallen into that trap, I know I have. My identity has also been only through Karim, but I've allowed it. I know I have. The irony is when we first got married it was all I wanted. I fell into conventional roles and expectations, I loved it. Then I began to see that Mrs. Karim was all I became. I lost me. Moving to Canada and being alone so much in the first few years forced me to assert myself."

"And," added George, "I think perhaps your, *I can take it or leave it* attitude was a defence mechanism for you to maintain your inner security."

"Yes, that's very true. It was like I buried my head in the sand when situations arose, it was easier than having to deal with the facts. I would minimize problems just to appease others. I avoided any kind of conflict. I was always accommodating everyone around me. I'd say *Yes* to things I didn't really want to do. Now I've come to see that the more I have developed myself as a person, I'm able to do more for others in a much healthier manner. I truly want to do things for others. Karim and I have talked about it, he encourages and supports me in every thing I do. He's one of the good guys! And the more solid I have become as a person, the better I can serve my students and meet their needs."

"I think in the past you've been complacent and you've underestimated yourself Negar, now you're flowering!" said George "Do you think life can be an internal battle between what I should be and what I am?"

"Yes ... I am Saffron the artist! I try never to use the word should, it's a terrible word!" laughed Saffron. "Some women are confused, they're looking outside for their identity, instead of inside. I know because I was caught up in all that myself. Now I'm just starting to feel more and more grounded in truly being me and I believe it's showing in my art. For the past month or so I've just been painting madly. I'm obsessed by my paint brushes and loving it! I have five months until the show and I'll be ready."

"That's great Saffron," said Manjira, then looking at Bermudadas in the mirror, she stated, "Some women can be so self-serving."

Catching her intent Bermudadas retorted, "Are you suggesting that I'm self-serving Manjira?"

"Yes, I am."

"Well, perhaps I have been, I agree, but I'm working on it. I'm examining the choices I've made." And she had been, she was working at becoming free from her addiction to experiences. She had started to realize how foolish she had been at times, but she wasn't going to beat herself up about it all. It had been fun, perhaps she was just moving onto a new way of looking at life, a new way of experiencing life. "And what about you? Has your husband allowed you back into the business?"

"I never left, I've always been in charge of the accounts and getting new clients," retorted Manjira.

"That's not what I meant, are you back working with your staff?"

"No, and because of that he has to work so much more and quite frankly it serves him right. Now perhaps he'll see just how hard I worked day in and day out. He told me that I don't care if I'm right or wrong that all I care about is getting my way."

"Well, that's probably true," stated Bermudadas, "You do always want your way, you can't deny that."

Glaring at Bermudadas she continued, "Well, I'm not making any apologies. He also said I have no problem reneging on promises I make to our staff and until I learn to be right with them I'm not welcome back. What does he know? I have worked for years building that company."

"Well, I can't imagine working for you, that would be worse than a prison sentence!" said Bermudadas.

Everyone had to stifle their laughter as Manjira continued, "I want total obedience. They can defend themselves if they want. I have no respect for softness in people. There is nothing wrong with me. The loyalty of staff is undependable, the only thing certain is money. Money is power. And I don't have to justify my actions to anyone."

"And face it Manjira, you just love power and now you're making yourself the victim, it's all about you," said Bermudadas. "And hey, if you're in charge of the accounts, how come you never pay your tab here?"

Everyone froze. Manjira took a deep breath and finally answered, "I was going to pay that today, thank you for reminding me."

"Aren't you enjoying your free time?" asked Negar hoping to sway the conversation to a more positive slant.

"Well, I am," Manjira admitted, "But I'm home spending too much time with my mother."

"Why don't you get a volunteer job?" suggested Rebecca.

"Volunteer!? Forget it, I'm not going to be away from the business forever," she retorted. "They'll figure out soon enough that they need me more than they think they do. I solve all the problems."

Rebecca thought about her neighbour Joy, they had had coffee the night before and she had mentioned how much happier everyone was without Manjira around. Joy said she actually enjoyed going to work again, in fact everyone did, and with Mr. Das they wanted to do their best. It was so refreshing to go to work not dreading and fearing what Manjira was going to rant about. And apparently business had picked up; they were busy and getting ready for the wedding season and all the graduation ceremonies coming up.

"Okay, you're done Rebecca," said George as he unwrapped the apron from around her neck. "Who's next? Let's see, I'll get Manjira ready for the dryer and then I'll take care of you Negar, Lucy can you shampoo Saffron in about five-ten minutes?"

"Sure George," she replied.

Rebecca got up and sat next to Saffron in the reception area, Manjira moved to George's chair, Lucy was studying the appointment book at the reception desk and everyone else stayed put for the moment.

"Listen to this everyone," said Bermudadas holding up a magazine, "It's a quote by Coco Chanel, I just love her new perfume, Chanel No. 19, did you know it was launched last August 19th, for her 87th birthday? She just passed away in January; anyway, this is what she said to Arthur Capel, her lover, 'I'll know that I love you when I'm not dependent on you anymore'. Isn't that perfect?! What a quote! Women everywhere need to hear that, in relationships people create so much dependency, that's not healthy."

"What do you mean?" asked Lucy.

"Well," she said putting the magazine down, "Lucy you're moving from dependency to independency right?"

"Well, maybe, I don't know," Lucy answered.

"Being independent doesn't mean you don't need another, it doesn't mean you don't love, or rely on someone, it's just that reliance doesn't take away your independency. If you're dependent on someone, you're a slave. You're not responsible for your life and there's no freedom in that." Looking at Manjira she continued, "I'm not professing to be an authority, but that's how I see it. Being independent allows me to determine my own future."

"I agree," said George. "I don't allow anything on the outside to influence my well-being. For example, it can rain, it can be sunny, I don't allow the weather to decide if I'm having a good day or not! It's okay for two people to dependent on each other, with each person capable to choose the way they want to exist, that's independency, that's personal mastery. A drug addict is dependent on drugs right? Without the drug he'll fall apart, that's not living."

"True," said Negar and everyone agreed. Lucy agreed outwardly, but privately she knew she liked smoking dope and chilling out.

George continued, "Independence means you are the creator, dependency means you are being created, get it?"

A unison of nodded heads prevailed.

"Yes, since the kid was born she's been dependent on me and Richard," said Bermudadas, "But now she's a young lady and she's moving towards her own independence, that's why we've raised her to make her own decisions. We haven't rushed it, its been a process, eventually we want her to be self-reliant."

"And that makes perfect sense to me," agreed George. "Let me ask you, what do all of you really want?" Looking at Lucy he repeated the question, "Lucy, what do you really want? What do you want to experience?"

"I want to be independent, I see that, I get what you say, but one day at a time."

"Good, what else do you want? Don't be afraid to ask for what you desire either. The tree has a desire to be a tree!"

Everyone laughed and agreed.

"It's okay to have some fun Lucy, be true to what you desire, and when your desire is fulfilled, it's a flowering. If you desire a relationship, that's great."

"We've been taught not to desire George," said Rebecca.

"I know and that just seems sad. If your desire is to have a bigger house Manjira, then have a big house. Why not? You will enrich others, inspire others that they can rise to be more too. It's not ego, it's like a vision for yourself, from one joy to another joy. When you really look at it, there seems to be an epidemic around the world that people have given up, they believe they can't grow. They seem to get stuck into believing they can ever be more than what they are currently experiencing. Then people get depressed, eat chocolate, go shopping, start drinking. People seem to have lost their vision for their own growth. People live without a vision of how they want to live. If you really want to grow Lucy, you have to take the information and really actualize it. It seems to me that you're on the path, you're in the trenches looking at it; the door is opening. You know your beliefs create your reality. When something happens and you're sad, it's a beautiful thing. Life is teaching you, it's telling you something you need to know about yourself. Now that you're on your way, don't give up on your vision over you."

"I won't George," answered Lucy, while in her head she silently wondered if she could ever really live the life she wanted to live.

"Slowly, slowly ..."

With that the discussion was over and the ladies started to check their May Day Parade *To do* lists. Everything was organized; they finished up at George's and carried on with the rest of their day.

The following day, as predicted, was sunny and the crowds had started to line both sides of High Street by eight o'clock.

"What a perfect day for a parade!" said George. Looking around he was pleased that everyone had showed up. Marthina was sitting comfortably up front next to Rebecca and Saffron. Manjira had taken charge of their baby and was sitting comfortably with her mother next to her.

He met Karim for the first time, he and Negar were wearing matching tennis clothes, they looked like high school students just having fun. Lance along with his children, Elizabeth, Keith, and Rachel were all sitting on the sidewalk laughing and teasing each other. Rebecca was over the moon to have everyone together and she was so grateful that Rachel had agreed to come and spend time together as a family. Rachel had admitted to Constanze that she missed being around her family, especially her siblings, but she was loving her independence and not planning on moving back home for a while.

Behind them stood Constanze, Bermudadas, and Richard. He had driven out to be with Constanze; the warmth between father and daughter was totally obvious. And then there was Karen and Lucy sitting next to Ned, he had brought lawn chairs and was dotting over both girls and attending to their every need. It was just so great to have everyone together sharing the spirit of celebration.

Looking up and down High Street everyone was jarring for position along the sidewalk as the first float was to be expected to be making its way from the staging area at the recreation centre at any moment.

From a distance they heard the Legion Pipe Band, "There they are!" exclaimed Karen as she pointed down the road.

The Legion Band led the way with the pipes and drums demanding full attention, behind them two RCMP officers on motorcycles with their flashing lights led the municipal float with Daisley and his council waving and smiling at the crowd.

As the municipal float neared, Bermudadas' heart gave a nervous flutter, it was the first time she was seeing Daisley since the end of February. She was happy to have her sunglasses on so no one could truly see her reaction; thankfully everyone was looking at the parade. In witnessing her reaction she was relieved that she felt nothing for him.

His float approached and Saffron called out, "Hi, Mr. Mayor!"

He blew her a kiss and the crowd whistled. Saffron blushed and waved earnestly for all to see. She was happy; things between them had improved. *I'm not living in a bubble anymore* she told herself, *right now for the moment we're getting back on track and happy, I'm just living in the present and doing my best not to project more on to him than what he is.*

Meanwhile Bermudadas was thinking, *Its only been three months since all that drama.* She was relieved when Daisley had passed, her heartbeat settled as she waved to Sebastian on the police motorcycle behind the mayor's float. *Soon, I'll have to tell Richard and the kid about him, but not yet. I'll wait until after the girls have graduated.*

From his motorcycle Sebastian saw Berumdadas standing there in her designer sunglasses and floral printed cotton summer dress. He was smitten. He wanted to marry her now. She had made it clear that her home life with four young women were her priority and he understood, he believed he just had to give it all time and eventually they'd be able to go public about their relationship. He wanted to tell the world he was in love.

He was eight years younger, but it didn't matter to him. He didn't care about her past, if anything he respected her lack of concern for what people thought about her. She had told him, *I disregard all approval and I disregard all disapproval. I don't allow myself to be influenced by society and what people think.* The older man standing next to her must be her ex-husband he thought. She had told him Richard would be there and although he did feel threatened, he understood he was there for Constance. But there was one thing always running around in his head, would she ever have an affair on him? They had only talked about her affair with Mayor Michael briefly. She had told him it was a drunken mistake. She said she wasn't blaming the booze, that it was a bad choice they both made. He had wanted to talk about it more, but he hadn't pushed it. She was a knockout, what man wouldn't want to be with her? He was afraid of falling in love with her and of the possibility that she may one day leave him. Recently he had told himself he was getting way ahead of things, they were taking it slowly, but he still couldn't drop his fear.

Next came the Riverville High School Band; then bowlers from the bowladrome dressed up to look like bowling pins drew huge laughter from the crowd; followed by long line of Brownies, Scouts, Guides and local businesses.

Then, representing Riverville's extended care home, the staff was pushing the old timers down the street in wheel chairs; sometimes the stronger old timers would switch places with their caregivers and push them! As soon as they saw Bermudadas they all waved earnestly, which drew surprise from everyone.

"How come they all know you?" asked Rebecca.

"Oh, I pop in from time to time," she answered evasively.

"Time to time," retorted Constanze. "Since I was a kid she's dragged me over there on Christmas Day, and for years every Saturday we would take Maggie over for the old people to pet. I have to admit; when I was younger it seemed like such a drag, but now I really enjoy spending time with all them."

"What?!" said Rebecca.

Everyone stared at Bermudadas. "It's no big deal Becs, don't worry, I'm not in competition with you for the volunteer of the year award!"

"I'm not, I'm just shocked. You? A volunteer at the care home?"

"Well, don't let it taint the image you have of me or you'll start thinking you can get me to that church of yours!"

Everyone laughed.

"No, I'm over that Bermudadas. I know better than to try and get you to do anything you don't want to!"

The Lions Club and the Rotary Club came and went; then the Fire Department arrived with their lights flashing and they drew huge cheers from the kids as they sporadically set off their siren. Clowns ran up and down the sidewalk while children squealed at all their crazy antics and Lucy got her candy.

Manjira's catering company with her husband, children, and staff waving from the float made her feel sad. She saw how much fun everyone was having without her, everyone was dressed up as different appetizers and her children were dressed up as cutlery, she thought it was very creative. Her mother was madly taking pictures, waving and laughing with them as they went by.

Next came Bermudadas' sports car. As soon as she saw her staff she started hooting and hollering, the crowd burst out in laughter as her staff all stopped and bowed to her on their way by.

Then came the May Queen float with the happy winner seated in her royal chair surrounded by her attendants. It was obvious how happy she was, the young lady was beaming and so excited to be waving to the crowd.

"See mom," said Rachel, "The perfect person was chosen to be the queen. Look how happy she is, its made her day and her happiness is infectious. I'm happy for her. If that had been me, I would have been miserable and everyone around me would have been miserable."

Before Rebecca could answer, a small voice piped up, "I'd like to be May Queen someday." It was Elizabeth, "Mom, can I be May Queen when I get older?"

Everyone sat anticipating Rebecca's answer. She chose her words carefully, "It's up to you sweetheart, and it has to be your choice."

Rachel couldn't believe it, she didn't say a word, in fact, no one did.

14

A month passed, it was now the end of June; Constanez and Rachel had graduated, more centennial celebrations were scheduled for Canada Day, and everyone's lives were about to settle into their summer routines once again.

"Hey, did anyone read this?" Bermudadas asked as she held up a magazine from the reception area. "Last Wednesday, June 16th, was the 50th Anniversary of the lifting of prohibition!"

"Only you would be interested in that fact," retorted Manjira from George's chair.

"Now, now woman," replied Bermudadas, her hair was done, she was just hanging out for a while before heading back to agency. Business was great and her staff didn't need her around. Besides, right now she was focused on making sure she was at home for the four young ladies she had under her roof. Constanze and Rachel would be gone by the end of the summer, they had decided to go to university in Victoria together. She loved having Lucy and Karen stay with her and she was hoping they wouldn't leave. She was so grateful for everything she had, all the drama with Daisley had created a whole new appreciation for living and everyone was kind enough to give her a second chance; she wasn't going to let anyone down. She knew she was blessed with life's sweetest pleasures and thankfully she had figured it out before she lost all that was precious to her. She felt that life had become holy, not in a religious sense, but she truly realized that life was to revered and respected. On some crazy level she was grateful it all happened because of the awareness it was creating in her. Getting back to Manjira she laughed, "I bet under that stoic exterior of yours you'd love to let go and just get hammered one night! Actually it would quite entertaining to see you loosen up a bit and have a couple of drinks!"

Everyone laughed and even Manjira had to let out a smile, "Hardly," came her answer.

"Look at the fashion for this fall," said Saffron holding up her magazine. "The midi-skirt is in, now the length drops just below the knee and fashion experts are saying this is the year of the sweater. Oh and look, the new *Maria Poncho*, it's so hot. It's made with black velvet and has a hot pink fringe! I have to get one."

"Imagine my concern," said a sarcastic Rebecca.

"Oh Becs," said Bermudadas, "We know that you're secretly sad because you missed out on wearing all those mini-skirts hanging in your closet!"

"Bermudadas," she smiled. "I must say that life is never dull when you're around."

"And you always thought I was here to be converted. I guess I've disappointed you!"

"You know, with Lance's help, I've started to examine myself and my motives for doing things for others."

"Good for you Becs," said Bermudadas as she put down the magazine and gave Rebecca her full attention.

"I never liked to accept my dark side, or my negative feelings. Now with Rachel gone I've really been forced to become honest with myself. Lance said it's human to have negative feelings and that we all have them."

"Of course we do," agreed Saffron.

"And I'm seeing from accepting myself as I am, I'm starting to accept others as they are; starting with you Bermudadas!"

"So does that mean you've finally given up on getting me to church?!"

"Yes, I think I need to focus on myself before I start telling other people what they should be doing."

"Good for you Rebecca. The more we get right, the more the world gets right," smiled George.

The phone rang. Lucy was busy folding towels, so George excused himself from Manjira and quickly strolled to the reception desk.

From the dryer Negar offered, "Do you want me to get it George?"

"It's okay, thanks Negar," he answered, "George's Salon."

"George, this is Constable Smith. We met a couple of months ago at the medical clinic," he reminded him.

"Yes, certainly," not wanting to alarm anyone George purposely didn't say the officer's name aloud.

"Does Lucy Cassidy still work for you?" he asked.

"Yes," said George.

"Is she there now?"

"Yes … "

"I have some shocking news, her father has passed away."

"Oh …" replied a calm George, turning to face the window, still choosing not to alarm anyone.

"He was at the Swinging Lantern, he went to the bathroom and it appears he had a heart attack."

Glancing at the clock it was almost one o'clock, *I guess he was there for lunch, thought George.*

"Right now we're conducting our investigation, we're chatting with the bartender and people who were present. There doesn't appear to be anything suspicious, there wasn't a fight or anything. He was dead when the paramedics arrived; however, they can't legally declare the body dead."

"I see," said George.

"Right now the body is being transferred to the Royal Columbian Hospital, from there the doctor will legally pronounce him dead and he or she will contact Dan Cassidy's family doctor, Dr. Petersen, to confirm if he had any medical history. He was overweight and a drinker, so I doubt there will be an autopsy. And from that point it will become the coroner's case. If Lucy is there, we would like to come over and ask a few questions."

"Of course," answered George.

"Officer Kitchen and I will be over shortly to talk to her, is her sister at school? Are the kids still in school?"

"I believe this may be their last day, I'll find out by the time you get here."

"Okay, well, we'll see you within the half hour."

"Thank you," and George hung up the phone. He looked around the room. Lucy was stacking the towels on the shelf and was laughing about something with Rebecca; Negar was at one of the dryers with the receipts and ledger spread out on a footstool; Manjira was in his chair; and Saffron and Bermudadas were seated in the reception area.

Manjira had been watching him in the mirror, "What's wrong George?"

Everyone suddenly noticed he was standing at the reception, eyebrows pushed together and looking at Lucy.

Manjira twirled the chair around and everyone waited to hear what he had to say.

"Lucy," walking over to her, "Have a seat." He indicated to one of the empty stylist chairs. She complied without a word. He sat down in the chair next to her while everyone waited for what he was going to say.

"Your father passed away …" as George relayed the facts from Officer Smith, she sat there numb, bewildered, and immobilized.

That evening everyone gathered at Bermudadas': the ladies, Ned, George, and the local funeral director Ralph Moon. They were there to help Lucy and Karen make decisions.

Manjira had already taken charge of the catering and she was making arrangements with the funeral home operator, "I'll take care of all the food, don't give it a second thought girls."

"Thanks Manjira," replied a grateful Lucy.

"I don't care what happens," said a defiant Karen. "I'm not going to his funeral, he wasn't a father, he was a mean son of a bitch and I don't want anything to do with him."

"He's still our father and we have to make the arrangements and do what we can," argued Lucy.

She had called their grandparents in Revelstoke and they were going to notify the rest of family so the burden of spreading the news wasn't all on her. Their grandparents said they hoped to arrive within a day or two.

"Well, you go right ahead. He was a vile man and I'm not going to pretend he was a good father."

"Fine, you do what you want," answered Lucy.

With that Karen stood up and went downstairs to the basement to get away from everyone.

Negar stood up and followed her, "I'll just go see if she's okay."

Everyone nodded and then Ralph spoke, *he was obviously well conditioned to emotional times and potentially hostile environments* thought Bermudadas as he took charge going through what had to happen in the next few days.

As he continued Lucy's head flooded back to her mother's funeral.

"Lucy?" he smiled gently at her.

"Sorry," she shook her head to bring herself back to the present.

"That's okay. Let's go slowly. If you like, we can take care of transporting your father's body from the morgue to the funeral home. We can obtain the death certificate, help you to choose a casket and a grave marker, arrange the service and prepare the obituary."

"Okay, I would prefer if you just did it all," she agreed. She knew Mr. Moon had managed her mother's funeral and everything had gone perfectly fine.

"Okay, now has his employer been notified?"

"I don't know," she said. "But I'm sure the news has spread by now."

"Okay, I can take care of that too if you like."

"Yes, please do," she nodded.

With everyone's support the arrangements were put into place and the date was confirmed for the following Wednesday. Negar had returned from downstairs and offered to take Lucy out to buy something to wear for the funeral and virtually everything for the moment was done.

Wednesday arrived and true to her word Karen refused to go. Much to Lucy's amazement the funeral home was quite full. The seats were filled with her father's work colleagues and several seedy looking characters who Lucy recognized from the party days and drug deals made at her house. To her surprise they were all there dressed in their finest, clean shaven, and looking quite forlorn. Lucy hoped her father's death wouldn't be in vain and that perhaps they would make changes in their lives, but it wasn't for her to preach.

While she waited for the service to begin she thought about her sister and how disappointed she felt that Karen hadn't come. But, she thought, *It's her truth, so it's probably better she didn't come.* And although she knew there was going to be a lot of legal issues and work to be done to finalize his estate, she knew they would get through it all one day at a time. Ned was seated next to her, looking around she saw all the salon ladies and seated beside George was Dr. Petersen and his wife. She smiled to her friend Sherry, she had been around all week helping out with anything she could. Looking at the coffin she felt his tortured life was over and maybe now he would be at peace. He had caused them all such great pain, but looking over at her grandparents she suddenly wondered what kind of life he had had a child. She wanted to believe that somewhere in there that he was a good man who just made some bad choices. She took a deep breath and just wanted this day to be over and for things to get back to normal, what ever normal was. She told her self, *It's not about me, today is about honouring our father, so just get through it.*

After the funeral, during the tea, one by one her father's work colleagues and friends came up to her and a stream of compliments poured from them, He did anything for his friends, his boss came over to her and said he had worked for the railway for almost 25 years, rarely took a sick day and was always willing to do what had to be done. Lucy knew underneath he had had a good heart, it was just sad for some reason his family was rarely on the receiving end.

By evening the turmoil was behind her, yet she knew the residue would take time to settle. Lucy knew the gig, she had been through it before when her mother died, it was a threshold of pain she had never felt before. But it was different this time, she was older and she was buffering the pain just to do what had to be done.

Although George had told her not to worry about getting back to work, she wanted to start back right away. Her relatives had left the day after the funeral and there was no reason for her not to be at work. As usual, when she arrived she found George in the reception area reading the paper, smoking a cigarette, feet up on the table.

"Hey," she said as she hung up her coat.

"Hey," replied George folding up the paper and pulling a drag on his cigarette.

Sitting next to him she didn't say anything, happy just to sit and take a deep breath.

"What a week," she said.

"Yes, it certainly has been," replied George.

"You know there were moments when he was alive that I wished he was dead. I feel terrible about that."

"Don't beat yourself up over that Lucy, given what you endured it's understandable. Can you imagine how your father must have felt when he would sober up after one of his episodes? His guilt, we will never know, but I'm sure he was a tortured soul."

"Yeah, I guess you're right. It's just that family, no matter how crazy, is important to me."

"I know Lucy. Your capacity to forgive and the love you demonstrated this past week by taking charge of the arrangements and spending time with your grandparents and relatives has been incredible. Look at what you did Lucy; you took responsibility, you made decisions and your rose above your own emotions."

"Well, despite the abuse, I can't allow it to determine the rest of my life. Doing everything I could this past week seemed like a healing of some kind. I'm not sure exactly, I guess I'll figure it out eventually. I just wish Karen had been there."

"Well, that was her choice and we have to respect that."

"I know, I just hope in years to come she doesn't regret it."

"Well, it's her journey. Perhaps in time she'll come to terms with her decision."

"I hope so. I'm just glad I reached out and saw him last week when we met for coffee at the café. We didn't talk much, but I believe I truly felt his remorse. He was sober and kind. I really enjoyed talking with him again. I couldn't get Karen to come with me, she just got angry because I contacted him."

"I know, that took courage and now it's a memory you'll have."

The two sat in silence staring out the window. Directly across the street the hardware store was opening up and Lucy sat there amazed at how the rest of the world just kept going on; the street lights changed from green to amber to red; the cars moved; people were walking up and down the street; the news still came on at ten o'clock; life had stopped for her father, yet it kept moving on for the rest of us.

A couple of hours later the ladies were all there; Manjira in George's chair, Lucy shampooing Rebecca, Negar doing the books and Saffron and Bermudadas hanging out in the reception. It was a regular scene and one everyone truly loved being there every Friday morning.

"Lucy, what are you going to do with the house?" asked Manjira.

"Manjira, how can you ask that right now?" scolded Rebecca as Lucy wrapped her head in a towel.

"Well, it's a huge house in an excellent location, we may be interested in buying it, that's all."

"It's okay Rebecca. Karen and I have talked about it and we don't want to live there again. We're enjoying living with Bermudadas, especially until Karen graduates.

The only thing we'd really like to keep is our mother's rose garden, it means more to us than the house."

"I'm sure dear," said Manjira. "Well, once you've decided let me know and I'll talk to my husband."

"Okay, Mr. Moon said when we're ready we have to get all our father's important papers together, his tax returns, his Social Insurance Number, bank account statements, we still have a lot to sort out. He's been really kind, he's coming over on Monday to get things rolling."

"Well, it's probably good to get started on it all," said Negar and the conversation fell to a lull.

"Listen to this headline," said Saffron reading a newsmagazine, "This is the first year that women in Switzerland have the right to vote."

"Really?" answered Bermudadas, "I'm surprised it took them so long to get it. Wow, we're living in transitory times."

"I wonder what are women evolving to?" mused Saffron.

"Well," said Bermudadas, "I think women are looking to be appreciated for what they are."

"I think we need to understand the depth of getting ourselves right, live it, believe it, actualize it. People always want a quick fix, quick results, I believe the journey is a life time commitment to rise. And we need to help each other, woman to woman. We need to find the sacredness in each other," suggested Negar.

"There's our peacekeeper, always wanting harmony," smiled Manjira.

"It's my belief Manjira. As I see it, the foundation for friendship is honour and I honour all of you. I appreciate coming here every Friday morning and seeing all of you. It means the world to me. We've all become friends and just think, if we hadn't all started coming to Huxtable's, we never would have met."

"That's true," Manjira agreed.

"Yes, and as I have learnt this past year," said Rebecca, "that we, or I should say I, have to stop saying what I think is right for somebody."

Bermudadas starting clapping her hands, "Alajuela Becs! I do believe you have seen the light!"

Laughter erupted as Rebecca just shook her head and smiled at Bermudadas.

"And as I see it lades," injected George, "That is success."

"Success?" asked Manjira.

"Yes, living in success is simply giving the best of you."

"It's not that simple George," said Manjira.

"Everyone is chasing success, people go to war for success. Look at the competition kids are driven into in regards to their education. They are conditioned to be number one; they are pushed, and pushed, and pushed to compete against their friends."

"That's so true," exclaimed Negar. "When I was in school the competition was absolutely brutal. I swore that when I became a teacher I would never create such an unhealthy environment in my classroom. I always tell my students that it doesn't matter to me who gets the highest mark in the class, that it's about them just doing the best they can do, without competition. Who wants to compete with their best friend? My heart goes out to those kids who may not do so well in academics, they get labelled and then they end up carrying that for the rest of their lives. It's just terrible."

"Good for you Negar, I always told the kid her marks are secondary, that as long as she did her best, that was good enough for me," agreed Bermudadas.

"That makes sense, that's what we teach our twins, but success is also money George," argued Manjira.

"Absolutely, and there is nothing wrong with money, thinking it will solve all your problems is the crazy part," explained George. "Then there are those out there who say, *Money isn't everything* and their psychology is warped. They use their belief as an excuse to remain in poverty. They have given up, why is that? With money you can do a lot of things; provide a good education for your children, drive a good reliable car, eat well, have a good life style, share."

"I totally agree George, I think some people enjoy the ego trip of being poor, *Oh I have suffered so much … blah, blah, blah*, who wants to listen to that victim state over and over again?" said Manjira.

"So true Manjira, and as I see it," George continued, "Success has no meaning if it's used to exhibit, show off or to be recognized, that's shallow. The success of someone should be for the whole of humanity."

"That's a romantic idea George," said Manjira.

"I don't see it like that Manjira. Success begins once you have discovered the real you, when you have accepted you as you are. Then after that healing and you have attained to an inner rest, it's about giving birth to the best of you – that ladies, as I see it, is living in success. You discover you are a creator and you quit comparing, right Saffron?"

"Yes, that's been one of my biggest lessons of late, I'm not competing or comparing with anyone anymore," she agreed.

"If we all look at what we have failed at, it tells us something about ourselves right?" he continued.

"Right," agreed Saffron.

"Look at all of you, Saffron being you is an artist; Negar, the teacher; Rebecca the mom; Manjira and Bermudadas the business women; and Lucy is figuring it out. Don't you think you're all doing exactly what you love to do?"

"Very true George," agreed Rebecca. "Since I was a young woman there was nothing that I wanted more than to have a family."

"What about money George?" repeated Manjira.

"Well, money is knowing the best of you and then making it economically viable," he said.

"And it's obviously working for you George, you love what you do and look at your success," said Negar. "I know ladies, let me remind you - I do the books!"

"Then I guess I'll be getting a raise soon George?" asked Lucy.

Everyone laughed.

"Why not?!" he answered. "And you see, my success is Lucy's success too. It's the ripple effect. I'm making money rightly. I'm taking care of my family, my business, and sharing."

"Well, that does make sense," agreed Manjira.

"Sure it does," said Saffron. "And for me, I see now that everything has been unfolding quite naturally since I've been able to let go of comparing."

"And for you Manjira," continued George, "You have a big staff and you have an opportunity to inspire them, not scare the living shit out of them every time you walk into the office."

"I know George," she said quietly. "My husband says the same thing. I just don't know how to do that."

Everyone went silent. Manjira had suddenly stopped defending herself.

"You have believed life is brutal and in making money you have lost you," he said.

"I know, since my husband kicked me out, I've been really looking at what is important in my life."

"I'd say it's something like living in synchronicity," explained Saffron.

"I like that," said Lucy sitting down on one of the footstools.

"Think about it," said George. "When you are living from your heart, rising to be the best of you, when you are clear on your beliefs, and step into being a creator how can you not be a success?"

"Makes sense to me," stated Bermudadas.

"And Manjira, when I say the success of someone should be for the whole of humanity; I mean that your success benefits those around you and everyone is enriched. When we rise as individuals, humanity will rise. When you and your husband started your business you became the custodian of the wellness of the people who work for you and for those who buy your product, correct?"

"Yes, that's true, it's something we take very seriously."

"That is the extension of you and it's the ripple effect, you have triggered an awareness in others that they can rise too."

"Yes, I get it now George," stated Manjira.

"If you look at the forest, when the fir tree grows, not only has the fir tree succeeded, the whole forest has right?"

"True," voiced Negar while everyone nodded their heads.

"We can all live in abundance," he stated.

"I see that, it's just that … as I have said before, sometimes I panic," she admitted.

"Well, that's being human Manjira. I believe as you learn to trust yourself more, the panic will dissolve. Operate from the thriving mind, don't allow the defeated mind to take over."

"I understand," she nodded.

"Be a success in everything you do, being a mom, live it, walk it, be that state. Not from an ego of trying; from a place of having recognized your personal power. And your effort is not just for you it's for another too."

Everyone sat in silence and then Bermudadas asked, "Have you heard that quote by Sophie Tucker?"

"Who is Sophie Tucker?" asked Lucy.

"Was, sweetheart, was, she died a few years ago. Sophie Tucker was a Ukrainian born American, she was a jazz singer. One of her most famous quotes is ... 'I've been rich and I've been poor. Believe me honey, rich is better'."

"I love it!" said Saffron.

"As I see it," said George, "Right living is to have an abundance of friends, of laughter, success, an abundance of love, that is quality of life."

"I think we all agree George," said Rebecca.

"Now we all must have the strength to live that," he added.

"True," said Saffron.

"My psychologist said something similar," offered Lucy.

"What did she say?" asked Bermudadas.

"She was talking about power ... that if I do something I don't want to do, I lose my power. Like with my father, I just wanted to please him because I was afraid of what would happen if I didn't. I became my mother. I was stuck, where as when I'm in my power, my energy flows. She suggested that I embrace strong living."

"That makes sense," agreed George. "If we want to live a particular life, we must participate."

"What else have you talked about? If you don't mind me asking," queried Negar.

"She said I need to be careful of sending mixed signals. That I have to learn to communicate my feelings, not my reactions."

"That makes sense," said Negar. "That's probably something we could all work on."

"To be honest, at first I was suspicious of Ned."

"Suspicious? Of Ned?" asked a surprised Bermudadas, "He's a darling!"

"I know, but I feared he would take advantage of me. I know I have to learn to communicate my feelings and not my reactions. And she also said that I need to be aware of the deadly cycle I could fall into of seeking reassurance that we're okay as a couple and then over compensate by flattering him or trying to please him."

"Have you discussed this with Ned?" asked Negar.

"Oh yes, he knows everything,"

"She said I need to learn to trust me and then I'll learn to trust others."

"Well, you're on the right path Lucy. You've witnessed a lot in your short life time, and you're moving forward, good for you, that takes courage," said George.

"Thanks and you know, thinking of my father … he grew up in a trailer park in a small town. He probably never dreamed he'd own his own house. After listening to everything you said about success; he could have been more, but when I see what he came from he didn't do too bad. He tried and I know somewhere in all of the sadness that he did love our mother."

"I'm sure he did Lucy," consoled Rebecca.

"What this town needs is a safe place where women can go if they feel scared of any violence against them," said Manjira.

Everyone agreed.

"Well, I have to get some errands done," informed Bermudadas looking at her watch.

"Yes, me too and then I have to get back to my studio," said Saffron gathering up her things.

"How is everything going for the show?" asked George.

"Great, we're down to three months and all the arrangements are coming together. At first, as you all know, I wasn't crazy about letting some people get involved as I felt they were using me to get to Daisley, but now, I say, *Knock yourself out.* It's their choice, they'll figure out that Dailey is his own person and when it comes to politics his beliefs can't be manipulated."

"That's why my husband wants to run for council," said Manjira. "He supports Daisley's vision for Riverville."

"Daisley is really excited about that, I hope he wins Manjira."

"Well, I wasn't crazy about the idea, but if it's what he wants to do he's going to do it! If he wins, he'll be the first Indo-Canadian to be on council."

"Let's hope he wins!" said Saffron.

"I guess the fall election will be the next thing on this town's agenda," said Rebecca.

"Yes, it will be," agreed Saffron. "Bermudadas are you ready?"

"Yes,"

"Let's go have lunch at the café, do you have time?"

"I certainly do Saffron," the two headed out the door, but before they left Bermudadas announced, "Just so you all know … Sebastian Kitchen and I have been dating."

"That's great," said Negar. In the brief moments when she had met him, she felt he was such an endearing man.

"Good for you," said George. He liked Officer Kitchen.

"Yes, it is," agreed Saffron. "Let's go and you can tell me all about him!" In moments the two were off and out the door.

"After this past winter I never thought I would see that," said Manjira.

.

15

Summer passed, September passed, and Thanksgiving weekend arrived. Fall came early, the mornings were cold, colourful leaves were starting to cover the ground, the robins had headed south ages ago, and another season was about to be embraced. The municipal election came and went, Daisley remained mayor and Manjira's husband became the first Indo-Canadian to be on Riverville's council.

At the inauguration ceremony Daisley reflected that it was history in the making and a reflection of Prime Minister Trudeau's declaration that Canada would adopt a multicultural policy. A policy where Canada would recognize and respect its society including diversity in customs, religions and so on - and in Riverville it was something he intended to uphold to the best of his ability.

"We're living in exciting times, it's great to be alive at this moment," said Negar as she put the paper down.

"Indeed," agreed George.

"And now it's Thanksgiving weekend already," she continued from George's chair. "I think it's my favourite holiday, it's a celebration I really love."

"Yes," said Lucy, "Me too."

"And speaking of holidays," she said, "Karim and I decided we're going back to Iran for *Norwuz* next year!"

"When was the last time you were back?" asked George as he was finishing the final touches on her Mary Tyler Moore hairdo.

"It has been almost three years, so it's time to head back for a visit, I'm really looking forward to it."

"I'm sure."

"How long will you be gone for?" asked Saffron from the reception.

"We'll probably go for two months, it's a long way to travel and Karim has business to take care of, so it will be a work holiday for him."

"Just make sure you come back!" said Bermudadas from the dryer.

A unison of *Yeses* came from around the room.

Laughing she answered, "Oh we will!"

"I guess we'll have to close down for two months while Negar is away George," said Lucy. "We can't run the salon without her taking care of the accounts."

Everyone laughed.

"Actually," he said seriously, "Why don't you take a holiday Lucy? Go to Hawaii or something."

"Yes, come and see me, we have some great deals going on right now," said Bermudadas.

"Let's see, maybe Sherry could come with me, I'll ask her. And it's okay to send the bill to you right George? A little bonus for putting up with you and all your moods!"

"Why not Lucy? Send me the bill Bermudadas and Negar will see that it's paid."

"Really?" she was shocked, "Are you teasing?"

"No, you've earned it, why not?"

The door opened and in strolled Manjira and Rebecca. They were laughing together as they entered the salon.

"You two look like two naughty school girls," said Bermudadas.

"You would be the one to recognize naughtiness now wouldn't you Bermudadas," replied Rebecca teasing her as she hung up her coat.

"Well, now I'm doing my best to convert you Becs!" she answered.

Everyone laughed.

"Okay Negar, you're done," said George as he held the mirror for her to see.

"Thank you George, now I'll get at the books."

"Okey dokey, so ..." George looked around the room as he unravelled the apron from around Negar's neck. "Lucy can you shampoo Saffron? I know you have to get going for the opening of your art show ..."

"Oh there's no rush George, we're all ready for this evening," she replied.

"Okay, first I'll comb out Bermudadas while you're getting shampooed, Rebecca and Manjira you'll have to wait for a little while."

"That's fine George," they both said in unison.

Negar got up out of the chair and headed for the reception desk to get the receipts and the ledger, Saffron stood up and headed to the sink with Lucy, and Bermudadas moved to George's chair.

"Is everything ready for your show Saffron?" asked Manjira.

"Yes, we were there until two o'clock this morning and everything is done. I'm meeting the other two artists at six o'clock this evening and the official opening begins at seven. We're so excited, everything came together so naturally, and we're all so pleased with the exhibit. There is nothing more to be done, tonight we smooze and have fun!"

"What an accomplishment Saffron, we're all so excited for you," said Rebecca.

"Yes, we are, it's a celebration. You know ladies, next month I will have been here for two years!" said George.

"That seems so hard to believe," said Negar.

"It sure does," agreed Lucy.

"I remember your first day George, I was your first customer!" said Bermudadas.

"Yes, you were. I must say its been an interesting two years," laughed George. "Life hasn't been dull with you ladies in my life!"

"You've become a good friend to all of us George," said Bermudadas.

"We're like one big extended family, bickering one day and happy the next," said Manjira.

"So true," agreed Saffon.

"Tell me ladies, what has been the biggest change in yourself in these past two years?" asked George.

"Well, for me, I'd say I've discovered that I can take care of myself, I know I'm not there yet; in fact I know I have a long way to go, but I will get there," said Lucy as she wrapped an apron around Saffron's neck.

"For me," said Saffron, "I've learnt to drop comparison, this art show has been a great opportunity for me to really live that."

"Well," said Rebecca looking at her hands, "I'd have to say I realize winning the Riverville Citizen of the year award means nothing to me. Now I have to really look at when I do something for another, I ask myself what my intent is … and just allow people to be themselves."

"Funny you should ask this morning George, because last night I was thinking about how much I've changed since I left Iran. So, I'd say for me …" mused Negar, "I've learnt that I have a voice too, I found my voice, and now I love my time alone, I'm actually grateful for it now."

"And," stated Bermudadas, "I've learnt to turn inside to find restfulness, I don't have to have all those outside experiences anymore. I'm not effected by the outside anymore, I'm an effecter."

"For me," commented Manjira, "I'd say I've learnt the true meaning of success and that I don't have to assert myself at every moment."

"Well ladies, good for you, now what will the next couple of years bring?!" laughed George.

"Okay, Bermudadas you're almost done," said George as he held up the can of hair spray to complete the job.

"Thanks school boy!" she laughed. Everyone had a puzzled look on their face. "That's what I called him the first time I saw him! You still look like a school boy!"

Everyone laughed and agreed.

"Okay, Saffron to the chair, who wants to go first, Rebecca or Manjira?"

"You go ahead Rebecca," said Manjira.

"Okay, thanks" as she got up and headed to the sink where Lucy waited for her.

"You're looking so pretty Lucy," said Rebecca as she got comfortable at the sink.

Blushing she answered, "Thanks," smiling at Negar she continued, "Negar gave me a make-up lesson and now that George is finally paying me a decent salary I have money to spend on clothes!"

Smiling at everyone George, with his sissors in hand "You're all flowering ...

and when all of you flower, you make the whole world a more beautiful place. It's a lovely sharing, not just for you but for others too. Just keep flowering and others will flower too."

"Flowers flowering …" mused Saffron.

"Do you think growth is instinctive or is it a choice?" asked Negar. "I mean, a seed was planted for that flower to grow. I believe in nature, growth is instinctive. That little seed can't help but grow. Do you think that is the same for people?"

"I believe so Negar," said George. "As I see it, that little seed wants to move forward, step by step, there's no choice. So perhaps as humans it's the same, your being wants to grow. As I see it, if we don't have the capacity to learn we are finished."

"That makes sense," said Lucy. "I certainly never saw life like that, that's for sure. Now I understand the danger of living in a conclusion of who I am. That's lunacy."

"It's something we all need to recognize Lucy," said Manjira. "Not just you."

At that moment, the door swung open and in walked Ned carrying two boxes of product.

"Good morning George, ladies," as he tipped his hat.

"Good morning Ned," came a unison of hellos.

Lucy didn't say anything, she just looked at him and smiled. Her world was getting in order she thought.

"Is something going on?" asked Rebecca.

"Actually," said George, "I do believe there is something special going on … Manjira, Lucy?"

The confused looks on everyone faces sparked a curiosity, suddenly Rebecca said, "Lucy, you're getting married!"

The immediate shock on Lucy's face revealed that Rebecca was wrong.

"No," she stammered. "Manjira …"

"Okay, but first George can you bring the cooler out from its hiding place in the back? And Lucy, can you get the champagne glasses?"

"Champagne?" said Saffron. "What is going on?!"

"Just be patient," said Manjira as she took charge of getting eight champagne flutes arranged on a tray while George brought out a couple of bottles from the hidden cooler.

"Here Ned," said George as he passed an unopened bottle to him, "I'll open one and you open one!"

"Okay," announced Manjira, "Before the champagne is popped, Lucy and I have an announcement. Go ahead Lucy."

"You do it," said Lucy.

"No, this isn't about me, this is about honouring and celebrating your mother, you do it." She was working hard to inspire Lucy, and break her own past patterns of how she related to others.

"Okay," she took a deep breath, "Well, Karen is in school or she would be here too."

She paused for a moment with Ned standing next to her, "Well, it's Thanksgiving and first of all I want to thank everyone for your kindness ..." she paused and took another deep breath, "These past few months while we were sorting out all my father's paperwork Manjira and her husband approached Karen and I with a proposal."

Looking at Manjira with tears starting to form in her blue eyes she continued, "Well ...," she took a deep breath while everyone waited patiently, "The Das' have bought our house and in memory of our mother are going to finance the first women's shelter in Riverville and ... call it *Pearl's*."

Silence filled the air, everyone's eyes in the room went glossy and everyone stared at Manjira. Not wanting the attention she said, "Okay you two, open the champagne!"

The corks were popped and as George and Ned went about pouring, everyone was hugging everyone. George and Ned handed out the flutes and Manjira proposed a toast, "Let us not only toast to *Pearl's*, but to everyone here and to Saffron's art show that is opening later today …"

"Thank you Manjira, I'll donate some art to *Pearl's* and I can help paint, this is going to be so much fun!" she said.

"Thank you Saffron … I have to admit," said Lucy, "When my mother first brought me here to have Huxtable cut my hair, I never dreamed that this place and all of you would come to mean so much to me. I want to thank you for your kindness and George, thank you for all that you have taught me and for always believing in me. And finally Manjira, I want all of you to know that this is her idea and she is going to be the business manager. She's already started on the licensing and getting it passed to meet the municipal by-laws. I've been in awe at watching how she gets things done."

"Well, having my husband on council is proving to do some good after all!" she laughed.

"Yes," encouraged Saffron, "And if you have any problems, just let me know and I will personally speak to the mayor!"

Nodding Manjira agreed, "I'm creating a business plan and once we get to the operation stage, I'm sorry … " she continued as she turned to George, "but you're going to lose Lucy. I'm going to train her to be the manager and together we're going to create a safe place for abused women and their children."

"That's just fantastic," smiled George.

"So," finished Lucy, "Let's toast to all we have to be grateful and thankful for!"

A chorus of *Cheers* followed as the crystal clinked.

"Gratefulness is a quality of seeing truth," added George.

After she took a sip Manjira announced, "I'm not going back to the catering company, Joy is going to be in charge of operations as my husband and I will both be busy. And I'm just grateful that I have the means to do something and participate in something that will serve others. I'm so excited about getting it all started."

"Well," said George thoughtfully, "I'm sure you will inspire others to accomplish more than they ever thought they could Manjira. You have found your passion, and passion is transforming your being into something you will love to do. When you discover your soul, your love, your passion, life is new, fresh, vital."

"Thank you George," she said. "It's going to be so exciting. I've come to believe that one of the highest values is to sense what is needed for another no matter what it costs you."

Everyone stood in silence.

"You are a blessing to this world Manjira," said George. "Let your vision reflect all that you can be."

"Thank you George ... and *Pearl's* will be place where women live in celebration of what their lives can be. We will introduce celebration to everything we do there, we will celebrate the possibilities that everyone can embrace in a safe environment. I know it will take time, but Rome wasn't built in a day ... in fact, I believe its still being built!"

Everyone laughed and Bermudadas added, "Let's rock this life, but with responsibility and awareness."

Looking around the room George continued, "As I see it, doing something one believes in is crucial to the manifestation of one's soul, for both men and women. Own your life. You have only one destiny; to realize you are a destiny maker ... let's celebrate!" and he held his glass up and continued. "Let's celebrate. Fulfil the promise of what you can be; recognize that you are a part of humanity. As pure individuals, remain uniquely you because the world needs more people living in love and when all of us are living totally, we will bring more light to this earth and as I see it that is the only way this world will get right. The world cannot be transformed, people need to transform. The moment you get beautiful the world gets beautiful. Be open to order in your life. There are two types of people in this world, the fallen and the risen, I hold my glass to all of you here, and you have all risen. Don't dwell in the fallen. And when you are rising, existence will bring all you need to remain risen. Rest in the risen state. Not just for you, for humanity's sake. It is up to you. By being creators we all rise consciously. Have the power to make choices, create your reality, give birth to a better world. The hope for humanity is in humanity. Let's participate as a friend to mankind. We have a choice to make a humane humanity. Life is liveable and then love becomes real. It seems to me love can only flower through humanity. Then love becomes your pulse."

"Here, here," said everyone with John Lennon's newly released *Imagine* playing in the background.

Janet Love Morrison was born in Toronto, Canada and grew up in Port Coquitlam, near Vancouver, BC. Janet's first hair stylist was a young man named Stan who started cutting her hair when she was three years old. In fact, Janet often fell asleep in the stylist chair; her mother would have to hold up her head in order for Stan to finish the job! Stan has been her mother's hairdresser for over forty-five years and as her mother always said, "Stan and Linda are like members of the family." Stan was an immense help in assisting Janet with the setting and character development.

Love Morrison spent a lot of her life travelling around the world doing a variety of jobs while living in Switzerland, Israel, India, Japan, and Malaysia. She has taught English as a Second Language (ESL) for many, many years and teaching has been one of her greatest joys. Work is Love Morrison's life, whether teaching, writing, editing, or speaking: all are her joy.

In the spring of 2012 she created an editing company and is currently living in Vancouver, BC.

Love Morrison is also an Ambassador for Friends to Mankind (FtoM), an international non-profit foundation that works with individuals, corporations and philanthropic organizations towards the betterment of humanity.

"If your work is just work, then you haven't found your work, but if your work is your life, then you have found your life."
Dhyan Vimal: Founder, Friends to Mankind
www.friendstomankind.org

If you are interested in inviting Janet Love Morrison for a speaking engagement please contact Elke Porter at admin@porterprconsulting.com

If you would like any further information on Friends to Mankind, please go to www.friendstomankind.org

If you are interested in any editorial services please go to Janet's website:

Janet Love Morrison
www.janetlovemorrison.com
janet@janetlovemorrison.com
604.561.2664

If you want to get on the path to be a published author by
Influence Publishing please go to
www.InspireABook.com

Inspiring books that influence change

More information on our other titles and how to submit
your own proposal can be found at
www.InfluencePublishing.com

CPSIA information can be obtained at www.ICGtesting.com
Printed in the USA
LVOW120853011112

305304LV00003B/2/P